Jodi glared at Daniel Gleason.

He was even mo⟨...⟩ ⟨...⟩en years earlier, an⟨...⟩

"You'll be glad to ⟨...⟩f it is empty-handed," ⟨...⟩

"I agree with ha⟨...⟩ ⟨...⟩ Daniel had charm and contacts, but she had the drive of needing something badly.

Daniel hopped up on his running board. "Guess we'll have to agree to disagree on that."

She raised an eyebrow. "It's not a matter of agreeing or disagreeing. We're not playing on the same team anymore."

"Have we ever?"

Their eyes locked for a breathless moment, both recalling when they had.

"This is different."

He studied her for a long minute then waved before sliding inside the truck. "I know."

As he began backing out of her aunt's driveway, his eyes on her, she heard him shout, "This is war!"

Dear Reader,

My most important career is motherhood. Now that my daughter is applying to colleges and ready to leave the nest, I've been reflecting on what it means to be Mom. It is a miracle filled with joy, despair, frustration and– ultimately–fulfillment. I have a deep appreciation for the indomitable will of mothers to protect their children, to love them and to always keep them safe.

My sister Cathy personifies this type of parent. When Cathy's daughter, Abbie, turned three, she was diagnosed with autism. I'm awestruck by my sister's grace, strength and determination in helping Abbie grow into the beautiful young lady she's become, a unique individual who takes me by surprise with her humor and outlook on life.

The idea that we do not need to meet society's standards of "normal" or "perfect" to find happiness plays a large role in *His Hometown Girl*. What matters most is that we find joy in the life we've been given. Jodi, the single mother of her autistic son, Tyler, certainly deserves that happiness, which is why I gave them Daniel, a man who is strong enough to fight for *his* idea of the perfect family.

I would love to hear from you and learn your inspiring stories of parenting a special needs child. To contact me, please visit www.karenrock.com. Thanks!

Karen

HARLEQUIN HEARTWARMING

Karen Rock

His Hometown Girl

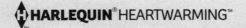
HARLEQUIN® HEARTWARMING™

Recycling programs
for this product may
not exist in your area.

ISBN-13: 978-0-373-36669-9

HIS HOMETOWN GIRL

Copyright © 2014 by Karen Rock

Printed in U.S.A.

KAREN ROCK

Since Karen Rock's grandmother passed her shopping bagfuls of Harlequin Presents as a teen, it's been her dream to add her voice to the romance genre. Now an author for Harlequin's latest contemporary line, Harlequin Heartwarming, Karen is thrilled to pen wholesome, tender, deeply romantic and relatable stories. When she's not busy writing, Karen enjoys watching anything starring Meg Ryan and Tom Hanks, cooking her Nona's Italian family recipes and occasionally rescuing local wildlife from neighborhood cats. She lives in the Adirondack Mountain region with her husband, her much-appreciated beta-reader daughter and two King Charles Cavalier cocker spaniels who have yet to understand the concept of "fetch," though they know a lot about love. For more information about Karen's upcoming books, check out her website at www.karenrock.com, or follow her on Facebook, at www.facebook.com/KarenRockWrites, or on Twitter, www.twitter.com/KarenRock5. She'd love to hear from you!

Books by Karen Rock

HARLEQUIN HEARTWARMING

13—WISH ME FOREVER

To the parents of children with special needs. You are mighty warriors and the most loving caregivers. Please know that you are special, too.

CHAPTER ONE

"TYLER, WHAT COLOR?"

Jodi Chapman peered from the blue card to the psychologist crouched before her autistic four-year-old, holding her breath. *Please get this, Ty.* A good evaluation meant entrance to this specialized school that would help him talk again.

But instead of responding, her towheaded only child yanked off his eyeglasses band and threw them at his feet. Her hopes fell with them.

"I'm sorry." Jodi slung an arm around Tyler before he bolted for the train table. She'd known it'd be hard for him to focus when he'd pointed to it after entering Wonders Primary's playroom. Her mouth felt like a desert as Beth's pen scratched across the evaluation sheet. After an hour of assessments, Tyler wanted out when they desperately needed in.

"May I ask what you're writing, Beth?" She struggled to put on Tyler's glasses with one hand while holding him in place with the other.

"Tyler, you can play with the trains in a little bit." As a single mom, she wished she had three arms instead of two. Yet even that wouldn't be enough some days. If only this wasn't one of them.

"Keeping his glasses on will be a behavior goal if he attends school here this fall." Beth lowered her clipboard, her khaki pants and green polo shirt lacking the wrinkles embedded in Jodi's suit.

Jodi dragged in a deep breath and held Tyler tighter as he escalated from resistance to flailing.

If. Beth had said "if." Jodi inhaled the childhood smells of crayons, apple juice and glue, her gaze darting around the vibrant room that'd be perfect for her son. Warm sunlight streamed from a round skylight, illuminating a large foam-sided circle that resembled a kiddie pool, filled with books and toys. A child-size cardboard castle stood beside a trunk overflowing with dress-up clothes. Floor puzzle pieces lead to its entrance. It was a far cry from the small apartment where her kind neighbor cared for Tyler.

Six children rocked and fidgeted on a circle of colored rug squares while their teacher read them a story. Aides walked the group's perimeter, pulling some of the children's hands away from their ears while others applied shoulder pressure to those flapping their hands.

"Show me the blue train, Tyler." The psychologist pointed to the table and held out a hand, but Tyler batted it away.

"No hitting, Ty." Jodi felt her lower eyelid twitch. The break in Tyler's daily routine unsettled and overexcited him, the perfect storm for lashing out, poor baby.

"Do you want to play trains?" Beth tried again.

The psychologist tucked her clipboard under her arm at Tyler's nod and headed toward the table. Before following, he squeezed Jodi's knees, the sweet, unexpected gesture catching at her heart.

She blinked back tears when he wobbled on tiptoe after Beth and picked up a green train instead of the blue. Green was his favorite color. It might be the wrong answer for the evaluation, but it was right for him. Her chest tightened when the psychologist frowned and scribbled something on her clipboard, a brief glimpse showing a heavily marked page. Jodi imagined the comments. If only Wonders Primary knew the boy who patted her cheek until he fell asleep, the one who dressed Ollie, his stuffed elephant, in different outfits every day, the child who'd cried for a week after his father had walked out, and then never spoke again. Guilt churned in her stomach like a live thing.

"MRS. CHAPMAN?"

Jodi turned and smiled unevenly at a distinguished woman with close-cropped brown hair and an arched nose, her picture familiar from the school's website.

She discreetly brushed her damp palm against her skirt and held out her hand. "It's Ms. actually."

"Ms. Chapman. Welcome. I'm Mrs. Garcia, school director." Her hand was gripped, then released. "Thank you for coming in so quickly. Hopefully our last-minute opening for this fall will work out. You've been on the waiting list for—"

"Tyler's doctor referred him a year ago," she answered, though it'd felt longer than that. It'd been an anxious twelve-month involuntary wait to see if her application would be approved. Given the number of children around the country who attended this highly recognized school, she'd been told Tyler might not have this chance for three years. Or at all.

"If you'll meet me in my office, I'll join you once I've spoken with Beth. It's the last door down the hall."

Jodi glanced at the train table where her son

ripped up tracks and smashed bridges. "Should I take Tyler with me?" Without her around, he might act out, give the wrong impression. Her heartbeat hammered.

"Our aides will watch him while Beth and I consult. Then Beth will take over when I join you." Mrs. Garcia studied Jodi over rimless bifocals. "He'll be in good hands."

Jodi hesitated, then nodded, feeling helpless. There was nothing more she could do. Fate had taken the wheel and would steer them where it would.

At the door, she called, "Mommy will be right back, Ty." But he continued playing without looking up and missed her reassuring smile. When he noticed she was gone, would he feel scared? Alone? With difficulty, she kept herself from running back to him.

She watched Beth hand Mrs. Garcia the clipboard, and their heads bent together. Jodi's grip tightened on the doorknob. What verdict were they reaching?

"I'll see you later, Tyler," she yelled, louder now. Several children in the reading circle looked up, but not her son. Her chest squeezed as he zoomed the green train around a wooden building. Did he care that she was leaving? The harsh truth was that she honestly didn't know.

She trudged down the hall and gave herself a

pep talk. From everything she'd read, Wonders Primary excelled at working with challenged students. Hopefully they'd see Tyler's potential. Believe in him the way she did.

Inside the wood-paneled office, she paced to the window and peered out at the foggy Chicago skyline, grateful to be here. Until now, the path to Tyler's recovery had seemed as murky as the weather, her despair darker still. She rested her head against the cool windowpane and tried not to worry.

"Thank you for waiting, Ms. Chapman," Mrs. Garcia spoke behind her a couple minutes later. "Would you have a seat?"

Jodi strode to a leather chair in front of an imposing desk and sat, her white knuckles contrasting against the brown upholstered arms. "How's Tyler?"

"He's in the right place at the right time." Mrs. Garcia smiled, her red lipstick matching her manicured fingernails, which were splayed against the desk calendar. "We'd be happy to welcome him at Wonders Primary this coming fall."

Jodi sagged in her seat. Finally. She wasn't alone anymore...and she wouldn't fail Tyler. His care would have the order and predictability they both needed.

"Beth and the rest of the assessment team

recommended that Tyler receive physical therapy, sensory-integration occupational therapy, speech therapy, social-skills training and behavioral training. We have every confidence that he'll make solid gains with us."

The news knocked the wind out of Jodi. She knew her son needed help. His therapist and doctor had said as much. But hearing the long list made his condition seem graver and more severe than she'd let herself imagine. She clamped a hand over her jittering knee. It was unfair. Tyler hadn't asked for this.

"I see," she managed at last.

"I realize this is short notice." Mrs. Garcia poured two cups of tea from an electric kettle on her credenza. "However, we'll need a ten percent tuition deposit to hold the spot." She offered Jodi a steaming mug. "Cream and sugar?"

Jodi shook her head and stared at the dark liquid, her wide eyes reflected back at her. In the excitement surrounding yesterday's surprise call from Wonders Primary, she hadn't asked about the cost.

She gulped her tea and the scalding liquid splashed down her throat. "And how much is tuition?"

Mrs. Garcia's brows met over her prominent nose. "Sixteen thousand. We don't provide that information on our website, but our secretary should have informed you when she called."

"She might have," Jodi admitted, her pulse thumping. Sixteen thousand? That couldn't be the price. "Tyler was having a tough time over...well...something and I'm afraid I only wrote down the appointment time. Did you say sixteen thousand a year?"

Mrs. Garcia scooped out her tea bag and laid it on her saucer. "No."

Air escaped Jodi in a rush. Thank goodness she'd heard that wrong. Her salary wouldn't cover such a large fee, even if her ex-husband contributed. And that was a big if....

"It's sixteen thousand a semester," the Wonders Primary director corrected, "and each semester runs six months."

Jodi splashed tea on her hand, too shocked to feel the burn when she set down her mug.

"But that...seems high." And impossible.

"Yes." The administrator's spoon clanked against the sides of her cup as she stirred in a packet of sweetener. "However, our board feels the fee is justified given our specialized work and reputation. Nevertheless, I understand if this is more than you expected and wish to look elsewhere."

Elsewhere? She'd tried everything and had nowhere left to turn. Jodi's hands twisted. She was failing Tyler and she couldn't let that happen. Not again. Disappointment settled around her slumped shoulders.

"I'm sorry to pressure you, Ms. Chapman, but there are many anxious families that would appreciate the chance to attend if you plan to withdraw."

"Please. A moment." Jodi strove to keep the panic out of her voice. She opened her purse to search for her calculator and found a Post-it note with her optimistic reminder: "Wonders Primary 10 a.m. J." How could she have been so naive? Expert care like this didn't come cheap. For people like her and Tyler, it might not come at all.

Her fingers encountered her cell phone and her screen saver flashed on. It was a picture of her and Tyler as she held him on her hip while he pointed at a hot air balloon. The festival had been a wonderful day, one of his better ones. They needed more of those after a year spent struggling through nightly therapy that ended with both of them in tears. Somehow this had to work.

"I'll take the spot," she blurted, then pressed her phone to her chest. What had she done?

Where Tyler was concerned, she tended to think with her heart.

"A wise choice," said Mrs. Garcia, her self-assured voice doing little to soothe Jodi's worries. "We'll need your deposit by the end of this week and the balance of the first half at the start of the fall semester. We split our tuition into biannual payments to make it more accessible to families."

"Yes," Jodi agreed, her voice faint. Her body felt limp and light, as though she could blend with the white clouds billowing by the *Tribune* building across the street.

"Excellent. We'll look forward to seeing Tyler in September."

Despite Mrs. Garcia's warm tone, Jodi shivered. September. Only three months to raise twice her current savings balance.

AFTER DROPPING OFF Tyler at her neighbor's apartment and returning to work, she sat at her desk, numb. Her ex-husband, Peter, hadn't returned her voice mails and her eyes lingered on her bare left hand, her mind inventorying her belongings. She shouldn't have flushed away her wedding rings—even though she'd been pushed to her limit by Tyler's wails for his vanished father. They would have helped to pay for the tuition to Wonders Primary.

Impulsive, her mother used to call her, just like her father. And look where that'd gotten him. How it had affected their family.

She shrank from the memory but it found her anyway. If she hadn't accepted a friend's last-minute invitation rather than going home for chores, she would have been there when a borrowed skid loader dislodged and the auger her father had been lifting crashed down. Because of her absence, he'd been pinned for two hours before her mother returned from work and discovered him, the delay costing him his arm and their family their livelihood.

She buried her head in her hands. Her parents hadn't blamed her, but she'd never forgiven herself. Never again would she put what she wanted ahead of duty. Yet when she'd tried keeping her failing marriage going for Tyler's sake, that had backfired, too.

Her phone buzzed and she snatched it off her desk when she recognized the number.

"Peter?" It was a rare day when he returned her calls. Thank goodness today was one of them.

"We need to talk." His distracted, impatient voice sounded as distant as ever.

"Yes. About Wonders Primary—" she began, knowing it was a long shot to ask, but for Tyler, anything.

"What? No," he barked, and she flinched, recalling previous times he'd used that tone with her. And Tyler. "I'm getting remarried."

Her mind skittered over that thought like a tongue probing for a cavity. After a moment, she relaxed. No pain. Tyler was her only priority, and the reason, according to her ex, that they'd split. For the hundredth time, she regretted her impulsive decision to marry Peter. On the other hand, that rash decision had brought her the greatest joy in her life: her beautiful boy.

"Congratulations," she said, hoping he'd found a partner who would give him a "perfect" child. He'd resented having a son who couldn't keep up with the other kids, who brought stares and snide comments from strangers. Her nightly research for autism treatments and insistence that Tyler's condition was beyond her or their son's control had only angered him further.

"I'm suing to lower my child support."

Her office seemed to tilt and spin. He might as well have reached into her chest and seized her heart.

"No!" she exclaimed. "Tyler needs more money to go to a school for autistic children."

"That was your label," Peter blustered. "Not mine. You spoiled him. All that coddling. That's why the kid wouldn't walk until he was two."

Jodi squeezed her eyes shut and counted

backward from ten. "It's a medical diagnosis, Peter. It's not my fault."

"Look. I don't have time for this. My lawyers are sending papers over this week."

She heard a beep, then silence, yet she kept the phone pressed to her ear for a moment, willing him to come back on, to say that he'd help.

Hands shaking, she dropped her phone in her purse and opened a file. Anything to steady her. At first she saw only a blur of numbers until her whirling mind settled enough to make out a purchase agreement. The Idaho farmers had agreed to sell their land to her employer, Midland Corp. Several families had even accepted her company's offer to let them stay in their homes, rent-free, as contracted workers. They'd farm their old land for a paycheck instead of profits.

Despite her day, she felt some satisfaction in this hard-won deal. It was one of several she'd made that had helped Midland become the world's largest food producer and owner of agricultural land.

"Ms. Chapman?" Her secretary's voice came through the intercom.

"Yes, Linda."

"Mr. Williams would like to see you in his office immediately."

Jodi rubbed her throbbing temples. Of all the

times to get a summons from her boss. "Please tell him I'll be right there."

The familiar sound of fingers tapping on keyboards, phones ringing and fax machines spitting out paper filled the corridor as she strode toward Mr. Williams's office.

"Hi, Gail." Jodi placed her hands on the granite counter before her boss's door, noticed her chipped nail polish and yanked them down to her sides. "Mr. Williams wants to see me?"

Gail slid a candy bowl her way and lowered her voice. "You might want reinforcements." She glanced at the door behind her. "He's in a tear."

Jodi's stomach twisted and she ignored the treats. Focusing on work instead of her crisis felt impossible. Facing an irritated boss on top of that might be more than she could handle.

Well. There was nothing for it.

She took a deep breath, put on her business face, knocked and then strode inside. Her boss half rose from his seat and waved her to a chair. He was an imposing, florid man whose white comb-over contrasted with his helter-skelter black eyebrows. His thick glasses made his eyes seem to look everywhere and nowhere at once. When she perched on the edge of her seat, he shoved a folder across his desk.

"Got another acquisitions deal for you, Jodi."

He tugged at the striped tie that half disappeared into his neck roll. "Espresso?"

Knowing better than to argue, she accepted the minimug and sipped, careful not to make a face. It sure wasn't chamomile, and she could have used the soothing blend to settle her jangling nerves.

"Good, eh?" Mr. Williams beamed and Jodi nodded, bolting back the rest of the foul brew.

"Did you mention something about a new deal?" It took every ounce of her dwindling energy to keep her voice steady.

Her boss held out the folder. "I believe you're familiar with this area."

Jodi grabbed the file while her mind replayed her conversations with the Wonders Primary director and her ex. How would she find a way to pay for Tyler's care if her husband wanted to contribute less?

She started when Mr. Williams cleared his throat, and then she flipped the file open and froze at the location typed on the cover sheet.

Cedar Bay, Vermont. She dropped it back on his desk, blinking rapidly.

"This looks like a large deal. Surely Jake or Micah—" She sought to rein in her rising voice. "Brady—" Logic, not emotion, she reminded herself. She'd made too many mistakes in life by ignoring that rule.

"Don't have the connections there that you do, and we need this land to stay ahead of the competition." Her boss twisted the end of a gold-plated pen, the point appearing and disappearing. "Besides, they already tried, with the exception of Brady, who's still tied up in Mexico. Look, Jodi, it's your hometown."

"I haven't been there since I left for college."

"You still have family there." Her supervisor pointed his pen at a nearby picture. In it, the executives mugged in red Santa hats or antler headbands. "I met your aunt at last year's holiday party. Grace, I believe?"

Of course Mr. Williams would remember that detail, just as he stored every tidbit, small or large. Her mind worked frantically. How could she get out of this? She needed to stay in town and sort things out for Tyler.

She rose. "I'm sorry, Mr. Williams. But Cedar Bay will be a conflict of interest."

"A conflict for whom, I wonder?" Her supervisor waved her to take her seat again. After a tense moment, he opened the file and read from it.

"Layhee, Trudeau, Drollette…" His voice droned on through the long list, each familiar last name making her pulse pound harder than the last. "…and Remillard," he finished.

His sharp gaze met hers. "Recognize any of those?"

All of them, Jodi thought. "A few," she said.

"Then that's the in we need. We've been trying to take over this prime dairy land for years. Put all of our best men on it." He pulled out his pocket-handkerchief and dabbed at his glistening forehead. "I mean, we put our best senior executives on it, but we haven't made any headway as a result of some fellow by the name of—" he glanced down at the chart "—Daniel Gleason."

Jodi wasn't surprised. Of course Daniel would be behind the resistance to Midland's buyout. His family had farmed in Cedar Bay for centuries, and if anyone could hold out against her corporation, it'd be charming, clever, stubborn Daniel.

"Says here he's twenty-seven. That's your age." Mr. Williams peered at her through his thick lenses. "A friend of yours?"

"Hardly." Irritation rose as she recalled how often her popular ex-classmate had bested her throughout their childhood, from being the first to cross the monkey bars to edging her out as valedictorian. Then there was that moment of weakness when she'd nearly fallen for him. "The opposite, actually."

Mr. Williams grunted, then nodded at a

painting of the company's former CEO. "I was once a junior exec like you, Jodi. But my mentor taught me the secret to moving up in life. Know your enemy. This Gleason fellow's our enemy. Who better to make our case than someone who knows him well? Plus, you can take your son with you. Stay at your aunt's for a couple of months and get Tyler out of the city for the summer. Fresh air and all that. Once you've acquired five thousand acres, you'll be back in time for the Bears preseason."

Five thousand acres? The small hairs on the back of Jodi's neck pricked. This was a large deal, a herculean task, even with her connections and a summer to accomplish it. And just how well had Mr. Williams gotten to know her talkative aunt? She always praised the benefits of country air in hopes of tempting Jodi out for a visit.

But Jodi remembered how unpredictable and dangerous farm country could be. It was the reason her parents had left town once Jodi finished her senior year in high school. As for why she hadn't accepted her aunt's offer to stay with her during college breaks, that story ended with a different kind of heartbreak.

More important than her tumultuous hometown history, however, Tyler did best with routines, things he knew and expected. She couldn't imagine a worse place for him.

She cleared her throat.

"I haven't spoken to Daniel Gleason in ten years, so I'm afraid I wouldn't be of much help." She edged toward the door. "If I may be excused, sir?"

Her employer intercepted her. "Jodi, I've seen your talent and ambition. In fact, you remind me of myself at your age. Look how quickly you wrapped things up in Idaho and every other deal we've given you. Succeed on this, and I'll give you a promotion to midlevel executive."

Jodi gripped the doorknob, afraid her weak knees would give out. Midlevel? Even her fellow junior executive, ambitious Brady Grayson, couldn't hope for such a steep corporate climb at their age. Her mind ran over the numbers that came with the promotion's raise, seeing that Wonders Primary would be in reach. Almost. If her ex's lawsuit failed, it might work.

"And of course there'd be a closing bonus of, say, five thousand." Her boss waved the folder beneath her nose like a matador.

Jodi blinked at him, disbelieving. Suddenly her dreams were within her grasp, the chance to provide the care her son needed, a brass ring at her fingertips. She wasn't going to fail after all.

"Fine." Mr. Williams sighed at her extended silence. "How about eight thousand? But that's my best offer, Jodi." Mr. Williams raked his fingers through his hair wisps. "You drive a hard bargain. Do we have a deal?"

She nodded and felt her palm pumped up and down. A tide of joy rolled through her before unease dragged it away. Going home meant returning to a place—and a person—she'd vowed to forget.

CHAPTER TWO

A WEEK LATER, at Burlington International Airport, Daniel Gleason shifted in his work boots and peered up at the arrival and departure board. Jodi's Chicago flight was on time, meaning it must be landing. Any minute now and she'd stride through the terminal gate and back into his life. A foreboding feeling settled in his gut. Would her local roots make the community trust her more than the other Midland suits? Sell their farmland to her? Worse, would seeing her rekindle his old feelings? He gulped back that bitter thought.

"Yep," a farmer beside him murmured. "The corn should be a foot taller by now." The man pulled off a John Deere cap and scratched his bald head. "Rain better slow up soon."

"Every path's got a few puddles," Daniel quoted absently, his mind focused more on the appearance of his lovely—and cunning—childhood competitor. The woman who'd walked out on their relationship ten years ago without a word.

"Heard you had some kind of socialist plan to get us out of this mess, Gleason." His neighbor's eyes slid Daniels's way.

Daniel waited a beat, then gave the man a reassuring smile. "A co-op isn't socialist," he said evenly. "It's practical. If we produce organic products from humanely treated animals, we'll get a higher price per pound of milk. It's our best strategy for making it through this economy, and the weather. But we can't apply for the upgrades grant unless we form the co-op."

The farmer spat chewing tobacco into a handkerchief. "Still sounds socialist. And I didn't fight in Vietnam to go commie now."

"But—"

A voice announced a disembarking plane, interrupting Daniel.

"That's my wife." The vet clapped a hand on Daniel's shoulder. "Look, kid. I served with your dad and I know you're trying to keep his farm going since he can't. But we've got to look at more realistic solutions. We'll talk more at the next town council meeting."

It's my farm, too, Daniel wanted to interject, though he knew better than to be disrespectful. Patience and persistence would win his neighbors to his cause. And losing was not an option. Like his ancestors, he valued a life shaped by his own hands and the independence that came with it. He'd protect his farming community's traditions, no matter the odds or the adversary. His pulse stuttered. Even if it was Jodi.

"Now disembarking, Flight 152 from Chicago, Gate A," a boarding agent announced into a microphone. Passengers streamed by her podium and Daniel stepped forward, his heart beating out a forgotten rhythm.

Then he spotted golden hair…and there she was, Jodi, more beautiful than he remembered. Thinner, the youthful roundness of her face replaced by finer contours of jaw and cheekbones, dressed up in a yellow tank top and a flowered skirt instead of the jeans he was used to, her waves smoothed straight. But she was still the gorgeous girl next door. His breath caught at the vision she made as her hair flowed around her face while she secured a struggling child in a stroller.

Tyler. Grace had filled him in on Jodi's son and divorce when he'd offered to pick her up at the airport. It was part of his "keep your friends close and enemies closer" strategy. He didn't have to worry about the "know your enemy" tactic, however. Every one of his earliest memories included Jodi—some of the best and a few of the worst.

"Daniel?"

Jodi's large blue eyes peered from him to the

handwritten sign he held and she frowned as she read it, her lips silently forming the words *Jodi Lynn*. He forced his eyes from her full mouth, the sight doing something funny to his heart until he caught himself. Those feelings were from a lifetime ago. One he had no intention of reliving.

"What are you doing here? And I don't go by Jodi Lynn anymore. Please put that sign away."

He lowered it. "I wasn't sure if you'd recognize me. You've been gone awhile." Despite his efforts, it sounded accusing and he hurried to continue. "And Grace had a DAR meeting, so I offered to pick you up."

She peered up at signs bearing the taxi symbol. "Thanks, but I can manage on my own." Her son began to cry, his voice sounding hoarse, as if he'd been doing it for hours. Maybe he had, poor kid. Grace had mentioned the boy was autistic and that keeping him calm in new situations could be a challenge.

Daniel took her carry-on so that she could attend to her child. "Jodi. Face it, you've got your hands full and your aunt wanted me to help you." After he'd convinced Grace not to miss her meeting, he added to himself. He needed to know what Jodi planned.

She sighed, although it was hard to tell if the frustrated sound was aimed at him or the plastic-framed glasses her son flung into the crowd.

A man in a business suit stopped short and spilled his coffee down his shirt. He snatched up the eye gear by its band and advanced their way, his scowl directed at Jodi until Daniel stepped in his path.

He forced an easy smile and held out a hand. "Thanks for that. Wouldn't want a child to lose his glasses."

The traveler opened and closed his mouth like the bass Daniel had hooked last Sunday.

He nodded toward a row of boarding-pass kiosks. "Looks like you'd better get going since you're in such a rush."

When the man scurried away, his tie flapping over his shoulder, Jodi turned to Daniel. "You didn't have to do that." She straightened her spine and looked him in the eye. "I can fight my own battles."

He didn't want to suggest that it looked like her hands were already full with her cranky preschooler, but that was the reason he'd stepped in.

He passed Jodi the glasses. "Like the one you're fighting for Midland Corp." He figured it was safer to put this conversation on professional grounds right off the bat. "Or is it more personal than that?"

Jodi's face remained neutral and he wondered if she felt guilty for coming home to sell out her former neighbors. It was one thing for her parents to lose their farm. Another matter for a community to lose its way of life. He wouldn't let her get away with it.

"This isn't personal, Daniel," she said at last, her voice muffled as she bent over her son and pulled the glasses over his head. "It's business."

His jaw tightened. "It involves people's lives, so I'd say it's personal."

"Baggage for Flight 152 now unloading on Carousel C," the overhead announcer blared.

When she spoke, Jodi sounded cool and matter-of-fact. A stranger's voice. "Let's table that if you don't mind. Now, if you're my chauffeur, we should get my bags. Oh, and this is my son, Tyler."

Amazing how much the child resembled his mother. "Hey, Tyler."

But the boy ignored him and gnawed on his stuffed elephant's ear. The kid looked stressed.

"Let's get your luggage."

Jodi rolled her stroller toward a moving conveyer belt sweeping dusty bags in a circle. "Once I've gotten the farmers to sell, those suitcases will be on the next flight. Promise." She pointed to a pair of large, plastic-encased bags and wheeled her son back from the jostling crowd.

He didn't doubt it. She'd done it before and it'd nearly broken him.

After hefting them off the moving track, he caught up to her. "That's a lot of baggage for someone who's not staying long."

"I'm planning on staying until I get the job done." She gave him a level stare. "Except losing."

The luggage wheels clicked as he rolled the bags toward the exit, his mind working just as fast. "You did a lot of that before you moved away."

"Emphasis on the word *before*." She stopped the stroller and crouched in front of Tyler, her hands on his kicking legs. "I'm not the same girl who fell for your games, Daniel."

"Maybe we've both learned some new tricks."

She straightened and stepped so close that he took an involuntary step back. "I conduct multimillion dollar deals while you..." Her voice trailed off as she looked from his mud-spattered boots to his faded plaid shirt.

"Earn an honest living." He adjusted his Red Sox cap. "You get your hands a lot dirtier than I do." Before her family's tragedy, she'd been proud to be a 4-H girl and farmer's daughter. Now she acted as if this life was beneath her.

Where had the girl gone who'd swung out on a rope over Cedar Bay farther than anyone, the young woman who'd walked the ridgeline of a barn on a dare and had raided Mrs. Tate's berry patches at midnight? The impulsive risk taker he'd known was replaced with a carefully controlled, polished version of herself. Yet he preferred her former warm glow to this reflective sheen that wouldn't let him see the real her. If that person existed anymore. Had she been this way all along? Was that the reason she'd left him?

The sliding doors opened with a hiss and they stepped out into the cool midmorning drizzle. Daniel breathed in the smell of exhaust and couldn't wait to get home, away from all this concrete. He needed to strategize. Regroup and think about how he'd handle this new, unflappable Jodi.

She raised an eyebrow and gave him a measured look. "Where are you parked?" Her stroller's plastic wheels swerved along the parking lot's asphalt.

So she was letting his accusation go, her self-possession unnerving him. Gone was the girl whose passion had once swept him away from his everyday life, her white-hot temper later imploding it. How things had changed. At least the temporary cease-fire meant he could find out her plans. Stop them before she put them in place. For that matter, the drive home might soften her up with a tour down memory lane.

"I've got a ground-level spot," he said, raising his voice so it'd be heard over a plane's roar.

"Great. The sooner Tyler gets his nap the better."

"Are you working right away or having some R & R first? I'll show you some of the old sights."

"I have to check in with my boss, then I plan to—" She stopped and shoved wet, frizzing hair from her face. "Why am I telling you this?" Her eyes roamed over him, mystified. Suddenly she looked like the girl he'd known years ago, the one who'd once worn her heart on her sleeve and had captured his.

"Because we used to be friends, Jodi Lynn."

"Friends?" She snorted and shook off the water collecting on the stroller's canopy. "And don't call me Jodi Lynn."

"Would you prefer 'ma'am'? Is that what country folks are supposed to say when a city girl comes to town?"

"Knock it off, Daniel." She nudged him, and the warmth of her bare shoulder through his thin shirt nearly burned.

"That's Mr. Gleason to you," he joked to hide the response her touch ignited. *Careful,* he warned himself.

Jodi shot him a level look, then picked up speed when her son started to kick again, his voice sounding like a teakettle about to boil. No wonder. Daniel would scream, too, if he was strapped in when he could walk instead. Parking lots were unpredictable, but with a firm hand and a sharp eye the little guy could have had his freedom.

"So why are you here instead of one of my aunt's neighbors?" she asked once they halted beside his muddy blue pickup. The misting rain had only streaked the dirt.

"We're all neighbors, and neighbors help each other." He tossed her expensive-looking suitcases into the open bed, an echoing *thunk* sounding when plastic met metal. "In case you forgot."

"I haven't. I'm helping my old hometown get a fair deal that will improve their lives." She spoke without looking up at him, her movements practiced and efficient as she swept up her thrashing son and secured him in the child seat she'd detached from the stroller, buckling him into the center of the truck's continuous front seat.

"If you want something, use your words, Tyler," she told her son.

The boy screamed and pounded his fists against the dashboard, but Jodi slid in beside him, looking as if it was any other day. And for her, maybe it was.

Daniel felt his resistance weaken until he caught himself. Her "fair deal" would only benefit Midland, not her former community. They'd either have to abandon their land or become corporate drones, working for a Midland paycheck. No. Jodi was the enemy. No matter that she made him remember good times he'd rather forget.

If he couldn't convince her that this was personal, not business, remind her of the good times she'd had here and the people she'd cared about, then he needed her gone before she wreaked havoc on his home and his heart.

She'd done the latter the last time she'd left town. He'd be a fool to let her do it again.

He wouldn't let himself, or his town, fall for Jodi Lynn Chapman.

No, ma'am.

JODI CLOSED HER eyes and rested her head against the seat as the truck accelerated out of the airport parking lot. Of all people, why had Daniel been the one to meet her at the airport? The unwelcome surprise had rattled her to the bone. It'd taken every bit of control to act professionally around him when she'd wanted to bolt from the emotions he'd shaken loose. Besides, personal spats wouldn't convince the local farmers to trust her professionalism.

But she and Daniel had been much more than enemies once....

Her eyes flew open at the unbidden thought and she peeked at Daniel's profile. He'd matured in subtle ways over the past ten years. His square jaw and broad cheekbones had filled out, balancing his strong nose so that his masculine features looked handsomer than ever. His left-sided cowlick pulled dark hair from his prominent brow and framed hazel eyes fringed with thick lashes she'd always envied.

Her face heated and she lowered her lids again as the truck took a couple more turns. No. She wouldn't let herself think of him that way. Not again. Not when she needed every bit of her focus on acquiring local farms, even Daniel's. And how would she manage that magic trick?

Then again, how could she not? Besides Mr. Tisdale's lakeside property, Daniel's Maplewood Farm had the most land in the area. With her target set at five thousand acres, success was her only option.

Her chest burned when she recalled being served with Peter's petition to lower child support payments yesterday. Despite everything, she still hadn't believed he'd do it. And now, on top of battling for tuition to Wonders Primary, she'd need to hire a lawyer to fight him.

She held in the sigh that'd give her inner turmoil away. This was the most important deal in her career and she had to think strategically and rationally. Use the skills she'd learned from corporate wheeling and dealing in order to win when she needed it most. Emotion or doubt couldn't cloud her judgment.

Her eyes slit open and flicked Daniel's way. Nor could she let their former relationship influence her. She'd been betrayed by men in her life and she'd never forget that Daniel had been the first. Her index finger tapped against the window, punctuating the thought.

When the truck hit another pothole, her eyes opened and teeth rattled. She glanced through the mud droplets and instead of seeing the tree-lined edge of I-89, she saw the Pearsons' stainless steel silo. The curved ladder they decorated with red-and-white light strips every December flashed by in a blur. Why had Daniel taken this slower, back-road route?

The answer came to her in waves of nostalgia.

A weakness.

He was testing her. Seeing if she missed the place. Felt sentimental. Hah. Tyler was the only one to whom she'd entrust her feelings again.

"I know what you're doing and I don't appreciate it." She crossed her ankles against the dusty floor mat and tried to blot out the memory of visiting the Pearsons' enormous lit candy cane; it had been a Christmas season tradition.

Daniel shot her a sideways glance, then said, "If you look over there, Tyler, you'll see Field Stone Farm."

Tyler continued pulling Ollie's tail, the hand stitches she'd used to reattach it last week nearly pulling free.

"I beat your mother at a stone-carrying challenge there. Hope she's still not holding that against me since I shared the prize with her— one of Mrs. Willette's raspberry cobblers." Daniel's vivid eyes sparkled when they met hers, the green-and-yellow kaleidoscope of color drawing her in until she shook her head and looked away.

"I hardly remember those times, so there's no grudge." Jodi shifted uncomfortably as she recalled too much.

Tyler jerked when Daniel ruffled his hair.

"Guess that means your mother's become the forgiving type."

"I've moved on and so should you," she muttered as she pulled out her smartphone and read an email from her boss to call him. "And would you please go a bit faster. I have to—"

"The speed limit here is thirty-five. Besides—" Daniel shrugged his broad shoulders "—I'm showing Tyler where he comes from. If you have your way, he'll never have this chance again."

Jodi tamped down her sudden spike of anger. "He's from Chicago, not Cedar Bay." She passed Tyler a Fruit Roll-Up snack, then sighed when her son flung it away. He really was hungry.

"There've been Chapmans here for over three hundred years."

"His last name is Mitchem. I changed my name back after the divorce."

Daniel shot her a speculative glance then continued. "Your last name might be different, Tyler, but you're still part of a large family that goes back generations." Daniel drummed along with the Eagles tune "Take It Easy," which was ironic. She noted his empty ring finger as it beat against the wheel, then chided herself for looking. What difference did his marital status make?

When the song ended, he pulled a bag of raspberries out of a dashboard pocket and passed it to Tyler. *No!* She lunged, too late, as Tyler squealed when he crushed them, the crimson color bleeding through his tiny fingers. Jodi's shoulders slumped and she reached for a Handi Wipe. What a sticky mess.

"May I have one?" Daniel held out a large hand in front of Tyler. Her heart squeezed when her son struggled, then plucked a berry from the bag. He would have won a gold star for that in physical therapy.

"Thank you, Ty." Daniel's white teeth flashed against the tanned skin of his face and her breath caught when his crescent moon dimples appeared. She forced her attention away and dabbed at the sticky berry juice dribbling down her son's face. "Careful, you'll choke," she warned as Tyler shoved in another handful.

Her son stopped chewing, but didn't look up. For Tyler, that was the most attention anyone could expect when he got fixed on something he really liked.

"Glad you're enjoying the treat, Tyler," Daniel said before continuing the kind of chatter that charmed everyone. "I had to ask my neighbor Mrs. Tate for some since the birds had eaten all of mine. You remember going berry picking on Blueberry Hill, Jodi Lynn, right?"

Their eyes caught and held over her son's head, a memory of their first kiss, berry flavored and full of sunshine, bursting in her brain. She stared at his mouth and turned away when it curved into a knowing grin. Her teeth ground together. He was trying to get under her skin and she'd be darned if she let him.

"Did Grace tell you that she got elected state regent of the Daughters of the American Revolution?"

"Yes. She told me. In fact, she keeps me up-to-date on all of the local news." Jodi crossed her fingers at the white lie. But she didn't want Daniel to think she had a special reason to avoid hearing about her hometown. Like a broken heart that had never fully healed....

"Is keeping tabs on your acquisitions part of your job description?" His dark lashes cast shadows over his eyes, but she detected sarcasm in his voice.

"Half of all New England farmers hold full-time jobs off the farm, then return home to farm," Jodi quoted from a survey she'd read recently. "The rest are full-time farmers. Their work extends year-round. Two-thirds of the farmers are fifty years of age or older. One-third are sixty years of age or older. Only a few farmers receive help from their adult children, and most farmers have difficulty finding farm labor, so many farms are kept to a size that the family can manage alone." She rolled down her window and let the warm, early-summer air flow over her. "Looks like the berries aren't the only thing ripe for the picking."

Daniel whistled long and low, making Tyler cup his hands over his ears. "So you think Cedar Bay's in a crisis."

Jodi tugged Tyler's hands away and danced Ollie across his lap. "Fortunately, I'm here to help so that no one becomes a charity case."

From the corner of her eye, she saw him wince.

"I never called you that," he said quietly.

"But you believed it."

Jodi remembered overhearing him agree with teenage friends who'd called her a charity case. He'd been unable to deny those feelings when she'd confronted him. Although it'd happened the summer she'd worked on Daniel's farm to pay for her father's medical bills, the memory still burned bright. She'd been falling for Daniel and hadn't seen the truth, had trusted him when he'd suggested keeping their relationship quiet until things settled down with her family. Her father's emotional distress and slow recovery meant her mother's every waking moment was spent caring for him. They didn't need any extra distractions or worries.

But when Daniel had admitted that he pitied her, she'd realized the horrible truth.

He'd only dated her because he felt sorry for her—a fact he hadn't denied when she'd accused him.

So when her parents had moved to Arizona, she'd left a week early for college without warning him. What could she have said that wouldn't have caused more hurt? Their original plan had been to maintain their relationship and see each other during college breaks. Instead, she'd vowed to never return home again. Until now... She'd reacted impulsively, she realized, looking back. But there was no sense in wishing for a chance to make things right. Especially not with both of them on opposite sides of this battle.

Besides, those were the feelings of an adolescent girl crushed by her failed first love. Not the woman she was today. Not even close.

"You said this wasn't personal." The timbre of his voice deepened.

She shrugged tense shoulders. "It's not." Not in the way he meant anyway. This was for Tyler, not revenge on an ex-boyfriend.

"Then it's for the bonus."

"That's none of your business." Heat flared along her upper chest and crept up her neck. She needed that payment for Tyler.

"Fine. You win." He sent her a sideways glance. "This time."

She unclenched her hands when Daniel clicked off his windshield wipers. The rain ceased its steady drum and sunshine splashed down where clouds broke apart and moved off, revealing patches of blue. She squinted out the window and breathed deeply. She had nothing to feel guilty about.

Until they rounded a corner.

"And this is where your mother used to live growing up."

Tyler kept eating and Jodi averted her eyes. She didn't want to see the scene of her father's accident.

"The next side road's a shortcut to Aunt Grace's house," she said through shaking lips. "Could we take that, please?"

"But you'll miss seeing Deep Meadows Farm. Remember the daisy chains we used to make?"

"Take us home, Daniel," she ordered, voice thick. She clasped her trembling hands in her lap, recalling the dash to the hospital ten years ago, and her remorse for not being there to help with the skid loader borrowed from Daniel's father.

"But, Jodi Lynn, you are home." Daniel's insistent tone softened.

"Home is Chicago." Jodi said it to remind herself as much as Daniel. "I meant to my aunt Grace's house. The tour's over."

Her voice was harsher than she intended and Tyler flapped his hands. He rocked forward in his seat and made a keening sound that pierced her heart.

"Tyler, I'm sorry," she crooned, regret filling her. "We'll be home soon and you can take a nap." She wedged his stuffed animal beneath his seat belt. "Ollie's tired, too." She tried pressing on his shoulders the way the therapist had showed her to calm him, but couldn't get the right angle.

Daniel turned off the radio and flicked his blinker on at the side road.

"No," she protested when Tyler's protests escalated to full-out screams. "Some noise is good. Do you have anything classical?" A familiar weeping willow flashed by along with a clearing that contained two grazing dapple-grays. Good. Getting closer now.

"Just 102.9."

But when he tuned into the local channel, they were running through sports news, the announcer's high-pitched voice making Tyler's legs beat against the seat, his small hands covering his ears.

Familiar panic set in. The juice box she of-

fered Tyler wound up on the floor beside the
Fruit Roll-Up. The back of her neck grew damp
and her eyelid twitched.

She knew she shouldn't feel ashamed of
her difficulty in controlling Tyler's outbursts,
but she did. It felt as if a marquee sign appeared over her head flashing Bad Mother...
Bad Mother.... And the disapproving looks she
got in restaurants or checkout lines confirmed
the fact that, yes, she was being judged and
found wanting.

How would they have handled this at Wonders Primary? She pictured the brightly colored
toys and equipment in the well-lit, open space,
the smiling, patient therapists who played on
their knees with the children. There this tantrum might never have occurred.

This was exactly why she needed to succeed
and head home as soon as possible. She wasn't
what was best for Tyler. They were. And the
thought made her want to cry along with her
son.

A few minutes later, Aunt Grace's cedar-
shingled house appeared through a row of blue
spruce. Behind the tidy one-story, the deep
navy of Lake Champlain shimmered. Tyler let
out a piercing scream when they bounced to
a halt.

"It's okay, Tyler. We're here," she murmured

as her hands struggled with the child seat restraints across his stomach. Her fingers tingled when Daniel brushed them aside. In one snap, he freed her son, lifted him out of the truck and carried him to the front porch steps.

Jodi freed the car seat, grabbed it and her purse and followed until a familiar voice stopped her.

"Welcome home!"

She whirled and sagged into Aunt Grace's outstretched arms, her face buried in her familiar, lilac-scented shoulders. Or maybe the scent came from the purple, white and pink blossoms in the basket she carried. Either way, the smell made something inside her loosen.

"It's so good to see you." She stepped back at last and admired Aunt Grace's soft pink blouse and gray slacks.

"I've waited a long time for this, Jodi." Her aunt's brown eyes, set behind skin folds and creases, were still as piercing as ever. "Wish you'd come home under better circumstances."

"A visit with you is the best circumstance." And it was.

"I agree. If only your parents would come back from Arizona, too." Aunt Grace wrapped an arm around her and led her toward the garden beds surrounding her porch. "How are you, Daniel? Would you like to come inside for some tea?"

"I think Jodi's had enough of me, Grace, but thanks." His eyes lingered on Jodi's for a long minute before he headed back to the truck, his movements easy and athletic.

No sooner had he grabbed their suitcases than he dropped them again to lunge after a bolting Tyler. A tern, Tyler's target, squawked and flew from Aunt Grace's dock directly behind her small house.

Jodi clutched her chest, grabbing the locket containing Tyler's baby picture, her heart beating like the frantic bird's wings. If not for Daniel's lightning reflexes, Tyler might have ended up in the water, or worse, on the rocks that flashed just above the surface before the lake bed dropped off. She'd been so fixed on watching Daniel that she'd missed her son's dash. Her "Bad Mother" marquee flashed on again.

"Daniel, thank you," she said when he deposited Tyler in her arms. Her son kicked and protested until Grace offered him a cookie and led him inside.

Daniel's face creased. "No need to thank me. It's what neighbors do, Jodi. Help each other."

And just like that her gratitude dissolved into irritation. She pushed back the strands a lake breeze blew in her face.

"Neighbors in cities support one another, too. My neighbor has been taking care of Tyler until—"

Daniel's biceps flexed as he carried her suitcases and placed them at her feet. "Until…?"

Her hands curled. Why did she forget herself so often around him? "Until he starts day care." There. It was the truth without saying anything that would connect it to her real reason for being here. Daniel needed to see her as a strong opponent, not a mother who was struggling to provide for her child.

He stared intently at her, then passed her a small bag. "You'll be glad to go back soon. Even if it is empty-handed."

"I agree with half that statement." Daniel had charm and contacts, but she had the drive of needing something badly.

Daniel hopped up on his running board. "Guess we'll have to agree to disagree on that."

She raised an eyebrow. "It's not a matter of agreeing or disagreeing. We're not playing on the same team anymore."

"Have we ever?"

Their eyes locked for a breathless moment, both recalling when they had.

"This is different."

He studied her for a long minute, then waved before sliding inside. "I know."

As he began backing out of her aunt's driveway, his eyes on her, she heard him shout, "This is war!"

CHAPTER THREE

AND WAR IT was, regardless of the fact that Jodi had been on his mind nonstop during his afternoon chores, his ever-present retriever, Goldie, at his heels. He could fool himself. Think he was strategizing. But the truth was he kept picturing the smile she'd given him when he'd rescued Tyler. And the way her blue eyes had warmed to him—even for a short while.

He cranked off the engine on his feed blower, stepped out and pulled off his hat, letting the fans sweep his damp hair away from his forehead. Who was he kidding fantasizing about Jodi? Their short-lived relationship had left scars. She'd been right to accuse him of pitying her. He had felt bad about what'd happened to her family. It was the reason he'd put a stop to their rivalry and started being nice to her.

But when their truce had turned to romance, it'd been hard to separate those feelings. To know where one emotion ended and the other began. When she'd asked him if he'd dated her out of pity, he'd struggled to express himself clearly.

Looking back, he understood that he hadn't been mature enough to handle the situation. It'd been complicated, and she'd run off, quit, before he'd figured out how to explain without offending her or revealing his own family's secrets.

Her father's accident had left Daniel's family in a bad place financially. Replacing the skid loader her father had broken had pushed Daniel's cash-strapped family over the edge. That was the real reason he'd convinced her to keep their romance a secret—he didn't want to give his parents another excuse to argue. After all, she'd been the source of his family's strain. He rubbed the back of his tense neck. But that was a long time ago; they weren't teenagers anymore.

In fact, like Jodi, he'd moved on. He had dated other women, although none as seriously. He had too many things to focus on before settling down, his updated farm being one of them. He looked on with pride at the orderly rows of newly widened stalls. Brown jersey cows stuck out their heads and nipped at his homegrown organic silage, their lowing filling the barn. Besides sunrise, this was his favorite time of the day, when the last of his herd had exited the mechanized, circular milking parlor and returned to stalls heaped with sweet straw bedding, their eyes drooping from a long day at pasture, many on their knees already.

"All set there, Daniel?" A gawky young man waved at him from farther down the center aisle. His hired hand was a decent guy who mostly kept to himself. Hopefully, this one would last out a full year. Colton was one of the best workers he'd found in a while.

"Pretty much. I'm about to head up. Are you coming for supper?"

"Yeah, if you don't mind. I've got to set the timer on the mister and change out of these." He plucked at his tan coveralls.

"Sounds good. We'll hold the meal for you."

A striped barn cat wound its way through Daniel's legs and touched noses with a tail-wagging Goldie. Cat and dog. Natural enemies. Yet they'd found a way to get along. Would he and Jodi ever find that peace? He gritted his teeth. Only if she saw the light—like the mellow gold shafts striping the sawdust-covered floors. No business office could compete with this. It was majestic.

And Jodi shared that quality. It had made her his fiercest enemy growing up, and the subject of many boyhood dreams—one of which had briefly come true. He paused to look at a mound of hay in the same place as the one where they'd kissed ten years ago. It was a memory best forgotten, especially now that they were locked in this "winner take all" battle.

If she had her way, his jerseys wouldn't be brushed nightly, given hours of outdoor time or slipped a carrot when they looked a little off, because yes, despite having three hundred head, he knew them all that well. Had birthed them and named them himself. They were a family of sorts and he never could look at them as pure dollar signs.

He slopped milk into a trough left out for the cats. The orange tabby had already been joined by three calicoes, a gray short hair, a tailless Manx, and a rag-doll cat he couldn't resist picking up and letting flop across his forearm. He rubbed its belly fast before its claws came out, then put it down where it shoved its way into the growing crowd. He noticed a Persian hanging back. Huh. He'd never seen it before. Must have been another midnight drop-off from a regretful pet owner.

The skittish cat raced from him as he approached, but in minutes he had it cornered and in a pet carrier. He strode up the small knoll to his gray, plank-sided, two-story farmhouse where the smell of pot roast and onions made his stomach growl. For a moment he imagined what it'd be like to have Jodi there, waiting for him, but shook off the foolish thought. As soon as she left town, she'd disappear for another ten years, maybe forever.

Feeling hollow, he trudged up the back porch steps, which badly needed a coat of paint, and pulled open the screen door. He shrugged off his plaid overshirt and stepped inside the narrow hallway lined with framed pictures of his ancestors, their smiles absent, but their eyes content. He grinned at his grandfather's 1957 tractors calendar, glad they'd never had the heart to take it down.

"Sue!"

His sister appeared in the door frame, her glasses askew on her narrow nose, her short dark hair standing up in odd places.

"Tell me you didn't fall asleep and forget to turn off the oven."

Her hazel eyes widened and she tugged at the collar of a top she'd probably crocheted herself. "I'm sorry, Daniel. You know I'm useless in the kitchen."

He passed her the pet carrier. "Did you start the water on the potatoes?"

"Ten minutes ago." She peered into the plastic container. "Who's this rapscallion? Don't remember seeing it around."

He glanced up at the worn edge of the Scrabble box perched on the hall-closet shelf and whistled. Last weekend, their traditional Saturday night game had ended after three hours and a few words that weren't allowed on the board.

"Nice word. A fifteen pointer. As for this guy, he looks like another drop-off. Thought you might bring him to the vet tomorrow. Get him checked out, shots, neutered...you know."

His sister heaved a sigh and poked a finger in the cage to stroke the cowering feline's nose. "Oh, I know. We're practically an animal dumping ground."

"It's not just us, Sue." He sniffed and calculated. He'd put the beef in the roaster when he got back from picking up Jodi, so it was probably burned on the bottom. And the potatoes he'd peeled would still be as hard as rocks. Another typical Gleason meal. "I'm going up to shower but I'll be down in ten to help finish."

His sister gave him a small salute and took the pet container. "Will do, Cap-i-tan." It was their inside joke from the days he'd earned enough badges to move on from Eagle to Life scout. "Oh, and is, uh...Colton joining us?" The toe of her flip-flop circled the rag rug in front of her.

"Yes." He kept his face neutral at her less-than-subtle crush on his employee and raced upstairs. After a quick shower he was back in the warm kitchen. He kissed his sister on the cheek as she stood by the stove, wearing his mother's old green-checked apron. Steam rose from the potatoes she whipped and turned her face a bright hue—that and a lounging Colton sipping coffee at the table.

"Smells good, sis. Hey, Colton."

The farmhand looked up from the sports section, his work coveralls replaced with a T-shirt and jeans. "Looks like the Hawks won again. They're moving on to the state finals. Sure wish I could go." When he took off his Hawks cap and studied the emblem, his light brown hair lay flat against his skull and curled beneath his ears.

"When is it?" Daniel asked.

"Next Thursday. But I can't bike to Rutland and back. The game starts at three."

A spoon clattered to their red-tiled floor. "I could drive you." Sue spoke without looking up as she grabbed the utensil. "I mean. You could use my car. Or I could come and you could drive, or—"

Time to leave before his sister's nervous flirting made him chuckle out loud. He headed for the double parlor at the front of the house.

"Hi, Pop." Daniel stopped and let his eyes adjust to the sight of his frail, trembling father seated in a rocking chair, an afghan of Sue's design across his lap. It was hard to reconcile the image with what he remembered— his hearty father overflowing the chair, two kids and a dog on his lap, his mother laughing at all of them.

But that was a lifetime ago. Or at least it felt like it.

"Supper's ready. Susie made a roast."

His father lifted his chin and sniffed. "Smells like she burned it again."

Daniel unfolded the walker in front of Pop's chair and helped him to his feet. "We'll cut off that end."

His dad laughed, a faint sound that ended with a coughing fit. "We always do," he wheezed out.

Step by step they made it to the kitchen.

"Smells good, darlin'." His father lifted a shaking hand to Colton and lowered himself into the chair Daniel held out.

"Thanks, Pop. I think everything's on. Who wants to say grace?"

"Good potatoes. Good meat. Good God, let's eat."

Everyone laughed at Colton and started passing the heaped dishes of mashed potatoes, sliced pot roast, bread, sweet pickles and boiled turnip—or microwaved, Daniel supposed, given Sue's last-minute rush. Even so, it all looked great.

"So I ordered that wind turbine today, Pop." Daniel scooped some potato onto his father's plate, waited for a nod then piled on more. "Between that and the solar panels, we should be set for power this winter."

His father nodded. "It's a good thing to be independent. Never regretted a dime on educating you and your sister. Though I wished you'd done something else with your life." He looked away, as he always did, when Sue reached over to cut his meat.

"I saved the farm from bankruptcy. That's doing something." Daniel kept the heat out of his voice, despite his words. Pop meant well and wished his worsening Parkinson's hadn't forced Daniel to take over the farm after college. Daniel would have chosen to return anyway. It'd just happened sooner than he'd planned.

"Bud Layhee stopped by today," Pop continued, scooping some potato with a shaking hand. "Says his son Ted can't keep the farm going with milk prices where they're at. They're borrowing thirty thousand dollars a month and he might have to sell out and put Bud in a nursing home."

His father's fearful tone made Daniel's fingers tighten on his fork. Wouldn't Jodi pounce on that news? "That's not going to happen, Pop."

Not on his watch. He'd known the weather was making more than a few farmers skittish. If Jodi got hold of some of the financially weaker ones, they might give into the pressure and sell out. Things were worse than he'd thought if a tough, retired old farmer like Bud would share that kind of news. Daniel needed to put his co-op plans in motion faster than he'd intended and send Jodi on her way before she did more damage than the relentless rain.

"Colton, would you like more roast?" Sue smiled warmly and passed more beef over Daniel's empty plate.

"So are you still going to Princeton?" Colton spoke through a mouthful of beef, then took a long drink of foamy milk, his Adam's apple bobbing.

Sue twisted her cloth napkin.

"No."

"Yes."

She and Daniel spoke at the same time and looked at each other. "Sue. You're staying at Princeton until you finish your Ph.D." He kept his voice low and eyed his father's bent head. As far as his father knew, Sue was on break.

"You stopped at an MBA," she hissed for

his ears only. "So why the grief? I'm already a certified psychologist." She spooned more turnip on Colton's plate.

"Because you're not a quitter."

"Mom was."

A hush came over the table as all eyes fell on Pop. Luckily he was tinkering with his hearing aid and seemed to have missed the painful reminder.

"Sue. Stop." Daniel forked a piece of beef and ladled more vegetables on top of a slice of bread.

"Oh, sure. Let's not talk about the fact that she walked out on all of us. Couldn't take farming. Hah. Couldn't take us!"

"Enough, Sue." Daniel's glass banged on the table as he recalled the painful summer he'd lost his mother and Jodi. When his father looked up, Daniel smiled for his confused-looking dad's benefit. "Got the fly! Hey. What's for dessert?"

"Strawberries and pound cake." Sue crossed her arms and leaned back in her chair, her eyes on Daniel. "Heard Jodi Chapman's in town."

"Jodi Chapman?" His father sat up straighter, his eyes sparkling. "No one said she was home. Now, that's a sweet girl. Remember how hard she worked in the barns after her father's accident? A spirited little thing. Is she visiting soon?"

His pulse sped. "Not a chance, Pop."

Sue sent him a warning look.

"I mean, I don't think so."

"Well, you'll have to invite her. I know she'd want to see me." His father pointed his turnip-laden fork at himself, then lifted it to his mouth and got his cheek instead. Sue reached over to wipe him but he brushed her aside and did it himself.

Daniel held back a groan. He'd bet Jodi would love to visit his father. Him and all the other farmers around town. And they'd welcome her, their reactions just like Pop's. His unease amped up another notch. He'd better nix whatever she planned pronto. If good guys like Bud Layhee could be turned out of their family's homes, then this wasn't just about a way of life anymore. It was about lives. Period.

"Will she be at your class reunion Friday night?" Sue asked.

"It's your tenth, right? Wow, that's old." A confused look crossed Colton's face at Sue's sudden frown. She was four years older than the oblivious object of her affection.

"I'm guessing she won't miss the chance to talk to some of the farmers attending. She'll probably be there." Daniel drained the last of his milk and wiped his mouth. "But not for long."

THREE DAYS LATER, Jodi stood on her aunt's back porch and hugged a quilt around her shoulders. The chill air was fresh with dewy promise and filled with birdcalls. It'd finally stopped raining and the rising sun changed Lake Champlain's rippling surface from onyx to periwinkle, and then a deep navy studded with white caps that glittered in the growing light. She sighed and wrapped the blanket tighter. It really was beautiful here. She eyed the lake again. As long as you only looked at the surface.

A door squeaked open and Aunt Grace joined her at the railing. "So did you miss your hometown?" She passed Jodi a cup of tea.

"No," Jodi answered honestly. And she hadn't. Since she'd left for college, she'd used the mental equivalent of a Magic Eraser and wiped her past clean. Yet somehow, Daniel had stayed with her. Her mouth quirked. Even his memory was stubborn.

Aunt Grace's wire-rimmed glasses fogged when she sipped her tea. One of her curlers dangled over her ear. "Well. I'm glad you're here, even if I wish you had a different reason."

She sighed. "Aunt Grace, you know it's

the only way I can get the money for Tyler's school."

"We've got perfectly good schools here."

Her hand covered her aunt's and squeezed. "Not the kind that Tyler needs." Her aunt meant well, but she was Tyler's mother and knew best.

"I like this," Jodi added after tasting the minty tea. "Peppermint Harvest?"

"Green Moroccan. Trader Mike's is carrying it now."

"Since when did Cedar Bay go international?" She couldn't resist teasing her aunt, although the inclusion of foreign products at the local mom-and-pop store did surprise her. Yankees weren't fond of change. Just look at Daniel. As the class valedictorian with a full ride to Cornell, he could have studied anything. Been anything. And what had he done? Gotten an MBA in agricultural economics and run right back to his farm. She took another sip of tea. Why did her thoughts so often turn to him?

Her aunt gave her shoulders a squeeze. "Stick around, honey. There's a lot that's changed. Not just you."

She rested her head on her aunt's shoulder. "And how have I changed?" It was clear that she had, but she wondered how people back home saw her. More confident. Self-assured. No longer an object of pity? And had Daniel noticed? Not that it should matter...but somehow it did.

A hand stroked the crown of her head. "Oh, honey. In lots of ways you're still the sweet, generous girl you always were, but now there's something a little—I don't know—hard about you. And please don't take that the wrong way."

She pulled back, stung. "*Hard* as in strong or *hard* as in mean?" The former she'd be happy with but the latter...

Aunt Grace's eye folds looked puffier than usual and she pulled a crumpled tissue out of the robe's sleeve and blew her nose before answering.

"I don't know, sweetie. It's like Chicago put a coat of varnish on you that I wish I could strip away. Uncover your natural self."

Jodi shook her head. Considering her aunt supplemented her deceased husband's retirement by refinishing antique furniture, it wasn't a bad analogy. It just didn't apply to her.

She spread her arms. "Aunt Grace, this is the real me. I was never myself here."

"It sure looked like you were enjoying those 4-H picnics, and no one's beat your record for bobbing apples. Not even Jimmy Terry. With his teeth, we all thought he'd best you for sure."

The competitor in her felt a flash of satisfaction, and then she remembered they were talking apples, whereas she'd closed multimillion-dollar deals. She'd definitely changed, and for the better. No matter what her aunt might be suggesting.

Aunt Grace lifted her tea mug while Jodi stared out at the red rowboat floating beside the dock. She remembered the gentle slide of the boat through Lake Champlain's water and yearned for such a peaceful moment. How long since she'd done something just for herself?

"Do you still take it out?"

"When the arthritis isn't acting up. Why don't you go for a paddle? Take Tyler. You haven't let him out of the house yet and everyone's asking about him…and you."

She glanced at the silent monitor perched on the porch railing. "He's got allergies like you. Maybe when he's better." She gulped more of the minty brew and refused to imagine why she felt reluctant for the community to meet her son.

"Well, you should get out at least. You've been working all kinds of hours since you got here. Mailing out letters. Setting up meetings. Talking on your phone steady. I feel like we've hardly had time for a good visit. And I don't think you've had a bit of fun."

"I'm not here to have fun. The sooner I get

this deal wrapped up, the sooner I can get Tyler home. The country isn't good for him."

"It isn't good for him, or it isn't good for you?" Aunt Grace's eyes peered into hers, missing nothing.

Jodi glanced at the lake when a trill drifted in the morning air, the melancholy sound echoing her mood. A pair of loons swam past the dock, a small V rippling behind them. They were one of the bird species that mated for life. She'd once expected the same for her and Peter.

As if reading her thoughts, her aunt asked, "How's Peter?"

"Suing to lower child support, actually." The words poured out of her, unbidden. Why had she burdened her aunt with that?

Aunt Grace's eyes sparked. "I don't mind telling you, Jodi, I never liked the guy. How he wouldn't accept Tyler's autism diagnosis and acted ashamed of his own son. You both worked the same hours, but he didn't lift a finger at home with Tyler's treatment. It wasn't right."

Jodi sighed, remembering how hard she'd tried—but it'd never been enough, especially when she'd "spoiled" Tyler, according to Peter, with the extra attention required by his therapy plan and "wasted" her time in autism chat rooms and doing research.

"So he's not going to help you pay for day care, then?"

She shook her head. "He won't admit Tyler has autism."

"Or visit him, either. And now he won't even support his son. The man is despicable."

Jodi agreed, though she wouldn't voice her complaints. She shouldn't have brought up the subject in the first place. He was still Tyler's father.

"Tyler's my priority now. There isn't room to think about anything else."

"Or anyone else." Her aunt gently turned her by the shoulders so that they faced each other in the brightening light. "Listen, Jodi. Take it from me. Life is short, and while I understand that Tyler's important, you're important to me. Since Charlie and I couldn't have any of our own, we've always thought of you as our kid, too." Her tissue reappeared and she dabbed at her eyes. "I only want the best for you."

Jodi caught her in a tight hug, tears pricking the backs of her eyes. It'd been a long time since she'd thought about herself, and it felt good to know her aunt cared. Since her mother had her hands full helping Jodi's father with the post-traumatic stress disorder he'd developed after the accident, Jodi hadn't burdened her mother with her problems. Their phone calls usually focused on lighter issues.

"Once I get Tyler settled and talking again, I promise I'll get out more."

But even as she said the words, she knew she never would. Her ex had accused her of caring more about her son than him, and maybe he'd had a point. When a child needed love and attention as much as Tyler, she couldn't make room for anyone else in her life or her heart.

Aunt Grace smiled. "There's my girl. And you can start tonight with your class reunion."

She blinked. "My what?"

"Your ten-year class reunion. Didn't you see your invite on the fridge? At least I think that's where I put it. Anyway, it came here since they didn't know your Chicago address. I was going to forward it until I heard you were coming."

"Oh. I don't know. I think I should stay home with Tyler."

"I can watch him, and it'd be a great way to get out like you promised." Her aunt rubbed Jodi's arm. "See your old friends, maybe make some of the connections you're fussing over for Midland."

Her pulse sped at the thought of facing those who had called her a charity case and others who'd thought it. But those were adolescent insecurities, not the fears of a mature woman.

She needed them to see her as a successful professional, someone they could trust and depend on to equitably handle the sale of their farms to Midland. Hopefully those old impressions hadn't lingered.

Aunt Grace had a point. It would push her Midland plans along faster than waiting for next week's town council meeting. Plus, she'd just been authorized to increase the offering price to a number they'd be crazy to refuse. But how to face all of them? See Daniel again?

A low snuffling cry crackled across the monitor. Tyler.

"I'd better go check on him." Jodi took her aunt's mug. "I'll leave these in the sink. Oh, and, Aunt Grace?"

"Yes, honey?"

"If it's not too much bother, would you mind looking for a copy of my old yearbook? I think I might have left it here."

"Of course, sweetheart. I just want you to be happy."

Tyler's cry turned into a full-out wail and she hurried to the door. "Me, too, Aunt Grace. Me, too."

CHAPTER FOUR

"GOOD TO SEE you, Melissa. How's Rex doing? Any better?" Daniel ladled punch into a plastic cup as a DJ blasted another 90s hit. His ex-classmates filled the veterans' hall with their excited chatter, scented candles on cloth-covered tables filling the muggy air with an evergreen aroma.

He peered around the tall woman and glanced at the empty doorway. When would Jodi arrive? Was she coming? He'd bet any money she wouldn't miss this opportunity to talk up her company. And he'd do everything to stop her. After hearing about Bud Layhee, he was more resolved than ever.

"Turns out Rex picked up a tick, so we've got to treat him for Lyme disease," the woman said, and moved aside to grab a napkin.

Daniel murmured something sympathetic, he was sure he did, but his attention was captured by the stunning blonde framed in the doorway. Wow. In a pink dress that showed off flawless skin and curves, she was more beautiful than he'd ever seen her.

An artificial rose pulled back her curls on one side, the gold strands gleaming under the soft twinkle lights strewn around the long, rectangular hall.

He tossed back a cup of punch, handed over the ladle and strode toward her. Looking that way, she wouldn't make it two steps inside without admirers surrounding her. He needed to head them off before she got her Midland hooks into them. He could speak from experience; farmer bachelors were a lonely crew. A beauty like Jodi was fresh milk to a barn cat. A hungry one at that.

He arrived just in time to hear her exclaim, "You're still pregnant?" to a nearly full-term Pamela Bates.

The glowing woman's complexion paled. "That was my first pregnancy—in high school. This is my fifth."

Jodi leaned in and murmured, "Then I suppose money must be tight on the farm?"

He shook his head at the frowning blonde as Pamela stomped away. "You're unscrupulous."

"And you're vexatious. Go away." She craned her neck to look over his shoulder, but he moved closer and blocked her view. At this distance, he could smell her perfume—something floral, but not anything that grew around here. It flooded his senses.

"Having fun?" He forced a light tone to cover the effect her proximity had on him. It was the best he could manage when her skirt brushed against his pant leg as she twisted for a better view of the crowd.

"Daniel. I've got work to do. Would you mind?"

He sidestepped with her when she made to walk around him. "Don't mind at all. In fact, I'll help." Keep your enemies close, he thought.

Jodi snorted. "Thanks, but I can manage on my own. What?"

"What?" Daniel blinked down at her.

"You're staring. Knock it off." With her hands on her softly curved hips, her blue eyes flashing, she was irresistible.

And right. He couldn't take his eyes off her. A song from their senior prom played, something acoustic and slow. He took her hand, loving the delicate feel of her fingers, the silk of her palm in his. She was a siren. Why was he answering her call?

"Dance with me and then I'll leave you alone."

"Hah," she scoffed, and yanked her hand

away. "I didn't come here to dance, Daniel." She pulled a yellow sticky note from the tiny purse that matched her dress and seemed to mouth the names written on it.

His eyes flew from the paper to Ted Layhee, one of the names she'd written down. *Oh, heck no.* The guy would be the first to sign up. He'd about said as much to his father, Bud.

"Let's get you some punch, then." He put a firm hand on her back and steered her through the crowd toward the drinks table. He could feel her toned back through the silky fabric of her dress and strove not to run his fingers up over her shoulder and bury them in that thick tangle of hair.

"Whatever game you're playing, Daniel, it's not going to work." She took the punch and stared at the dancing, chattering throng over the rim of her cup. He followed her gaze and watched the former head cheerleader trying to rally her old squad into doing the Macarena, his old football buddies laughing and fist-pounding each other.

"Hey. I come in peace." He forced his hand away and spread his arms wide. His eyes drank in the gentle cast of her features that glowed pink then orange in the revolving strobe light, her generous upper lip that begged to be nibbled on, her short, straight nose and her large, wide-spaced eyes.

"Said the big bad wolf." She laughed, the throaty sound of it setting off alarm bells inside him. He knew he needed to leave her for his own sanity, but she'd only cause trouble on her own. Especially if she talked to Layhee.

"Evening, Daniel." He tensed at the voice. Ted. "And if my eyes aren't lying, this is Jodi Chapman. How are you, darlin'? You're breaking my heart in that dress."

"Oh." She squinted at him for a moment, and then asked, "Ted?"

"That's right! Knew you'd remember me from science class."

"It was social." Jodi's eyes met Daniel's over Ted's shoulder and her mouth hitched up at the corners.

"Whatever." Ted shrugged. "It was all the same to me. Hey, listen. I heard you were buying farms and wanted to talk."

"Perfect." She arched a triumphant brow at Daniel, Ted's hand at her waist as he guided her away.

Daniel's pulse picked up and he tugged at his tie. *Not so fast, Ms. Jodi Lynn.*

"Ted, isn't your pickup the red 150 with the flame decal on the sides?" he called after them.

Ted turned. "Because its lights are on. Meant to mention it earlier."

"Darn. Had to give the batteries a jump just to get here." Ted hurried off and Daniel unfurled his hands.

Jodi tapped her fingers on her hips and glared at him, her nose scrunching in a way that got his heart thudding.

"Was that the 'help' you mentioned earlier? Scaring off every person I talk to?" Jodi pulled her note out and scanned the list of names, her eyes lifting from it to the crowd and back again.

"I think you did a good job of that on your own with Pamela Bates. Plus, you should be glad I rescued you from Hands." It had been Ted's nickname in high school—earned for a reputation Jodi should keep in mind. "And who else is on that list?"

She turned her back, but he peered over her shoulder, the brush of her hair soft as satin against his jaw. He forced himself to focus and noticed a number written at the bottom of the list. That couldn't be the price she was offering per acre.

He swallowed hard. With a number that high, who'd say no? This was worse than he'd imagined. Midland had put the best person on the job and armed her with an irresistible deal. He had to stop her. Now.

"Care to dance?" asked one of their classmates, a part-time crop duster and farmer, Frank Trudeau. Jodi smiled and Daniel recalled seeing Frank's name on her list.

"Actually, I'd rather talk if you have a minute...Frank."

Frank, one of his bowling team members, caught the small shake of Daniel's head and took the hint.

"Uh, that's okay. I was just looking for a dance."

"Oh." Jodi's mouth turned down in disappointment. "Maybe another time."

"How about a dance with me?" Ted reappeared, out of breath. "Came back as quick as I could before another fellow got you. Oh, and it turns out you had the wrong truck, Gleason."

Jodi extended her hand. "I suppose this is the only way I'll get to speak with anyone."

Daniel paced as he watched her smiling and talking a mile a minute. Ted's eyes looking unfocused; his hands drifted lower and lower until Daniel couldn't take it anymore.

"Time's up, Ted. She's dancing the next one with me," he grumbled when he reached them.

He forced his face to relax when Ted immediately gave way.

"Of course, Daniel. If I'd known…"

"We have a conversation to continue, Ted. Remember? My offer?" Jodi asked, insistent.

But Daniel held Ted's eye until he shuffled away.

"Later, Jodi," Ted muttered.

"Phone me at my aunt Grace's," she called, her business card disappearing back into her purse. Her eyes leveled on Daniel. "There's no reason to behave unprofessionally. And, despite what you said when you dropped us off, this is not a war. It's business. Big difference."

He looked down at her and shook his head, unable to resist tucking a strand behind her ear. "Keep telling yourself that."

When the music switched up to something low and smooth, he pulled her in close, every inch of him aware of the feminine beauty he held in his arms.

"Regardless, he said he planned to sell and knew other farmers that would hear me out. Oh. And he liked my offer. See? Not personal."

His body tensed as he looked around at the many people who had traveled less than a few miles to be here and at all of their community events. This was their hometown. Who'd be left if Jodi had her way? Pamela Bates?

Frank Trudeau? He'd grown up with them. Had imagined them all farming and growing old together. Yet with one check, Jodi would destroy that future. Old men who'd fought to preserve their legacies for the next generation would finish their lives in nursing home corridors instead of on their farms' front porches. It wasn't right.

"Look around you." He gestured at their classmates. "These are people, Jodi, so it's personal. How can I get that through to you?"

"You can't. This is a business transaction. Plain and simple."

A spotlight stopped on them, blinding him before he could insist that it was the end of a way of life. He'd thought the old Jodi might still be reachable, but now he knew the truth. Another Midland suit stood before him. The only difference? She resembled someone he used to know.

"And now it's time for a speech from our valedictorian," boomed Frank. "Daniel Gleason."

Raucous applause exploded around him and he reluctantly let go of Jodi's hand and took his place on stage. When he looked out at the smiling, cheering audience, the group that had voted him class president, he knew what he had to do. With old men about to get turned out of their farms, and Jodi's offer too good to turn down, desperate times called for desperate measures. Her refusal to consider others meant he'd run out of options.

He held up his hands until they hushed, and raised the microphone.

"Folks. Looking out at all of you, I see family, friends...Layhee." He paused for the ripple of laughter to die down and Ted's attention-getting protests to end. "I see a community of people I've known all my life, whose parents grew up together and their parents before them."

Lots of smiles and nods erupted around the room as well as a few cups of punch raised his way.

Daniel yanked at his tie. It was hot under these bright lights, especially with Jodi's narrowed eyes fixed on him. He gave her a look that he hoped expressed his silent apology for what he was about to do.

"Farming and family-run businesses have been a way of life in Cedar Bay since our ancestors struggled, sacrificed, fought and died to make the independence we enjoy today possible."

"Hear! Hear!" someone hollered in the back. Bobby, another one of his bowling pals.

"Our teachers gave us extra time to turn

in work during harvest or when we had to get the fields ready in the spring, but they understood—like the rest of our community—that we're in this together, helping one another. We're here for each other, whether it's taking over someone's milking to give another a vacation, bringing meals every day if someone's ill, joining forces to repair and rebuild when tragedy strikes." He avoided Jodi's eyes. If he met them, he knew he wouldn't have the heart to go on.

"And that doesn't even take into account the good times like our potluck dinners overseen by Grace Chapman, Mary's line dancing, hay-bale mazes at the Darbys', the Winches' sleigh rides, our tractor races and watermelon-eating contests and all the other things that go into making our daily challenges worth it."

"I'm ready to line dance right now!" roared Ted, whose wandering hand moved toward Jodi before she shook it off. She was pale under the lights, her stare unwavering.

"We'll get there, Ted." Daniel shifted in his tight dress shoes. "I wanted to bring this up because this is the first time we've all been together since we accepted our diplomas and faced a future that, for many of us, was already a given. We knew we'd take the torch our farming families passed us and keep it safe."

"We love you, Daniel!" shouted a female voice. By the set of Jodi's face, it wasn't hers.

"We've done a good job so far, weathering one of the worst economic times and coming through intact. Yet some would like to take advantage of the cracks in our foundation. Midland Corp, for instance."

Several boos erupted in the audience and he saw Jodi flinch. He had to swallow over the lump clogging his throat and force himself to keep going.

"We've resisted their attempts to steal our livelihoods from us—our communities, our traditions, all that we have to pass down to our own kids. Yet they've devised an even more sinister plan than I could have imagined."

He had the room's full attention now. Many leaned in or stepped forward. You could have heard a pin drop.

"They've sent one of our own against us. Jodi Lynn Chapman." He gestured toward her and while everyone turned to stare, no one clapped or smiled. In fact, many who had been cordial before now looked hostile. Guess word hadn't reached everyone about her real purpose for coming home until now.

Jodi's face turned bright enough to look sunburned.

"Let's show her the door. That's all the welcome she's getting if she's with Midland instead of us," yelled someone from a shadowed corner.

Murmurs of agreement rippled through the crowd, their angry babble rising until it drowned out his attempts to quiet them. He had more to say, but they weren't listening. In fact, they'd turned their backs on him and were closing in on Jodi. Her face contorted and she pressed a napkin to it before pushing through the crowd and out the door, her rose hair clip loose and flopping on her shoulders.

He turned away from the microphone and muttered a word not for public hearing. After hopping off the stage, he shoved through the crowed in pursuit of her.

"Great speech, big guy." One of his friends slapped him on the back.

Daniel nodded to the well-wishers who swarmed him, angry at himself for stirring this already boiling pot. Jodi's motivations were wrong, and the sooner she realized it the better, but he'd underestimated the crowd and he owed her an apology. He'd wanted to get through to her, not drive her to her breaking point. The thought filled him with regret.

"Jodi!" He cupped his hands around his mouth and belted her name across the parking lot before she slipped inside her car.

"Leave me alone, Daniel." Her keys fell from her shaking hands. "You've done enough." She crouched down to search but ended up putting her fingers over her eyes, her shoulders quaking.

In a flash he was by her side, scooping up her keys and the flowered hair clip that'd fallen before pulling her upright. Her damp hair clung to her temples when he pushed it away from her face, and his hands cupped her cheeks, his thumbs brushing away the moisture gathered in the corners of her eyes.

"I'm sorry, Jodi. I didn't mean for it to turn that ugly."

"Didn't you?"

His stomach clenched. Hadn't he? Yes. In a way. But he'd never imagined the aftermath would affect him this much. He had her on the ropes, but he felt as if he was the one down on the mat. Yet it'd always been that way between them. Each swinging until they couldn't raise an arm, the wounds they inflicted staying long after the contest was over. His chest constricted when he recalled their squabbles over the years, from who'd win the blue ribbon for best pumpkin at the county fair to who'd win class president.

Even their temporary truce, called when they'd given in to their feelings, had ended badly. She'd disappeared from his life for ten years. And now she looked ready to quit again. It was what he wanted. So why, then, did he suddenly wish she'd stay?

He pressed his forehead to hers, but she jerked away. "Please believe me. I'm not out to get you. I meant it when I said this isn't business, it's personal. I'm fighting for my life. Mine and others'."

Suddenly her face regained its composure. If anything, she looked stronger and more beautiful than ever. She took his breath away.

"So am I, Daniel," she said after a long moment. "So am I."

He started to ask her what she meant, whose life she fought for, but she held up a finger and the words dissolved on his tongue.

"You're right. It isn't just business. It's personal. Like you said, this is war, and I'm in it for the long haul."

And with that she grabbed her keys, unlocked her car and roared into the night, leaving him with thoughts and emotions as scrambled as the dust cloud she left behind.

Despite his turmoil, however, he grinned. The old Jodi was back. She drove him crazy, but he'd rather have a clean, honest fight with the firecracker he remembered than mince words with one of those polished suits he'd feared she'd become.

He stared down at the rose she'd left behind, then tossed it skyward. When it returned, he snatched it out of the air and tucked it into his pocket.

"Now, that's my girl."

CHAPTER FIVE

A DUCK CALL woke Jodi the next morning, her uneasy sleep clinging to her like the muggy air. She peered at the sunlight filtering in around the edges of the opaque window shade, then at her alarm clock.

It was 10:00 a.m.

She bolted upright, her quilted coverlet pooling in her lap. How could she have slept so late? Usually Tyler's monitor sounded by six. But when she glanced at it, the light was off, the battery dead. She lunged to her feet and stumbled down the narrow hall lined with pictures of her father and Grace as kids and Grace's wedding photo.

"Aunt Grace? Tyler?"

Her heart pounded as she peeked into Tyler's room, then her aunt's. Last night at the reunion, she'd broken down and admitted to Daniel that her fight wasn't business. What he didn't know was that her personal reason for returning to Cedar Bay was Tyler. Yet how noble was her fight to help her son if she couldn't keep track of him?

She swerved into the kitchen and spotted a cartoon-patterned cereal bowl, a cup and a mug drying in the dish rack beside her aunt's porcelain sink. Evidence that they'd eaten together. Jodi's chest loosened and her breathing eased as she stood beside the potted geraniums lining her aunt's open windows. Okay. So he was supervised. But where was he?

A distinct belly laugh followed another duck call outside. Tyler?

As she pushed out onto the back deck, a fifty-state spoon collection beside the kitchen door swung wildly.

"Tyler!" She lowered her cupped hands and squinted into the midmorning light. The slanted roof shaded much of the narrow back lawn, its shadow reaching to the uneven rock wall and the stone staircase that led to a wooden dock. Lake Champlain sparkled brighter than a sapphire and for a moment the reflective, rippling waves blinded her.

She clutched the rail and groped her way down the steps, blinking the spots out of her eyes.

"Jodi! We're over here," called Aunt Grace.

Relief filled her as she jogged to the dock where her aunt cradled her son on her lap, a familiar young woman with short dark hair and hazel eyes lounging nearby.

"Sue?" Amazement pulled her up short and the rough planks scraped against her bare feet, her sleep shirt flapping in the lake breeze. She hadn't seen her since the day they'd bet on which egg would hatch first on her father's farm.

Sue lifted a carved duck whistle and blew, making Tyler bring his hands close to his ears and laugh again.

Warmth radiated through her at the sight of her animated boy, his head swiveling every which way, his cheeks flushed and mouth parted in a smile as he chuckled. The moment rejuvenated her more than a cup of Mr. Williams's espresso and eased the heaviness Daniel's speech had put in her heart. Seeing Tyler like this convinced her that she was on the right path, no matter how many cuts and bruises she got along the way. Daniel may have won last night's battle, but the war wasn't over.

And her enemy's sister was in her backyard. Coincidence?

"I heard you were in town and wanted to come over and say hi." Sue's wide smile made her look more pixie-like than Jodi recalled. Sue shoved her glasses higher on her delicate nose and peered up at Jodi. "How are you?"

Jodi swallowed. How much had she heard from her big brother?

"I'm fine. Tired, I suppose." She laughed self-consciously and plucked at her sleepwear. "Good morning, Tyler, Aunt Grace." She leaned down to kiss his cheek, and he turned and caught her on the lips instead.

Happiness filled her. Tyler loved her. He might not be able to say the words, but his actions spoke for him.

"Morning, sleepyhead." Her aunt's eyes crinkled. "That must have been some reunion."

"Something like that." Jodi avoided Sue's assessing stare. "If you don't mind waiting a minute, I'll grab Tyler's glasses, change and be right back."

"Sounds good." Sue blew the duck whistle again and the memory of Daniel whittling them chased Jodi to the house.

Inside, she leaned against the shut door, the glass knob digging into her spine. What was Sue's real motive for being here? They'd grown up together, had been in the same 4-H groups and riding club. The two-year age difference meant they'd spent time hanging out, but had never been close friends. Was she the next weapon in Daniel's arsenal?

Five minutes later, Jodi rejoined them on the pier, her tank top the same emerald as the Adirondack Mountains across the lake, her jean shorts practical in the rising heat. When she kneeled on the dock, she twisted her hair in a high ponytail, earning it a tug from Tyler when she pulled his eyeglasses band over his head.

"Hey!" She untangled his fingers, then lifted them to her lips before he could swat her. Prevention like that was pure autistic mother instinct. "Hands to ourselves, Ty."

"Ah!" He kicked off his sneaker and it arced into the lake, where it bobbed on the surface. Jodi smothered a sigh and kept her face neutral as Tyler watched her. At least it wasn't his glasses.

"Got it!" Sue slid onto her belly and snagged the shoe when it drifted close. She pointed the dripping sneaker at Tyler before handing it to Jodi. "Sneakers are for feet, not fish," she said with a smile.

Tyler's improbable, deep chuckle was infectious. His head pivoted on his shoulders, his eyes wide. When he reached for the band behind his head, Jodi tugged him into her arms. "Glasses don't swim either, Ty."

"Want to go in?" Sue lifted the hem of an open-stitch crochet half shirt to reveal a bathing suit underneath.

"I don't have my suit." But she wished she did. The morning had turned up the heat another notch. Sweat pooled at the base of her neck and trickled down her back. The sound of children splashing and calling from a neighbor's private beach filled her with longing. Farther out, blue and yellow kayaks sped by, paddles flashing, while a cormorant nosedived from a nearby spruce then resurfaced, gulping a briny-smelling fish.

She and Sue swapped grins, probably both recalling the many times they'd run to the end of the dock and dived into the jewel-toned water, the cool wet washing away many hot summer days. Seeing her was a nice surprise. But it was time to ask a few questions and find out her real reason for the visit.

"How's Princeton?" Jodi asked casually and looked over at her aunt. "Aunt Grace mentioned you'd finished a doctorate."

Sue polished her glasses with her top. "Almost."

"That's great. Amazing. Should I practice calling you Dr. Gleason now? I heard you were studying—" What had Aunt Grace told her? Or had she? Most of the Cedar Bay chatter went in one ear and out the other. It produced too many bad memories otherwise.

Sue hung her head and, to Jodi's surprise, the upbeat girl seemed at a loss for words.

Aunt Grace slid nearer. "What's wrong?"

"Everything," Sue said after a moment, her voice uneven. She folded and unfolded her glasses with trembling fingers. "My advisor rejected my dissertation and Daniel's furious."

Sympathy welled up in Jodi. Daniel was a relentless fighter. She imagined that Sue, who took after her softhearted father, was no match for her bulldozing older brother.

Aunt Grace pulled the slender girl close. "What terrible news. Is it too late to redo the paper?"

Sue's red-rimmed eyes peered across the lake. "No. But if I want to stay in the program, I have to rewrite it so that it supports my advisor's research and present it at the end of the summer. He basically said my ideas were too controversial and wouldn't be approved by his golfing buddies on the panel."

"We support you, Sue. That's a tough break." Jodi leaned forward and rubbed Sue's arm, wishing she could help more than just comfort. Tyler's rough face pat was a little more like a slap, but Sue didn't seem to mind.

She put on her glasses. "Thanks, everyone. Really."

"What are you going to do?" Aunt Grace held out a bowl that contained granola, dried fruit and nuts, but Sue shook her head.

"I know what Daniel wants. He said I should

follow my advisor's suggestions, finish my Ph.D. and make Pop happy."

When Tyler made a grab for the bowl, Aunt Grace pulled it out of reach and passed him a cashew.

"But that's not what you want." Jodi stretched out her sticky, damp legs. It figured Daniel would advise her like that. Anything to win.

Sue's shoulders rose then fell. "Publishing a paper I don't believe in is intellectually dishonest and I won't do it."

"Good girl." Aunt Grace offered Tyler a dried apricot next.

A flapping wind sail glided by, its driver dressed in a wet suit and gripping a long bar. She and Sue gazed after the splash of color as it skipped across the water and she wondered if Sue remembered the time they'd borrowed a couple from Frank Trudeau and spent the entire day up to their waists, falling in and out of the deep water. It'd been their first and, for Jodi, her last attempt. A failure. The thought brought her back to the present.

"So you'll drop out?" Jodi looked at Sue in despair. She could imagine how much effort hardworking Sue had put into the project. She'd always been one of the brightest kids in school.

"Looks like it unless—" Sue broke off and peered at Tyler as he rested his head on Jodi's lap, his eyes tracking the heavy-bottomed clouds moving sluggishly overhead.

"Unless?"

"Forgive me, Jodi. But I have another reason to visit and it has to do with Tyler." Sue pushed to her feet and paced the deck, her rubber soles squelching when they hit a damp spot. "I need a research subject."

"I don't understand." Her grip tightened on her son. Tyler wasn't anyone's lab rat....

"My doctorate is in child psychology. If I have research on a test subject, I'll take my chances and go before the committee and present the paper I believe in." Sue turned and looked across the lake at the distant green peaks of the Adirondacks. "Show them that an organic diet combined with real-world sensory integration experiences will produce significant improvement in appropriate reaction, verbalization and attention."

"But Tyler doesn't need—" Jodi trailed off as he pointed at a bottle of bubbles she'd grabbed on her way back. "Use your words, please."

He shook his head and strained for it.

Sue knelt in front of Jodi, her hazel eyes wide and apologetic. Earnest. "Sorry. That was a lot of technical jargon. The bottom line is that I can help Tyler. Please forgive Grace, but she came to me a year ago for advice about

Tyler's diagnosis. I'd wanted to help then and this could be my chance. A chance for both of us. Tyler would be helping me as much as I hope to help him."

Jodi met her aunt's concerned gaze and nodded her head in understanding, her mind swimming with possibilities. Her therapist had warned that Tyler would regress without his normal treatment regimen and here was a certified psychologist, almost a doctor, offering to help. The only catch? She was the sister of Jodi's enemy.

Jodi covered Tyler's ears. Inattentive as he could be, she wouldn't let him hear this. "He might not be the best subject." Her heart hurt, but she forced herself to continue. "A year ago he stopped talking. Completely. And each day he gets more and more withdrawn. I'm sorry. But if you want to prove your thesis, he might not be the ideal candidate."

Tyler wiggled out of her grasp and flung himself at Aunt Grace. His large blue eyes stayed on Jodi, however, and she wondered if he'd heard some of that after all. If he had, how much had he understood? She never wanted him to feel like a failure. Her sweet baby.

Sue eyed him as a motorboat zoomed by pulling two shrieking teens on an inflatable raft. The exhaust-scented air temporarily blotted out the smell of fresh water and cedar mulch. Aunt Grace blew a stream of bubbles from a plastic holder and Tyler clapped his hands around any he could catch.

"I believe in him, Jodi." Sue's sudden intensity caught Jodi off guard. "I can see his potential. Please give me a shot at proving my theory and breaking him out of his silence."

Tears stung Jodi's eyes. It was exactly what she needed to hear. But Wonders Primary had a proved track record and they'd promised her the same.

Sue scooted closer, the sun glinting off the gold studs in her ears. "I'm not an expert. All I'm asking for is a chance. I know you and Daniel have this thing going on, but that's between you two. Will you at least meet me after the class-reunion pig roast tonight? I'd like to show you the alpacas."

"Alpacas?" Jodi echoed, feeling overwhelmed by more than the heat. They definitely weren't on the Wonders Primary treatment plan. And no one had mentioned a pig roast. Then again, she hadn't left last night's party on good terms… with anyone. She shuddered. Somehow she had to earn back the community's goodwill. And the promotional party she'd been organizing for Midland tomorrow already seemed like a bust. If she hadn't booked the entertainment and facilities she would have canceled.

Sue nodded, her smile back but tentative. "They're the gentlest animals." She poked a large bubble that got away from Tyler and earned another belly laugh. "Their wool makes great thread for knitting. But in grad school, I realized they could help autistic children, as well."

"That's amazing, Sue." Aunt Grace gave her an approving nod and a handful of granola.

"Find me before Daniel's co-op presentation and I'll show them to you," she spoke through a mouthful of crumbs. "Plus, I'll have a formal outline of my treatment plan for Tyler."

"Co-op?" Jodi's head swam. First Daniel's crushing speech last night and now this? If he convinced the farmers to join him, her acquisitions bid would be over before she started. Her son's laugh rang out as he grabbed at bubbles in midair. That couldn't happen. Not a chance.

"He's going to explain his plans for a co-op that produces organic products from humanely treated animals." Sue's eyebrows came together. "I thought you would have been invited."

Jodi's mind reeled. She'd dealt with co-op resistance before. The fact that Daniel hadn't invited her showed he wanted it kept a secret.

Good thing Sue had stopped by, a visit Daniel clearly knew nothing about. A plan took shape. She wouldn't be crashing the party if Sue invited her over. And if she found the opportunity to speak, it'd be Daniel's turn to feel the sting of her words. Her shoulders straightened. Time to head back into war.

"If you tell me what time, I'll come." She'd like to hear what both Gleason siblings had to say and lend her own voice to the mix. It'd be an exciting night. Adrenaline surged through her and her fingers flexed. She'd be ready for the fight this time.

Sue brightened. "Great. And you'll love the alpacas. They're goofy and harmless."

"Yes," Jodi agreed. If only Daniel was harmless, as well.

"WHAT'S JODI DOING here?" Frank Trudeau asked later that night as they stood behind Daniel's house at the pig roast. "I thought you said she wasn't coming. Some of us wanted to apologize for yesterday." Chattering ex-classmates sat at food-laden picnic tables, a pig on a spit in the back corner of his lawn. Daniel's friend Steve played old-time rock while the salty tang of pork filled the evening air.

"I didn't know." He glanced up from his overloaded supper plate and watched Jodi wave to his sister and start down his back-porch steps. His gut clenched. He'd been so busy outside organizing this part of the class reunion weekend, he'd missed her arrival. Pop had probably been the one behind Jodi's invite. He'd suggested asking her for dinner at least twice now.

"You don't look happy to see her." Frank's dark eyes slid from Jodi to Daniel.

Daniel blew out a breath. "I'm not. She's here to spy for Midland. It's why I didn't invite her," he admitted.

"Well, that was a dumb thing to do." Frank tossed his plate into a nearby trash can, then rubbed a hand over his crew cut. "Have you heard the saying 'May the best man win'? Make it a fair fight, buddy."

"Midland could throw their corporate muscle around and interfere with the co-op upgrades grant."

"And she wouldn't have found out about the grant—ever?" Frank shook his head.

Daniel rubbed his neck. "I needed to get the co-op going before she found out. A head start."

Frank cuffed his arm and chuckled low and deep. "Then you'd better start running because it looks like she's coming our way."

His appetite gone, Daniel put down his plate and watched Jodi as people stopped her to chat.

Her sleeveless red-checked halter top and jean shorts showed off a strip of taut, tanned stomach and a tiny waist that made him stare longer than he should have. Her long, lean legs ended in a pair of scuffed white cowboy boots that shone in the deepening twilight.

His best friend of twenty-some years studied him closely. "Are you going to apologize?"

He gave a slow nod. Frank had a point. He hadn't made it a fair fight. Worse, he'd been cruel. After seeing her vulnerable side in the parking lot, he'd felt guilty and more. What that "more" was, he wouldn't imagine. He pictured the rose he'd tucked into his nightstand drawer and wondered why he hadn't given it back to her the night before.

Yet standing under the oak tree where he'd once pushed her on a tire swing made him recall happier, less complicated times with Jodi.

Tonight, he'd apologize and ask Jodi to stay. Mingle. She'd leave soon to put Tyler to bed anyway—given her protectiveness, he didn't believe she'd let Grace put her son to sleep. After that, he'd give his speech.

Fingers snapped before his eyes.

"Earth to Dan. You in there?"

He turned his head but kept his eyes on Jodi's delicate face. "Sure."

Frank's deep laugh sounded beside him. "You didn't hear half of what I just said."

"I—"

"That was a statement, not a question. Go get your girl." Frank slapped him on the back. "And apologize," he reminded him before sauntering away.

So he did.

"Daniel. Hello," she greeted him when he drew near.

The brilliance of her smile and her sparkling blue eyes stole his breath.

"What's the matter? Cat got your tongue?" challenged Mary Spellman, a classmate who hadn't made last night's party. There'd been a bachelorette party at her business, The Lounge, he recalled. When she wrinkled her nose, a diamond piercing flashed. "I heard you had plenty to say last night, though. Sounded brutal."

Mary's naturally red hair gleamed under the lantern lights he'd hung from the porch, her eyes just as fiery.

Jodi put a hand over Mary's gold bangles. "It's okay. All's fair in…"

"War," Mary snorted, her purse snapping open then closed as she took out a wand of lipstick. She glanced between them as she applied the color. "Because this definitely doesn't look like love."

He stepped closer and put out a hand. "I'm sorry, Jodi. I meant my apology last night and I wanted to say it again but thought I'd give you a day to cool off."

Now, why did his explanation make her straighten her back and lift her chin? Had he made her angrier? Impossible. He was sincere…for the most part. He also hadn't wanted her to know about the co-op.

"I'm fine. In fact, I'm so good that I thought I'd stop by the party your *sister* invited me to. She wanted to show me her alpacas."

He followed her gaze around the crowded green lawn between his barns and house, noting the alpacas as they milled inside their pen. Of course, Sue was free to invite over whomever she wanted. He just wished she'd chosen any other night but this one.

In a far corner, men whooped when a horseshoe hooked around an iron nail with a clang. In the middle, a small crowd line danced to a rockabilly tune played on an iPod dock belonging to Mary's brother, Steve. By Sue's rose garden, people crowded on picnic tables. They slathered butter on biscuits he'd baked this afternoon and shoveled in the salty crisp pork he'd sliced off the rotating pig an hour ago. The music floated across the lawn and was echoed by birds wheeling in the sky.

"I'm glad you came." And he was. When she'd stepped out of his house, the world had turned up its dimmer switch.

"Are you?" Mary rolled her eyes, then moved off with a jingling wave. "I'm going to help my brother with the music. See you tomorrow, Jodi."

"Bye," Jodi called before turning back to him. "And I'm glad to be here, too." Her straight, light eyebrows rose and he found himself staring at the splatter of freckles across her pert nose.

A strange feeling overtook him, a sense of rightness, of homecoming. The way she looked tonight, standing in his backyard, made it hard to imagine her as his enemy. It was easy to remember the girl he'd once fallen for.

"What I did was wrong. Crossed the line. If there was a way I could make it up to you…"

"Actually, there is." She cut him off smoothly and he glimpsed the businesswoman in her again, the images of kissable girl and formidable woman warring in his mind's eye.

"Given your compelling speech yesterday, I'd like a chance to talk. It's only fair."

He couldn't argue with that. It was fair. And he owed her. Besides, what could she possibly say that would change anything? After last night's speech and tonight's presentation, he had this.

"How about ladies first, since I'm sure you'll want to get home to tuck in Tyler."

Her lips curled at the corners, and unease twisted in his gut.

"Perfect. Hey, Goldie!"

Her cool demeanor transformed into the relaxed, friendly smile he remembered, the effect making his pulse speed.

His retriever barked and jumped like the youngster she'd been when Jodi left. After getting her ears and chest fur ruffled Goldie presented her rump for a rub, tail beating the mosquitoes from the air.

Jodi's laughter rang out and he joined in, enjoying this temporary truce. It felt great to be around her this way. They swapped grins over a wriggling Goldie, their hands brushing as they scratched and petted his overexcited dog. When Jodi's palm accidently slipped into his, he laced his fingers with hers and heard her gasp. Her eyes met his.

"I mean it, Jodi." Her hand twisted in his and he let her go. "I wish I could take back what I said yesterday. Hopefully this will show you that I want a fair fight." He neglected to mention the part about his own, upcoming speech.

There was fair and there was naive. Besides, she'd have a chance to talk first.

Her cheekbones lifted and the left-sided dimple he'd once loved to kiss appeared. "That's all I want, Daniel."

At his gesture, Steve cut the music and Daniel stepped up on the porch.

"Hey, everyone." The talkative group quieted. "Thank you for coming out today and taking a tour of my upgraded barns. I also want to publically apologize to Jodi for not making her feel welcome yesterday at our reunion. I know you feel the same way."

A weak chorus of "sorry" sounded in the fragrant evening air, the last of the lilacs mingling with the earthy, early-summer smell of growing things.

"Jodi has something to say and I know you'll give her your respect and attention." He nodded encouragingly. "Take it away."

"Thank you, Daniel. And hello, everyone. I didn't get a chance to say hey to all of you yesterday and I'm glad I've got that opportunity tonight."

Some put down their forks and turned to face her, their eyes as wide and surprised at her gutsy move as he'd been.

"Yesterday Daniel spoke movingly about the importance of community. Of supporting one another." A night owl hooted from near his barns followed by a flutter of wings in the darkening night. After hearing her opening comment, many went back to eating and a few resumed their chatting. Daniel felt torn. He'd brought out this unneighborly behavior by speaking against Jodi last night. He stepped forward to intervene, force them to pay attention, but stopped at her next words.

"Tonight I'd like to talk about something bigger than community. America." Jodi's glowing face seemed to shine with a light of its own, the golden swing of her hair and her vibrant smile drawing the crowd, and him, closer still.

When she tightened the little knot on her shirt and turned out her foot to better show the flag decal on her cowboy boots, he had a strange feeling that maybe her talk wasn't as spur-of-the-moment as he'd thought. Had he been set up?

She leaned against the beveled post and her face grew grave. Not a sound rose from the assembly. Even Goldie sat at attention at the bottom of the porch, her ears pricked forward.

"My ancestors, like yours, fought and died in the Revolutionary War that established our individual freedoms and rights."

"Woo-hoo!" cried Doug Utzler, a descendent

of the Green Mountain Boys and a Revolutionary War reenactor.

Daniel shifted to his left leg and tried to keep himself from throwing her over his shoulder and stomping away with her...to do what? He could think of a few things, but mostly to stop whatever bad thing he sensed she was about to say. What had he unleashed? He hung his head. Duped.

"America is now the most powerful democracy in the world."

"You got that right, honey!" someone yelled. Sounded like Ted Layhee. He crossed his arms and stared down his former classmate. The guy would go along with anything to get closer to Jodi.

"And we've become the greatest country in the world, refusing to give in to threats to our freedoms." Jodi put a hand up to her mouth and coughed delicately. For a moment it seemed as if everyone leaned forward. Maybe they did.

"Like terrorists. And communists," she continued.

"Reds," hollered someone from the back of the crowd.

Where did people come up with this stuff? Luckily his father had gone to bed shortly after dinner and was missing the commotion. What would Pop think when he heard his son's plans for cooperative farming? It was one thing to go green and organic—another to go "commie" as his father would put it. It was a point that would resonate with the vets who'd come out tonight.

"Thank you, Jodi," he called out, and kept his voice congenial though there was electricity in his gaze. "We appreciate the history lesson. Been a long time since we've had one. For some of us, this may be the first one we've listened to." He paused and flashed a grin. "Ted."

Yet the crowd didn't laugh with him and an uncomfortable feeling settled in his gut. Was he losing them?

"I wasn't actually finished, Daniel," Jodi said, her eyes wide and innocent. Only he wasn't fooled. Not anymore, at least.

"Let her talk," Frank shouted, and Daniel shot his bowling buddy a glare that was returned with a scowl.

"Thanks, Frank." Jodi inclined her head. "Now, the reason I brought up this 'history lesson' was to remind us of how important it is to preserve our right to make our own choices, to pull ourselves up by our own bootstraps, to be the boss of our life, rather than fall to the collective will of others. However, Daniel is about to propose this."

She reached behind her and held up a chart he'd made of the upgrades needed in order to form the co-op. His throat trapped his breath and held it hostage. How had she found out about his plans? The grant? Would Sue or his father have told her? He hadn't warned them not to, but he hadn't imagined them meeting. He frowned. The minx. On her way through the house, Jodi must have swiped it from his kitchen and now used his labor against him. If he wasn't fuming, he'd admire the tactic.

"Daniel got you out here on the pretext of an all-American cookout. Once he filled you with pork, he planned to throw in some slop—namely these mandatory changes to your farms." Her finger ran down the list that looked long now, even to his own eyes. He should have consolidated some categories, made it look less complicated.

"But they won't be your farms anymore if you join the co-op. How could they be when you'll no longer call the shots?"

A collective murmur rose from the group and a couple of classmates crowded him.

"Is it true?" asked one.

"I'm my own boss," hissed another.

Daniel shook his head and held up a finger as if to say "wait." He needed to hear the rest of Jodi's speech in order to plan a counterattack.

"The collective will of the co-op will decide when and how many changes you'll be required to make on what was once your and your ancestors' farms," she continued, a moth banging on a light behind her. "Before you so much as change your feed order, you'll have to check in with the new authority. Not you. No." She hoisted the chart so that she had to peek around the side. "The co-op will decide that, along with each of these areas."

Several boos erupted and Daniel flinched. He itched to put a stop to her speech, but any move he made would cast him in a worse light than she already had.

She underlined each category with a yellow highlighter that glowed in the gathering dark. "So if you join this co-op, I ask you, haven't you just signed away your freedom, your rights, your individuality? The American Dream?

"Heck, yeah!" several shouted, and he could hear a few bottles clink.

"America is the mightiest nation on the planet because we have the freedom of choice. The decisions we make, *as individuals,* directly impact how much we improve. Please come to the village green by Fellowship Church after services for fun, patriotic games, food and entertainment sponsored by one of America's biggest employers, Midland Corp. I'll explain exactly why Midland will guarantee your freedom to choose your future, rather than have it controlled by a co-op, as Daniel is about to propose."

Cheering broke out when Jodi stepped down after a quiet smile and a thank-you.

"It's all yours, Daniel," she whispered in his ear as she passed by close enough for him to smell her perfume.

His chest burned when he mounted the steps and saw that the party had largely broken up; many had followed Jodi down his long driveway toward their cars.

He opened his mouth, then closed it at Frank's smirk.

"She got you good," his friend chuckled before flipping his hand up and disappearing into the night.

Daniel walked among the tables and picked up his old plate, his brain feeling as muddy as the ground. He gave Goldie a piece of pork, then took a bite himself. But instead of the crispy, salty goodness he'd anticipated all day, he tasted something unfamiliar and bitter.

Defeat.

CHAPTER SIX

DANIEL INJECTED A dose of antibiotics into a restless cow, her tail whipping his face as his mind replayed Jodi's antics last night. She'd seemed sincere. How had he misread her? Must have been wishful thinking, hoping she'd become the person he used to know. Care about.

"Pinkeye?" asked Sue as he capped the needle and stepped out of the stall.

When he turned, she was folding a rain slicker over her arm, water dripping from her short hair and streaming down her cheeks. The smell of wet dog drew his eye to Goldie, who showered them with a powerful body shake.

"Infected leg." He wiped the spray from his eyes and pointed to the brown cow that stomped and lowed in the infirmary pen.

After feeding her a carrot, he scratched the white diamond on her forehead and unhooked her. Cows could be unpredictable and it paid to be careful. This one was the oldest in his herd and though she'd quit producing two years ago, he'd found it hard to part with her.

If only he'd been less softhearted around Jodi yesterday. Wasn't that what his mother had accused his father of when his habit of loaning money and equipment had nudged them near bankruptcy? He shouldn't have let down his guard. It'd allowed her to come back, harder than ever, after his speech at the veterans' hall.

"So are we talking again?" Sue pulled back a soggy cloth to reveal a mound of flat, brown cookies in a wicker basket. "I'm sorry about what happened with Jodi. I invited her over to talk about treating Tyler—"

"You're treating Tyler?"

How had that happened? The idea of seeing Jodi here every day filled him with anticipation and dread. But if it helped Sue, how could he argue against it? Besides, Jodi knew his secrets now. With nothing left to hide, he needed to work twice as fast to get the co-op going before Midland found a way, through high-level connections, to interfere.

Sue shrugged, "You want me to finish my Ph.D. so I asked Jodi if I could work with Tyler for my dissertation."

"But you're proving your advisor's theory. Correct?"

Rain drummed on the tin roof and he positioned a couple of buckets beneath ceiling drips.

"No. I'm proving mine. Tyler quit talking when his father left them over a year ago. I know that if I can get Tyler to speak, the committee won't reject my theory."

He looked at her, surprised and dismayed. "I can't believe a father would abandon his child." He'd supposed Jodi's split with her husband had been a mutual decision. This information put things in a new light. Jodi's husband left, not the other way around. It showed a more mature side to Jodi that challenged his memory of the teenaged girl who'd run from their problems.

"Yes. It's horrible," Sue continued as she stroked Goldie. "She told me about it before we joined your party. Tyler was traumatized and I want to help him."

She put a hand on his tense arm. Now both their fates were tied to Jodi.

"Why won't you believe in me?"

Her large eyes implored him, her passion reminding him of his feelings about organic farming. Many were reluctant to trust a new method. Maybe he shouldn't be so hard on her and give her a chance.

"I do. I just don't believe in those jerks on the committee. But if you want to go for it, then I'm here for you. As long as you're not quitting, I'm proud of you."

Sue's face lit up. "No. Not that. And I hope

you won't give up either, after Jodi's speech last night. Trust me, I had no idea. I'm not getting in the middle of this, but I would never set you up."

He nodded and flexed his sore back as they headed toward the milk parlor, his pride smarting more than his muscles. He and Jodi had declared war, yet he hadn't seen her maneuver coming. Irritation fueled his stride as he passed tributaries running down his windowpanes, the barn's pungent smell strong and close. "I know."

Sue handed him a cookie. "Good. We bicker, but we wouldn't betray each other like that." Her eyes followed him as he circled the milking carousel, inspecting the equipment. "Except Mom."

Her words clutched at his throat. "Let's not talk about that," he said, his voice tight.

"When do we ever?" She dropped the basket on a ledge and grabbed a hose hooked to a cleansing solution tank with a Green Certified emblem, her movement jerky. "She walked out ten years ago and you've never mentioned it. Pretended like she didn't live here. Raise us."

He studied a broken machine's underbelly. Better to find faults here than focus on his family's. Results mattered, and in the end, Mom's leaving had broken Dad's spirit, but not their home. He'd made sure of that. When Goldie nudged the back of his leg, he patted her wet nose. Now, that was loyalty.

"It's easier." He straightened and pulled off his hat, the moist air doing little to cool his damp forehead. Why couldn't Sue let Mom go? His mother hadn't looked back. Hadn't contacted them.

"Only if you're in denial." She squeezed the nozzle and water jetted across the round, raised platform, white foam chasing away the dirt and other matter left behind from this morning's milking. An odorless mist filled the air.

"What do you want me to say?" Daniel pulled out a paper pad and wrote down the model number for the broken machine. "That I miss her? Wish she'd come home?" He thought of Jodi and how she'd walked out on him that summer, too, but pushed the thought aside. No sense wishing for what he couldn't have.

"Yes. And more." Sue used her forearm to slide her glasses into place as she doused the area. "You've been so focused on fixing the farm and keeping us out of bankruptcy that you barely talk about anything else. And you only hang out on bowling or Scrabble nights. When was the last time you went on a date… college?"

He avoided her eyes. They saw too much.

Besides, he'd needed to earn his bachelor and masters degrees in four years instead of six to help Pop. The pace had made only casual dating possible. Not that he'd been interested in another serious relationship. Not after his summer with Jodi.

"What are you so afraid of?"

"Don't psychobabble me, sis. I'm fine." He smiled to take the sting out of his words.

Sue stopped the pulsing water and aimed the nozzle his way. "Keep telling yourself that, Daniel, though you'll never believe it. Not really."

The hollowness that made falling asleep by eight impossible and midnight improbable made him wonder. But once he saved his community from Midland, from Jodi and any other threats, he'd rest easier. Families would stay together, their farms intact. It was worth this fight. No matter the cost. Speaking of which...

"Do you think Jodi's Field Day is still on?" He glanced out the window as a ray of sunshine poked its way through the heavy cloud mass.

"I hope so! Was planning to stop by now that morning chores are done," exclaimed Colton as he joined them. "Hey. Cookies!" He snatched one out of the basket before Daniel could warn him and bit in. "Ouch! Think I lost a filling!"

Sue jumped and smoothed her shirt, her

rounded shoulders back for once. "Sorry. I might have overcooked them."

Colton beamed and Sue blushed. "Extra-crispy, then deep-fried. That's how I like my desserts. You ever have deep-fried Oreos? Better than anything they make in Par-ee."

Daniel fought back a smile and turned to flick off the parlor's lights. His sister responded and Colton laughed, the mingled male and female sounds reminding him of his time here with Jodi the summer before things went bad.

"Let's all go into town." Sue's eyes sparkled behind her square lenses, her face as lit as a Christmas tree. "What do you say, Daniel?"

His mind searched out options and settled on only one. Jodi had made her move last night and now it was his turn. And this time he'd be prepared.

"WE HAD A late start, but we'll make up for it with lots of fun," concluded Jodi as she stood on a wooden dais in the packed village green an hour later. Finally, her plan to acquire Cedar Bay farms felt back on track.

Cheers erupted from picnic tables and activities stations, and folks waved the American flags she'd passed out, a Midland card attached by red, white and blue ribbons.

She lowered her megaphone and hopped

off the raised platform, her heels sinking into the spongy ground. Her navy dress slacks and white-and-blue polka-dotted shirt felt sticky in the humidity, but she'd dressed to impress. At least her pinned-up hair left her neck cool.

Thank goodness the weather had improved. A few puddles spotted the grass, but they only added extra fun for splashing children. The adults seemed more intent on the elaborate spread of food Midland had provided. The table laden with roast turkey and beef had the longest line, a hired chef in a tall white hat behind it. Her stomach grumbled at the succulent smells of yeasty sweet rolls, buttered corn and the greasy goodness of fried chicken legs.

But she had no time to eat. Not when she needed to mingle and set up private meetings with the farmers in attendance. When she'd given her speech earlier about Midland's buy-out price per acre and the opportunity to re-main in their homes as contracted workers, there'd been smiles and applause all around. The afterglow still filled her, buoying her spirits with the belief that she and Tyler might be back in Chicago within a couple of weeks, the five thousand acres acquired faster than she'd dreamed. Hopefully, that amount of time would help out well-meaning Sue enough. Then again, after her speech at Daniel's gathering, perhaps

Sue wouldn't want to treat Tyler. All the more reason to get her son home and into his therapy routines until Wonders Primary took him in the fall.

"That was one heck of a speech."

She pivoted slowly and her lips twisted. Ted. She inched back from the grinning man who, despite a few facial lines, looked like the same kid who'd thrown spitballs at her in elementary school. As they'd gotten older, he'd earned his nickname, Hands, and she'd learned to stay just out of his reach.

"Thanks. Would you be interested in setting up a time to meet and discuss Midland's proposal?"

Ted's laugh sounded like an innuendo. It turned a few heads their way, especially Aunt Grace, who cradled Tyler and read him a picture book.

"You bet." He scribbled his name and number on the sheet but wouldn't let go of her hand when he passed her the pen. "So when are we getting together?"

"I'll call you." She fought to keep the exasperation out of her voice as she freed herself. "Thanks, Ted."

When he didn't take the hint, she smiled politely and walked toward a weeping willow where a clump of farmers she recognized from childhood hay-bale rides gathered.

"Rains practically every day," she heard one of the older men say as he scratched his grizzled jaw. "We're not going to get much corn out of this year, and then what are we going to do with milk prices where they're at?"

The rest nodded as she joined them.

"Hey, Jodi Lynn Chapman. How are you doing? How are your folks?"

Archie Remillard's bear hug squished the air out of her. He'd been her school's afternoon custodian as long as she could remember. But he must be retired now—though not from farming by the faint, familiar smell coming off his shirt.

"They're doing okay. Still living out in Arizona, but now they've moved in with my grandmother. Mom wants to help her out since she's having trouble managing on her own."

Sympathetic noises all around.

"Your dad doing all right these days?"

Jodi's eyes wandered skyward and tracked a bird winging over the canopy of trees shading the boxwood-enclosed area. These were the kinds of questions she'd dreaded when she'd agreed to come home.

"He has his bad ones and his good ones."

It was as close to the truth as she could manage without mentioning his latest rehab stint, the slur in his words when they'd spoken last week. The guilt she felt when she thought of her formerly hardworking father reduced to post-traumatic stress–induced alcoholism and bitterness.

"As for me—" she cleared the lump in her throat "—I'm raising that little guy over there." She pointed at Tyler and her heart skipped a beat when she saw Sue Gleason kneeling in front of him. Tyler held out Ollie dressed in a pink tutu and a Chicago Bears jersey. Daniel wouldn't come today, would he? Her lips pressed together. Of course he would. Her heart sank.

"Heard the boy's no-good father skipped out, huh?"

"Bill. Shut it," growled Archie. He gave her a sympathetic look. "Sorry to hear about that, Jodi. You're a nice young woman and any idiot should know that."

Her eyes pricked at Archie's unexpected kindness. In fact, all five of the men nodded, their jowls bouncing for emphasis. The solid support propped up something in her she hadn't known was in danger of falling.

To stop emotion from clouding a business event, she held out her clipboard.

"Thank you, Archie. I'd love to talk more about all of your farms. If you'll write down your information, I'll take you to breakfast at the D & H." It was a local diner and the best greasy spoon in the area. Maybe in the country, now that she thought about it. Before they left, she'd take Tyler. He loved bacon and hash browns, a runny egg yolk coloring his plate bright yellow.

Bill pulled his cap lower and shifted on his feet. "No offense, Jodi, but I'm hoping to convince my boy to give up selling satellite systems and come back to the farm."

"Oh." She forced a bright smile. "I hope that works out. Anyone else?"

"I guess I'd be interested to hear more about that. Cousin-to-cousin."

She blinked at Archie, relieved and grateful for family, no matter how distant. "I'd appreciate that."

"Yeah. Add me."

"And put my name down, too. I'm in the phone book."

The remaining farmers jerked their chins in her direction and it was all Jodi could do not to ask, "Really?" Much better to take the clipboard and walk away, even if it was on wobbly legs. Sweet relief. This was going better than she could have imagined. And since she hadn't spotted Daniel, yet, today could be a home run.

"Thank you. I'll be in touch!" she called over her shoulder before stopping by Tyler for a quick smooch that left her cheek sticky.

"You just missed Sue." Aunt Grace passed Tyler a daisy-chain headband she'd woven for Ollie. "She wanted me to tell you to bring Tyler over tomorrow morning anytime after eight."

Jodi twisted her locket, her gaze darting through the thick crowd. Thank goodness Sue wasn't holding a grudge. But what about Daniel? A few people stood by the potato sacks placed by lines chalked on the grass while others looked down into a large bucket filled with water, apples floating on the surface. The whirring of a cotton-candy machine permeated the air with a syrupy aroma. Midland sure knew how to throw a down-home party.

Her stomach churned. Where was Daniel? His stunned expression during last night's speech haunted her, filling her with mixed emotions. It'd felt great to pay him back for his speech at the dance. Seeing him look so defeated, however, filled her with remorse. Not that she wanted a fight, but she didn't dislike him enough to see him demoralized.

"Cedar Bay. Are we ready to rumble?"

boomed a deep voice she recognized. Her body felt hot, then cold. Daniel.

He stood on the dais, his long muscular legs planted apart, a megaphone lifted to his mouth. What the… It was her party. But after last night's speech, she saw exactly what was coming. He wanted to take charge of her day and that was not happening. She unclenched her teeth and smiled instead as she handed her aunt the clipboard and strode his way.

"Why, thank you, Daniel," she called, and the buzzing assembly quieted. Her eyes locked with his until he passed her the megaphone and stepped back with a wink that shook her confidence. He looked anything but demoralized. Worse, his mischievous expression meant he had a plan. What was it?

"I've been having such a good time chatting with everyone, I nearly forgot that it's time for Cedar Bay's Midland-sponsored Olympiad." Her voice didn't shake and for that she was grateful. "All competitions will be performed in teams of two. The winning pair of each game will get fifty dollars to split and the pair who wins the most events will receive an all-expenses-paid weekend getaway to Montreal, Canada, or a thousand-dollar gift card. Pairs sign up on the sheet by the tree and attach your number stickers to your shirts. May the best team win!"

The crowd surged toward the sign-up sheet, a tried-and-true business tactic since she'd use their names to follow up as cold calls. She tried focusing on that, rather than the smell of Daniel's musky cologne and the warmth of him beside her.

His eyes searched hers. "What do you say, Jodi Lynn? Want to partner up?"

She lurched backward, stunned, her heel then toe encountering air until Daniel grabbed her. The firm planes of his chest and stomach pressed against her and her knees felt weak. His grip tightened and for a moment she imagined his broad hands running through her hair as they once had, bringing her face closer until...

"We'd better hustle or we won't get a spot." He tugged her down the stairs.

On the ground she dug in her heels and he stopped, his dark hair casting a shadow across his brow. "We're not competing together. It's not professional."

He released her hand, but his handsome face, all man and no longer boy, made it hard to draw in a full breath. "It'd be more professional to show everyone we can put our differences aside. Just this once."

Jodi opened her mouth, then closed it. There

was nothing she could say that wouldn't sound childish. Of course she needed to participate. It would help reestablish a sense of camaraderie with her former neighbors, although she wouldn't really be competing for prizes since she worked for Midland. Yet she'd been hoping to partner with Mary, who—Jodi sighed—already seemed to have paired up with Frank. Darn.

"Fine. Let's do this." She strode toward a table where a temporary worker hired by Midland signed her and Daniel up and gave them numbers. Twenty-five. They were the very last.

"Want me to put your sticker on?" His slanted eyebrows rose, the challenging spark in his eyes making her rip the number from his hands and plaster it on her abdomen.

"I'm sure I can do as much, thanks." She turned as Aunt Grace and Tyler joined them. "Hi, baby." Tyler held up his arms and Jodi hoisted him, wrapping his legs around her waist. "Help me hold you, big guy."

Aunt Grace eyed their matching numbers. "This is unexpected." Her lips pursed as though she held in a smile, her brown eyes twinkling. "Tyler and I will cheer you both on."

Don't bother, Jodi thought but instead she said, "Wish Mommy luck, Ty." She gazed down at Tyler's upturned face, his back arching so far he nearly fell out of her arms. After a beat, she settled him on his feet and tamped down the familiar disappointment of being ignored. If Wonders Primary could help him—help them—it would be worth a hundred potato-sack races beside Daniel Gleason.

Fifteen minutes later, her arms wrapped around Daniel's muscular torso as they stood in a burlap bag, she almost took that sentiment back. His steady heartbeat pulsed against her and the warm rush of his breath by her temple sent shivers down her spine. There wasn't an inch to spare and she was excruciatingly aware of every place they touched.

"Put your feet on top of mine," Daniel's voice rumbled low in her ear.

"Why?" she muttered into his shifting shoulder muscles.

"Trust me. Without your heels, your toes might get trampled."

She had forgotten about that. Her feet slid on top of his, the action feeling intimate despite the thick leather of his work boots.

"Hold on," he shouted when the whistle blasted, and he turned so that her back was to the finish line. He sprinted them across the field, her teeth rattling and her fingers digging into his shoulders. How had she let him trick her into looking like a frail woman in need of a man's help—Daniel's, to be exact?

Around them teams stumbled and fell but Daniel charged as if he'd returned to his high school quarterback days, six foot three inches of solid muscle focused on reaching the end zone. In an instant, she felt the tug of a string against her back and they collapsed on the ground.

Daniel gazed down at her and spoke. But instead of words, she recalled the first time he'd held her. How that embrace had turned from comforting to caring to passionate in a breathless, stolen moment.

"What?" she asked when the memory drifted away, leaving the sweet scent of berry fields behind. She pushed against his chest and scrambled to her feet.

His handsome face glowed. "I said, we won."

"Let's donate the money to the second-place finishers."

"Sounds good." He stood and stretched, his crisp polo shirt stretching across his flat stomach. "Ready for another round?" He gave her a long look.

"I'm always up for a challenge," she snapped. He would not put her in a bad light again.

"Good. Wouldn't want you to run again if the going got tough." He strode to the Kan-

Jam area where sets of buckets separated by thirty feet were lined up in a long row, a disk by each bucket.

Jodi narrowed her eyes and watched him go, his body moving easily through a crowd that was eager to clap him on the back or stop him to say hello. She followed, silently fuming. How dare he insinuate that she ran from her problems? She needed to set the record straight. As an adult, she understood that she'd acted immaturely by running from Daniel ten years ago. But this was business and had no connection to their tumultuous past.

When she reached him, she tapped his shoulder and pointed to a pine copse. "A word?"

Daniel scraped a hand over his thick brush of hair, his cowlick springing back into place. Good. She'd caught him off guard for a change. Time to put things back into perspective.

"Yes?" he asked once they'd reached the green, feathered boughs.

"This—" she gestured from him to her "—thing may be personal. But our battle for Cedar Bay is not about us. Got it?"

When she turned to stomp away, he neatly caught her elbow. "I never said it was."

"Then why were you bringing up the past? And I don't run from my problems."

"Sure looked like you did when you left ten years ago."

"I had no choice." Her voice hitched, despite her best efforts to stay calm. The smell of Christmas enveloped them, but the mood was anything but festive.

"Life is full of choices." He lowered his head until their noses nearly touched. "You just didn't choose us."

Jodi pressed her palms to her eyelids for a moment. "There was no 'us' then, not after what you said."

"That's the way you wanted it." He looked at her intently until she dropped her eyes, his vulnerable expression nearly undoing her. "I wanted to make things right. Have a second chance. But you left before I could figure out how to do that."

A whistle signaled the start of the next game and she jerked away. "I don't want to talk about this," she said as they strode to the cans. "In fact, let's forget it ever happened. We were just kids."

"Kids, huh." He paused and nodded. "That was a long time ago. We were different then."

She took her place behind her bucket as Daniel stooped to pick up the flying disk beside his.

"The first team to hit twenty-one points wins," hollered their referee. "One point for hitting the bucket, two if your partner hits your disk off the side of the can, three points if your partner bats it into the top of the bucket. If your throw goes directly through the front slit, it's an automatic win. Everyone got that?"

"Yes!" roared the lined-up teams. *No!* thought Jodi. She'd played Frisbee in college but never like this. She glanced at the tangle of trees and saw Tyler and Aunt Grace push through to join the watching crowd. Her aunt caught Tyler's shirt, pulling him back before he bolted for the field.

At the next whistle blast, Daniel side-armed it and it thudded against the bucket. Point. Jodi picked up the disk and tossed it back, her throw wide enough to evade Daniel's lunge. When the next throw winged back at her, she swatted it into the top of the bucket. Four points now! But all from Daniel. The old feeling of their childhood competitions took hold.

A familiar screech sounded to her right and her throw went wide again. Tyler. The man beside her swore and kicked a soda can. Since she didn't recognize him, she wondered if he was visiting or a spouse of someone. Either way, his anger at her son's yell was out of line.

Jodi turned her back on the rude man and waved at Tyler and her aunt, trying to not feel self-conscious as others stared. He strained in

Aunt Grace's arms, his hands grasping the air in her direction. Were others judging him? It had been her biggest fear about bringing Ty to Cedar Bay. He didn't deserve for anyone to think that he was less than amazing.

"Ready, Jodi?" She nodded and swatted another of his throws into the side of the can. Five points. But surely they were way behind now.

She didn't care if she won the game, although she'd like to outscore Daniel.

"Go Mommy," she heard her aunt Grace call. When she looked up, her aunt waved Tyler's hand in the air, his fussing noises growing louder.

"Could someone get that kid under control?" shouted the man beside her, and Jodi cringed, frozen by the insult despite her burning heart. Before she could react, Daniel ambled over, his athletic gait looking more dangerous than easygoing.

"What's the problem?"

"How am I supposed to concentrate when that kid's making a racket?" The man threw up his arms but took a step back at Daniel's cold expression.

"It's just a game," Daniel surprised her by saying, his tone making her shiver. "That's not more important than a child."

"Well, someone had better teach him how to

behave," the red-faced man muttered, his voice muted as he stared at his feet.

"He's autistic!" Jodi fumed, joining the two. She didn't care if this guy was a farmer who owned a thousand acres. He would not insult her darling boy. She pulled out a card she'd gotten from her parent support group, the printed rectangle trembling in her grasp. Hurt and anger returned to her like old friends.

She glanced at a teary Tyler, then shoved the card at the insensitive man. "If you want to know more about his condition, read this. But do not say another *word* about my son. Got it?"

"I...ah... Yes," he stammered as he looked from Jodi to a stone-faced Daniel. "Will do. Thanks." He pocketed the card in his jeans and tossed the disk to his partner before slumping off the field.

Daniel whistled. "Nice."

Jodi put a hand over her rapidly beating heart and tried to slow her breathing. People could be so ignorant. And cruel. Yet Daniel...

"Thanks," she said, meaning it. She looked at the cheering teams around them. "Although I'm sorry for losing us the game."

Daniel angled his head, his eyebrow quirking, his handsome face making her pulse speed. "Haven't heard the ref call a winner. We've still got a shot." He tossed her the disk and returned to his can, his flexed knees and widespread hands making him look like an action-figure version of himself. "Are you going to throw that thing or what?" he called, his expression so full of play, she couldn't help but laugh.

"What," she answered when she reached her bucket, one of their old jokes. His bark of laughter was infectious. The camaraderie felt good, and for a moment she wished things could have been different but...she looked at Tyler. He'd stopped fussing and now tossed pinecones with Sue. The smile on his face was all the motivation she needed to stay focused.

She blew Tyler a kiss, waved to her aunt and took her place. Daniel's eyes urged her on and she focused on the slit, lined up the disk and positioned her arm before letting it fly.

The blue dome whizzed through the air and slid through the bucket's front slit.

"Winner!" Daniel hollered, and the referee blew the whistle, ending the game.

Cheers rose up around her and her family rushed the field. Tyler patted every part of her he could reach and stuffed Ollie in her hand. His most precious gift of all.

She cupped the soft underside of his chin. "Thank you, Ty. That was for you." And it was. Every single bit.

The rest of the afternoon flew by with a

spoon-and-egg race and other events that she and Daniel excelled at. Then again, it seemed their natural competitiveness motivated them to win more often than not. In fact, she was so determined not to lose that she hadn't realized they'd won the grand prize until the DJ announced it.

"I'm sorry, folks. As a Midland employee, I can't accept. Guess I got caught up in all the fun," Jodi shouted to the crowd who applauded as if they didn't hear her turn down the prize. And many probably hadn't since there was a pie-eating contest going on that had Tyler's face looking like a blueberry.

"Daniel, would you please call up the second-place winners?" She handed him the megaphone. He couldn't possibly want the trip to Montreal any more than she did.

"Sure." He held the amplifying device to his mouth, then lowered it. "Only—"

"Only—" What now?

"I wonder if, after yesterday, you'd indulge me in one thing."

The hairs on her arms rose. He was planning something to get back at her for last night. But if Daniel insisted on going to Montreal with her, she'd take her chances with whatever he was about to propose.

"Please." She smiled graciously. After all,

she was winning over the farmers and that was the big picture, no matter what Daniel did. Today was a win for Midland. Besides, after the way he'd helped defend her son, she owed him. It'd meant a lot.

"Friends and neighbors." Daniel strode to the edge of the podium, his tall form commanding as much attention as his voice. The babbling assembly hushed and the pie eaters stopped chewing. "For our last activity, we need everyone to assemble in the games area, find someone to whom you are related and hold their hand. This will only take a moment and I appreciate your cooperation."

And there it was, that trademark Daniel Gleason charm that had swept her off her feet once. He both exuded and attracted energy, like iron to a lodestone. She watched, stunned, as everyone did his bidding. His effect on people was terrifying.

She trailed behind the group, watching in amazement as everyone seemed to find someone to hold hands with, the links of people growing until they created a looping human chain. Even Aunt Grace and Tyler held hands with Archie who extended another hand her way.

In an instant she saw what Daniel had done, and the crowd oohed and aahed as they realized it, too. Her heart squeezed at the beautiful moment. It touched her to see Tyler in awe, his face attentive, head swiveling from person to person as he seemed to connect with the world around him instead of being apart from it. She remembered the day she'd left him by the train table at Wonders Primary, how alone he'd looked and, worse yet, how he hadn't seemed to mind. Yet here, in Cedar Bay, she felt as though he belonged, that he wasn't isolated. She grasped her locket with Tyler's picture, feeling the warm metal against her chest. For the first time in a long time, neither was she.

"Amazing isn't it?" Daniel called, one hand laced with Sue's and another with his great-aunt Mrs. Dubrey's. "We are all connected, either through blood or marriage, and this is our living family tree. It's a reminder that, as a family, we need to stick together."

A drop of rain fell and then another, and Jodi felt like crying along with it. It touched a chord in her to see familiar people who were related to her in ways she hadn't realized. Funny. She'd been looking for Daniel's next sharp jab. Instead, he'd blindsided her with such a sentimental gesture. It cut deeper than anything else he could have thrown her way. Yet she couldn't find it in her to hate him for it. Quite the opposite in fact.

"Raise your hands, family," Daniel shouted through pelting rain, and when Archie threw his hands up, Jodi's went along with them.

CHAPTER SEVEN

THE DASHBOARD CLOCK flicked to 9:00 a.m. as
Jodi drove to Tyler's first therapy session with
Sue the following day. Getting him out of the
house had been a struggle, and the soft classical
music that played soothed her jumping nerves.
Aunt Grace had loaned Jodi her car, since she
rarely used it. Midland would have paid for a
rental, but her aunt wouldn't hear of it, insist-
ing they were expensive and unreliable.

She turned off I-89 to the road leading to
Maplewood Farm, her palms slippery on the
steering wheel, her mind as snarled as the tangle of weeds sprouting by the roadside.

While her field day had been a hit, thoughts
of Daniel had lingered as she'd drifted off to
sleep. Their day competing together had resur-
rected feelings she'd thought were long buried.
As far back as her memory stretched, they'd
battled, made up, competed, forgiven, fought
and excused each other. Jodi turned up the air-
conditioning and angled it toward her face. She

wouldn't let their old cycle begin again. She'd come too far to go back.

Yet Daniel's living family tree demonstration had moved her more than she dared admit. No matter the distance, he'd proved that Cedar Bay was still her family. A sliver of doubt pierced her confidence. Was she right to help Midland break up her hometown?

A glance in her rearview mirror, however, bolstered her. Tyler, secured in a car seat in the middle of the backseat, hummed and flew Ollie by her ears. The toy's pink sequined top reflected the morning light, her camouflage pants and ballet slippers making Jodi smile. Tyler certainly had a way with style. She looked down at her functional gray business suit. Maybe he'd give her some tips one day.

"Cah!" Tyler's feet smacked the back of her seat, his body wiggling in excitement when they passed a field of grazing animals.

"Can you say *cow,* Tyler?" A cherry air freshener swung as she swerved to avoid a pothole, the fruity scent making her sneeze.

"Cah!"

She reached back and rubbed his soft knee. "Coooow." When she returned her hand to the wheel, a memory of his third Christmas came to mind. Tyler had ripped off the wrappings

KAREN ROCK   145

to a farm-animal light-up board and screamed "cow."

Today *cow* was *cah*.

Heaviness filled her heart. Hopefully she'd been right to accept Sue's therapy offer. Tyler needed help, but what if Sue grew impatient with him? Wanted more progress for her dissertation than Tyler could give?

A sob signaled Tyler had dropped Ollie and she reached behind her, groped for the elephant's tail and passed it over. Tyler kicked her seat again and she smiled. She'd take any form of thank-you she'd get.

"You're welcome," she called, and peered at Tyler's reflection again. One day, Wonders Primary would help him say the actual words. And the sooner she met with farmers and bought some land, the better. Once she dropped him off, she'd phone the farmers on her list and set up times to get together.

"Bah!" Tyler shouted, and pointed at a herd of white lambs grazing on a shorn green hill.

"Sheep," she said. "Baaaaah."

Tyler clutched his belly and laughed, the deep sound making her lips twist despite her rising nerves. That pasture meant Daniel's farm would be around the next corner.

"Baaaaaaah," he called. "Baaaa—" he started until a giggle fit overtook him.

She recognized the fields of stunted corn flashing by and her mouth went dry. Any minute now and they'd arrive. Before the field day, she'd felt like she knew Daniel. Could handle him. As her boss pointed out, he was a familiar enemy. But now her image of her "nemesis" seemed blurred and tattered around the corners. She couldn't get a clear picture of how to act with him.

His protective defense of her son on the Kan-Jam field impressed her. Even more surprising, he hadn't cared about losing the game in order to stand up to that ignorant man. It was a grown-up, less competitive side of Daniel she'd never seen before. The fact that she admired it, and him, unsettled her.

The silver glint of a silo made her pulse speed. A sign that read Maplewood Farm loomed, followed by a rambling two-story farmhouse, as she turned onto a long dirt driveway lined with sugar maples. A green canopy arched overhead, spots of light splattering the packed roadway like crystals. Too bad the pretty surroundings hid a potentially dangerous way of life. Even before her father's accident, the hard labor of farming had taken a toll on her family.

Goldie bounded out when Jodi pulled around

back and turned off the engine. It ticked in the quiet until she gathered her courage.

"Ready to go, Ty?" She slid out, gave Goldie a head rub and opened the back door.

He covered his ears at Goldie's exuberant barking and shook his head.

"We've got to go, babe." She unsnapped the seat belt and Tyler scooted to the opposite door, his face buried in his stuffed animal.

To both their surprise, Sue opened the door behind him and he tumbled out into her arms. "Way to make an entrance, Tyler. You get a fist pound for that."

She set him on his feet and held out her hand. Tyler looked from her to Jodi, then yelped when Goldie bounded around the bumper.

Jodi's stomach twisted. Hopefully Sue could handle this or she'd be taking Tyler home in a few minutes instead of a couple of hours.

When Sue held out her hand, Goldie sat, tongue lolling in the early heat. Tyler's tears dried to a sniffle when she offered him Ollie.

"Would you like to see my playroom?"

Tyler stared at a field of Jersey cows. "Cah!" His blue eyes swerved from the stomping heifers to her.

"Is that a yes?" Sue smiled.

"He means *cow*." Jodi took Tyler's hand. "But yes, the playroom sounds great." The sooner she inspected the facilities, the better she'd feel about this.

To her surprise, they walked away from the house and crossed the wide dirt area that connected the barns to the field. The pungent scent of cow manure filled the air and a wave of nostalgia overtook her. She wondered, as she peered into the field, if the cow that she and Daniel had birthed together, Jodi he'd named it, was still there. Dairy cows usually dried up before ten years and were sold to slaughterhouses. Sadness for the big-eyed brown cow with a white diamond on her forehead flooded her.

She sighed and looked around the bustling farm for signs of Daniel. The lanky young man she'd spotted with Sue yesterday strode by wheeling a stack of cement bags. He jerked his chin, smiled but didn't stop. Yet Sue blushed to her roots and fumbled with her glasses before they resumed walking. Cows mooed in a fenced-in pasture while hens pecked and clucked behind chicken wire. Large, wooly animals in a pen, alpacas, lifted graceful necks and peeked at them through long eyelashes.

Sue opened the main barn's side door and gestured for them to enter.

"This is my temporary office."

At the top of a staircase, Sue unlatched a gate and they entered a spacious area with a slanted roof. Light poured from large skylights and windows at each end of the room. The warm tones of the natural pine walls and roof, combined with the colorful toys and children's furniture, made Jodi's breath catch. Pretty.

Tyler toddled toward a train table, his fast gait making him stumble. Sue caught him as he passed by.

"Steady, kiddo."

His eyes stayed on the trains and he tiptoed over at a slower pace. Jodi's heart swelled. If nothing else, he'd enjoy his time here, and Aunt Grace wouldn't need to watch Tyler while Jodi worked.

"Thanks so much, Sue." She watched Tyler sit Ollie on top of a large, semicircular, wooden train station. "He loves trains."

Sue nodded. "Good to know." She gestured to a pair of rocking chairs that held cushions with blue-and-green crocheted coverings. "Let's talk while Tyler's playing, okay?"

"Sounds good."

"Juice?" Sue gestured to a minifridge and Jodi shook her head.

"You've thought of everything."

"No. Daniel did. He built this for me as a graduation present in case I wanted to do some private practice work here. Only…"

On impulse she leaned forward and grasped Sue's cold hands. "You will graduate."

Sue raised her head, her eyes bright and focused on Tyler.

"I will."

A fierce wish for Sue to succeed overtook Jodi. Not just for Tyler's sake, but for this capable young woman. She remembered how Sue, an advanced math and science student, had spent time tutoring Jodi through the final exams she'd missed when her father had lost his arm. Instead of kicking off her summer with the rest of her friends at a lakeside party, Sue had pored over note cards, quizzing Jodi so late that one night they'd both fallen asleep in a clean, empty stall. She smiled at the memory and at the young woman who'd once treated her like family.

Sue handed her a folder. "Here is what I observed with Tyler during our first meeting, and I'll be conducting more evaluations today."

Sue must have read the expression on Jodi's face because she hurried on. "But they won't be like traditional tests. I'm going to bring him out on the farm a bit, not near any, um, equipment." She cleared her throat as Jodi tried to snatch a full breath. Tyler outside? On the farm? This room she liked. The farm, not at all.

"I'd rather he stayed in here."

Sue's mouth turned down. "That's what my advisor would say. But I believe that, supervised appropriately, autistic children need to be immersed in the everyday world. Contributing to it as much as learning. It gives them a sense of purpose, even at Tyler's age."

Jodi rocked her chair and tried not to look as skeptical, or fearful, as she felt. "What can he do?" She glanced over at Tyler and watched him fly a green train over the tracks.

"He's going to help me raise my alpacas, weave cloth, make things." She gestured to a wooden loom in a corner.

Jodi held up the pot holder maker Sue passed her. "He'll use this to make cloths?"

"Yes. But more important, he'll make gains in fine and gross motor skills, his attention will improve and vocabulary enrichment in real life settings will occur."

"I'm not sure about him being around the alpacas." The sweet-looking animals had seemed placid enough, but appearances could be deceiving, like the time she'd mistaken a placid cow's grazing for acceptance into her field. But the heifer had charged her all the way to the goose pond where Jodi had cowered behind an enclosure until Daniel's father rescued her. The unpredictability of such situations made her shiver.

"I promise they are the gentlest creatures, but to be safe, I'll have them in a separate pen when I clean out their areas and feed and water them."

"Tyler won't be able to do all that," Jodi exclaimed. At Wonders Primary, he'd play dress-up and make puzzles. Here he'd be shoveling out pens, or trying to, if he didn't get distracted by a nearby chicken, a wind gust or even a passing cloud....

Sue nodded, her hazel eyes certain, her mouth firm. She straightened the elastic bottom of her sleeveless yellow top. "He can do something, even if it's handing me the shovel. I know it's unconventional, Jodi, but I promise you that I will keep him safe and I'm certain it will bring results. My research shows that working and playing outdoors, selective indoor therapy and the organic diet that's outlined on the purple sheet you're holding will do more than help Tyler behave appropriately. He'll gain control of his responses to the environment, lessening his fear and increasing his willingness to interact with it and people."

Jodi twisted her locket's chain. Tyler was everything to her. Did she dare leave him?

As if reading her mind, Sue rushed on. "I won't take my eye off him for a second. I've devoted my life to working with children and

I would never put him in harm's way. Believe me, Jodi, it's not just because my dissertation depends on it, but because I care about ensuring Tyler's well-being and helping him progress."

Jodi nodded at Sue's contagious excitement, taking in about every other word. It would be nothing short of a miracle if she proved her thesis. Imagine if Tyler regained his speech? Her pulse sped until she tamped down the false hope. Sue was well-meaning and brilliant, but her theories were untested.

"Sounds great." She stood and put a hand on Sue's shoulder. "I'll leave you to it." It took everything she had not to show her reluctance to leave Tyler. On a farm. Surrounded by all kinds of dangers. Yet she'd known Sue all of her life and trusted her.

"He'll be safe, Jodi. Promise."

"Of course. Thank you."

She strode to the train table and squatted beside her son. "Mommy's going to leave you with Sue for a while. Okay?"

Tyler continued waving the train in the air and smashing it against Ollie's round belly. She squelched her familiar disappointment at his dismissal, kissed the top of his head and made for the stairs. "When should I return?"

"I'm just evaluating today, so an hour."

"Okay. Call me if anything comes up and I'll drive back sooner."

"Will do."

Jodi trod down the stairs, her fingers massaging her aching temples. *Please let Tyler cooperate and behave.* Both he and Sue deserved this opportunity.

DANIEL LATHERED HIS hands and face in the barn's sink and flinched at the ice-cold water. But he had to hurry if he meant to intercept the lithe gray-suited form passing by.

"Leaving already?" he called, and Jodi turned, her golden hair swept off her face and pinned up in a simple style that emphasized her slim nose and delicate jaw.

"Morning, Daniel." Her voice was as smooth as her skin, her expression impersonal. It made him want to shake her, remind her of who she was, where she'd come from. And here was the perfect opportunity.

"Morning. Since you're waiting for Tyler, I thought I'd show you my barns."

A telltale pink rushed along her cheekbones and he wondered if she thought about their secret trysts here. He had lately.

"I mean the changes I made," he added, assessing her, noting her wide blue eyes that darted everywhere but in his direction. "Lots of improvements. Even Midland would approve."

"Maybe another time."

"No time like the present." His smile faltered when she stepped back from him. "Please, Jodi. Don't you at least want to see co-op farming in action, know firsthand what it is you're discrediting?"

It was a bit of a low blow, but then again, her ambush at his pig roast the other evening had been below the belt.

She cocked her head, her eyes considering.

"Besides, it makes good sense to know your enemy."

Her gaze met his and, to his relief, she nodded.

"Fine, but just a short tour. I've got some people to call." She stepped out of her heels and slid into calf-length rubber boots by the doorway.

He tried and failed to stop the smile at seeing her perform that simple, familiar move.

"I'll show you the milk parlor first. We get a lot done in there, and then I'll show you the stall-cleaning system. And the stalls are wider. Gives the cows more room. The silage is different, too. It's my own blend of organic grown crops and—"

"Oh—" Jodi stopped short and stared at the

cow in an isolated stall, her leg bandaged, the white diamond on her forehead against her brown hide unmistakable. "Is that—"

Daniel looked down, and then to the side. How much would she read into what he was about to confess? "Yep. That's Jodi."

Jodi stepped closer and ran her hand over her namesake. "Are you still milking her?"

Daniel shook his head. "She dried up a couple years ago," he admitted. "Now if you'd like to see the—"

"So why haven't you sold her?"

He blew out a breath. Since he hated lying, he had no choice but to speak the truth. "I should have, but I didn't want to lose her." The cow held too many memories for him to let go of her easily.

"Oh."

For a breathless moment they stared at one another until a whistling Colton passed by and stopped, took off a glove and held out a hand. "I'm Colton, and you're Jodi, right? Nice to meet you. I'm Daniel's farmhand. Been working here since—"

His voice trailed off when he caught Daniel's eye. "Was I interrupting something?"

"Not at all. Actually, Daniel was just giving me a tour. Would you like to come along?"

Colton's shoulders lifted then lowered.

"Can't. I usually help Sue with the alpacas after my morning chores."

"I didn't know Sue had help with them." Jodi's face relaxed and her shoulders lowered.

Daniel had assumed he'd been the reason for her nervous behavior, but now he saw that she was anxious for her son. Beneath her city suit and designer look, she was a mom. A good one. He shifted, unsettled at this positive view of the new Jodi. Could he admire his enemy?

"Yep. They're nice animals. Nicer than cows, even. Well, see you." Colton strode off, his coveralls billowing around his narrow frame.

Daniel cleared his throat. "Guess that just leaves us."

"Guess so."

Her soft voice did something funny to his heart, and he tried focusing on her bid to destroy his community, how her plan would banish elderly farmers to nursing homes. Anything but how much he wanted to feel her full lips against his.

"The milk parlor?" she prompted, and he gave himself a mental shake. *Get with the plan.*

He gestured. "It's this way."

They passed rows of roomy stalls with wide head openings for feeding. Since the cows were outside, the stalls were raked and lined with sweet, fresh-smelling hay. With the sun sluicing through the oversize windowpanes, he could tell that Jodi was impressed. He felt his chest swell a bit when her face swerved from side to side, her expression astonished.

"All of these improvements were done to meet the standards for the ethical treatment of animals." He couldn't keep the pride out of his voice if he tried. As a kid, it'd bothered him to see the cows penned in narrow spaces, enduring freezing winters and stifling summers.

"But you don't make more money for this." Her voice sounded hollow, surprised. Her eyes met his and he leaned his hand on the beam beside her head.

"Yes and no. Mostly it makes me feel better about my job. That's all you can ask for in life, right? To know that you're doing the right thing?"

Her eyes dropped and he gazed down at her golden hair, wondering. Did she ever have second thoughts about her work?

"Do Midland barns look like this? You've seen one, right?"

Her lower lip dropped and her chest rose and fell. Surely she'd seen one of their barns, knew everything about the company she represented....

"No." She ducked beneath his arm and strode ahead. "I haven't."

He caught up to her and slowed his long strides to match hers. "Aren't you curious about your company? What they do once you've bought up the private farms?"

"I—I—" She stopped for a moment, shook her head, then hurried on. "No. It's not my part of the job. That's a completely different department."

"But it's still part of the, what did you call it the other night, American dream that you sell to the farmers." Daniel shrugged, irritated that she'd kept herself in the dark. He'd heard plenty of disturbing rumors of these industrial-size farms. "You owe it to every farmer to know what happens to their farm once they leave it."

They walked in silence and his gaze flicked her way, noting the clash of her eyebrows, the paleness of her skin. He had her on the ropes, and took another jab. "I challenge you to visit one."

Her head whipped his way, eyes wide. "What?"

"With me," he added. He'd always wanted to tour one, and they wouldn't deny Jodi access.

"Don't be crazy." She stopped and stroked a cat lounging in a pool of sunshine.

"It's reasonable. Practical, even. What are you afraid of? Is there something that you'd rather not know?"

She straightened so fast he had to take a step back. But that was Jodi. Whenever you thought she was down for the count, she fought back the hardest.

"I'm not afraid of anything." Her blue eyes sparked like the center of a hot flame. "And there's nothing to hide, if that's what you're suggesting. A tour can be arranged."

"For both of us," he added, his smile wide.

She sighed and tapped her fingers on her slender hips. "Together. Happy?"

"Like a pig in—"

"Did you say something about a milking parlor?" She cut him off and pulled out her cell. "I only have a few more minutes before I need to get some work done."

He could imagine the kind of work she had in mind. Especially given the sticky note with names and phone numbers attached to the back of her phone. He was in no rush to hurry Jodi along. In fact, it felt good having her here. And for personal reasons, if he was honest.

They walked to the milking carousel, their shoulders brushing in a way that drove him crazy with awareness. He couldn't stop picturing the times they'd spent together here and how much that'd once meant to him.

When they arrived, the repairman finished tinkering with one of the machines and stood.

"You got it figured out, Bill?" Daniel called.

"Replaced a faulty valve, so it should be good to go." Todd left with a wave and they were alone once more, a state Daniel was growing more and more conscious of.

He tried not to stare at Jodi as she gazed around the room. Yet even with his eyes closed, he'd be able to conjure her features, the symmetry of her large eyes and heart-shaped face. It was as if she was burned into his retinas.

"This is impressive." Her voice had lost its coolness and sounded awed instead. Impressed. "Daniel, you've done a good job."

He fought and lost the battle to keep the pride out of his voice. "Thanks. Things were rough for a while but we're back on track now."

"Your parents must be very proud."

He flinched. One was anyway.

"Daniel?" A soft hand descended on his arm and his biceps tightened. "When I...ah...came by the other night, Sue said your dad was sleeping, but she never mentioned your mom."

Daniel watched the whirring ceiling fans and fought to control his voice before using it.

"She left shortly after you did." His voice cracked and he strode to the room containing the milk tanks, needing a moment to get ahold of himself. He'd tried not to blame Jodi, and realized that, after all these years, part of him still did.

"I'm sorry, Daniel," she said when she joined him inside the dim, close room. "I didn't know. No one said." Her sympathetic tone made him blink back a sudden sting in his eyes. Why was he letting the past get to him like this?

"Grace didn't tell you?"

"No." Jodi's eyes looked navy in the gloom. "Why didn't she tell me?"

"Maybe because it had to do with you," he blurted, and then wished those words back again. It didn't pay to get that personal with her. Not again.

Jodi looked at him in shock and she gripped the edge of one of the large milk tanks. "How did I have anything to do with it?"

He looked at her, considering, then decided to tell her the truth and spare Grace the tale. "She didn't like my dad loaning our equipment out since it often came back broken. Mom accused him of being too soft and letting our farm get in financial trouble."

"And that has to do with me because—" Jodi's features scrunched and he imagined the wheels turning in that sharp mind of hers. "Because you loaned us the skid loader that crushed my dad's arm and it broke," she finished in a breathless rush, realization coloring her voice like dawn on a stormy day.

He didn't speak, his mind recalling the bitter arguments leading up to the divorce, how working with Jodi in the barns, their friendship and romance, had helped. Only, his latent anger at the situation had led to a moment of cruelty he'd always regret.

"So replacing it made your mother decide to leave your dad? I was so focused on my own family's problems that I didn't think about that." A fine line appeared between her eyebrows.

He nodded. "We've had to replace lots of parts and entire machines that Pop let neighbors use. Sometimes they had the money to pay for the repairs, but most times they didn't. But he never quit wanting to help and my mother didn't understand. She wasn't from around here.... Look, Jodi, it wasn't your fault."

A breathy exclamation escaped her. "But you resented me anyway. That's why you agreed when your friends called me The Charity Case. And when I asked, you admitted that you pitied me and my family. Worse, you never denied dating me because you felt sorry for me. I couldn't understand how you could have real feelings for me when you looked down me. I didn't want that kind of relationship."

He held her hands but she yanked them away. "I cared about you. Being together helped me get through that tough summer."

"Me, too," she whispered, her eyes searching his. "But I didn't put you down, label you."

Her words stung and he flinched. Echoes of the argument that ended their relationship sounded in his head. "I should have told those guys off for calling you a charity case and told you the truth about my mixed-up feelings. You were everything to me then, but I blamed you, too—for my parents' arguments—and that was wrong." There. It wasn't the best speech, but he'd needed to get it out. An apology long overdue. Saying the words made something inside him lighten, release and drift away.

"Thank you," Jodi murmured with her eyes lowered. He wished he could see her expression. Know if she really understood and forgave him. It still bothered him that she'd left without a word, but he now saw that he'd had a hand in that.

"Well." Suddenly her voice sounded crisp again, detached, as she studied a picture of herself and Tyler on her phone. "That's water under the bridge. I'm sorry for your parents' divorce, Daniel. Had I known—"

Her voice trailed off and she scrolled through

the contacts on her cell, the action sparking his temper.

"Had you known, what would you have done? Left a note before you walked out on me? Or, I don't know, maybe warned me?"

She lowered her phone. "Daniel. This is old news. Ten years ago. We've moved past it. Now. If you'll excuse me." She brushed by him, then turned in the doorway, the outside light illuminating her silhouette but casting her features in shadow. "It was a lovely tour."

And with that she walked away, leaving Daniel too drained to chase after her. Not that it would have done any good. Jodi left when she pleased, causing destruction without a backward glance. It was true in her personal life and it was true when it came to business. She hadn't cared enough to see the new and "improved" Midland farms—at least until he'd challenged her. Why would she want to continue discussing how they'd both felt that long-ago summer?

She might have moved past it, but suddenly, he realized, he had not.

CHAPTER EIGHT

LAKE WATER SPLASHED Jodi's face three days later, a wild screeching filling the late afternoon air.

"Tyler, stop." She reached for his fingers but they evaded her, churning Lake Champlain's cobalt surface to silver. Droplets sprayed into a cloudless sky. The vibrant sun kissed her son's face, and his happiness and the water's cool caress refreshed her. It soothed the ache of Daniel's revelation and the sting of another canceled meeting today. Her tenth this week.

"Roooooo." Tyler formed his mouth into an O and imitated one of Daniel's farm animals, his favorite new trick. He giggled so hard that he quit splashing and Jodi pulled him close, his swim vest and armbands making them buoyant. If only her problems felt this weightless.

Her toes dug into the soft sand and she bounced them up and down in the chest-high water beside her aunt's dock. Overhead, shrieking white-and-gray-feathered terns wheeled and Tyler cawed back. And then it hit her.

Why hadn't she noticed before? He might not be speaking, but his silent life had turned on its speakers.

Elation made her twirl them until silt rose around her knees. Could the shift in his daily routine have helped? Wonders Primary would be impressed at his new verbalization. Was there a chance they might get him to say words by the holidays? Her heart flew with the soaring birds. It would be the greatest gift of all.

Yet her happiness was tempered by the anguish she'd felt in Daniel's barns. She'd called their former relationship water under the bridge to keep herself from revealing her true feelings. His unexpected apology had touched her and it took everything not to tell him so. If only he'd said all of this to her ten years ago. Now it was too late and they were locked in a battle where the lines were clearly drawn. She couldn't cross them.

"Caw!" Jodi shouted to the chattering flock, startling a heron fishing off the end of the dock.

"Caw!" Tyler called, his eyes tracking the long-billed bird as it flapped away.

She cupped the back of his small head and pressed her nose to his, uneasy but happy for this time with her son. The feeling of failure over today's lost meeting and her inability to open up to Daniel receded. Unexpected moments with Tyler were precious and meant so much. He was her priority.

She tossed a rainbow of plastic rings onto the rippling surface and Tyler wiggled free.

"Find green," she suggested, following Sue's advice for continued, real-world motor skills work. So far Sue's therapy sessions had gone well—meaning no meltdowns or injuries. Better yet, Tyler handled the transition of being dropped off and picked up with less fuss than he had when she'd brought him to her Chicago neighbor's apartment. Another improvement: he went down for his naps easier, his eyes fluttering closed, head drowsing as she carried him to his bed. Maybe not huge progress to some, but to Jodi, every positive change, no matter how slight, felt like a victory.

Tyler slapped the water and strained toward a bobbing green ring, his legs scissoring, his voice rising in agitation.

She lifted his belly and pulled up his legs so that his thrashing propelled him forward. When he grabbed his prize, she let go and clapped.

"Good job! Now stick it on your vest." Using the Velcro she'd glued onto the ring, she helped him adhere it to a similar patch sewn on the swim garment. It rode high on his chest like a medal. And maybe it was. Great deeds were measured by effort in Jodi's book. "Now get the yellow one."

This time Tyler pushed his feet against her thighs, making her stumble and lose her hold on him. When his head dipped in the water, he resurfaced coughing and crying.

"Shh. Shh. It's okay, Tyler," She caressed his blotchy face. "You're okay. See. Safe. And you still have your green ring."

Tyler sniffled and patted the plastic on his vest, his eyes wide and questioning. His quivering lower lip steadied.

"The yellow ring is right there." She pointed to a nearby ring and helped him onto his stomach with his legs stretched behind him.

Patience. Perseverance. Persistence. Her mantra.

She needed to apply it to herself and her worsening Cedar Bay situation. The local town hall meeting tonight felt like her last chance to undo the fallout from Daniel's "living family tree" exercise. She'd been touched by that unforgettable moment; it haunted her still. But after farmers who'd agreed to meet and discuss selling canceled, she'd known that it'd hurt her sales.

One had told her outright that he couldn't sell his farm when his neighbors felt like family. Daniel's demonstration had been a powerful reminder of Cedar Bay's roots and how they connected the community. His talk with her in the barn had also been powerful, but in a wholly personal way she needed to stop thinking about.

Tyler butted against her and pushed the yellow ring in her face, pulling her out of her reverie.

"Gentle touch, Ty." She moved the plastic away from her cheek and guided it toward his vest. "Stick it."

Tyler's eyes narrowed behind his prescription swim goggles and his tongue appeared between his teeth. He struggled, then succeeded in attaching it, his smile lighting him up from the inside out.

"Good, little man! Now go for the red." She guided him to the left and was blinded by a spray of water as he kicked in that direction. She wiped the blur from her eyes and blinked until her vision cleared.

Disoriented. That was how she felt around Daniel lately. Seeing the confident swing of his arms, the pride that firmed his square jaw, his earnest expression when describing his farm improvements, and his heartfelt apology, had moved her in a way she refused to think about. He'd matured and changed, but so had she.

She flipped onto her back and floated, the

sun's rays warming her face. She kept her eye on Tyler, who grabbed at the bobbing red ring, missed and lunged again. She smiled at his perseverance. It ran in the family.

She trailed her fingers in the water and glimpsed Tyler snatch the ring and jerk it aloft. Victory. One step at a time. It was an important reminder when things seemed more lost than ever.

A few minutes later, all four rings swung from his swim vest, his "medals" lifting and lowering as he bobbed. She smiled despite her work and personal worries and was contemplating another round of ringtoss when she heard her aunt's voice.

"Jodi, phone call!"

Aunt Grace waved her cell from the porch and Jodi made out her boss's ringtone, the ominous chords of Beethoven's Ninth Symphony. Her chest tightened.

"Would you answer it?" she called in a breathy rush. "And tell Mr. Williams that I'll return his call in a minute?"

Her aunt nodded and disappeared into the house, the phone to her ear.

"Okay, merman. Time to go." She swam Tyler over to the rocks rather than hoisting them both onto the dock. Her feet scraped against shale but she was in too much of a hurry to watch her footing as she carried a protesting Tyler.

He reached for the lake over her shoulder and cried, wanting more swim time, maybe more *Mom* time, since they hadn't been together this much in…in…she couldn't remember. Maybe not since the six weeks' maternity leave she'd had to cut to four.

The thought saddened her, but that was the reality of being a single mother. Occasional choices that involved food on the table versus play on the floor.

Aunt Grace handed her a towel and the phone when she burst into the kitchen. With the wave of a Sue-recommended organic cookie, Tyler quieted and her aunt took him into the living room.

Jodi wrapped herself in the oversize terry cloth and returned to a canopied porch swing outside. She curled up against a cushion and hit the redial button on her caller ID.

"Hi, Gail. It's Jodi. Mr. Williams called me."

"Hi, Jodi! How's Vermont? Better bring us back some maple syrup and cheese."

She laughed, her fingers tracing the towel's zigzagging stripes. "I will. How's everything?"

"Insane. I mean, the same." Gail's chuckle snuffed out. "Oh, hello, Mr. Williams," Jodi heard her exclaim. "I've got Ms. Chapman on the line for you." In the brief pause that followed, Mr. Williams's low voice rumbled. "Of course. I'll put her right through," Gail said briskly.

"Bye, Gail." Jodi could barely hear herself over her thumping heart. What good news could she share with her superior regarding her progress in Cedar Bay? "See you soon, I hope."

"Hope so, too." Gail cleared her throat then whispered, "I heard the quarterly statements came in. Not good. See you."

Jodi's fingers tightened on the phone. A bad financial report meant Midland would be counting on this deal more than ever. Yet she couldn't reassure her boss. Would he yank her off the project, force her home before she'd had the chance to earn the promotion...and figure out her strange feelings for Daniel? She shivered as a breeze ruffled the lake's surface and tossed her drying hair.

"Jodi," Mr. Williams's voice barked in her ear. The seat swung at her startled jump. "I'd like a full report. How many acquisitions have you made? Acreage totals..."

"It's good to hear from you, Mr. Williams," Jodi stalled.

He snorted. "Sorry, Jodi. Things around here are a little tense right now. No need to worry on your end, though." His rough tone sounded off, however, and Jodi's anxiety rose.

"I'm making solid headway, Mr. Williams. Over a hundred people attended our Midland Field Day."

"Good." His voice brightened. "I saw some of the pictures the photographer sent back for the company newsletter. Was that the Gleason fellow standing next to you with the megaphone?" A swirling, swooshing sound carried through the phone followed by an "Ouch. Darn machine."

"Espresso?" she asked, desperate to make this conversation veer in any direction but sales transactions.

"Yes. Now, back to the photo…"

"You said 'know your enemy.'" Daniel's warm smile and easy way around Tyler came to mind. It was getting harder to see him as her nemesis, despite her words.

A chuckle carried through the receiver. "Right. Keep them close. Now, about your sales… What preliminary numbers can I run by the higher-ups?"

Higher up than Mr. Williams? Jodi couldn't imagine those individuals except that they lived overseas and only appeared on holiday cards. She gnawed on a fingernail.

"I don't have any, sir." Her halting voice

frightened her. Where was the confident junior executive she'd been in Chicago? Had a week and a half in Cedar Bay eroded her self-assurance? Her ability to get the job done?

A tapping pen or pencil broke the prolonged silence. "I see," Mr. Williams said at last. "That's unusual for you, Jodi. Anything the matter?"

She nearly choked on the bitter laugh that swelled. How could she admit that she was failing? That Daniel was besting her, getting under her skin as he had for most of her life. Worse, she was letting down Tyler, who deserved her success more than anyone.

She straightened her slouch and projected confidence into her tone. "Not at all. Things move a bit slower in Cedar Bay. The farmers need to be treated with special care. It's the reason the other executives failed and I'll succeed."

Mr. Williams took a noisy sip. "Fine. But the sooner you can get me firm figures the better. There's some noise about sending Brady to help now that he's wrapped up the Mexico deal, but I vouched that you'd manage fine on your own. I know how much you want that promotion, Jodi. But you need to get those five thousand acres on your own to earn it."

Jodi swallowed over the painful tightness

in her throat, then blurted, "Of course, sir." Brady? The junior executive nicknamed The Rainmaker for his incredible sales record? If he came he'd edge her out and steal acquisitions wherever he could. Worse yet, his shark-like tactics meant he'd mistreat the people who, she couldn't deny any longer, were important to her. She didn't want to undercut anyone and she knew he wouldn't deal as fairly with her hometown as she would.

"Good. Then I'll expect an update on Monday with sales data."

Four days. Under normal circumstances she should have no problem bringing him good news in that time period. But Daniel was anything but a typical sales obstacle. However, with Brady's presence threatening like a thunderstorm, she had to show central office she could succeed on her own.

"Understood. I'll speak with you then."

She clicked off the phone and slid lengthwise onto the swing, her stomach clenching. She had to make this work. Fast. Her eyes closed when a gust ruffled the swing's canopy, her mind as unsettled as the flapping material.

DANIEL PEERED AT the men and women packing the town hall later that night, their bodies filling up rows of folding chairs while others lined the walls. Impressive. His adrenaline rushed at the thought of laying out his co-op plans to such a large group. The only hitch in his plan was the beautiful blonde striding his way, her tailored black skirt and jacket looking sharp and professional in a way that his all-purpose suit never could.

He straightened his green tie and rubbed the back of his shorn neck, glad for the haircut Sue had given him after dinner. Despite the dry heat stirred by ceiling fans, he felt cool. Under control. As long as he didn't look too long at Jodi. He couldn't resist a peek as she sat down a few chairs away, his eye drawn to the swing of her curved calf and tapered ankle, the arch of her foot as it disappeared into impossibly high heels. How did women walk in those things? Yet she'd waltzed in here as if she owned the place. And that was not a foregone conclusion. Not as long as he had something to say about it.

The president of the council stood and the murmuring crowd quieted.

"Tonight we'll present our community with a couple of proposals to bolster our economy. Each speaker will have fifteen minutes to give a presentation." Richard Goddard's red-lined eyes meandered Daniel's way and narrowed sternly. "A fifteen-minute question and answer session will follow. Daniel Gleason, you're up."

He slung his data posters under his arm and avoided the triumphant gleam in Jodi's eye. She'd get the last word tonight when the home-court advantage should have been his. Well. He'd make the best of it.

Thirty minutes later, his knee jittered as the assembly burst into thunderous applause at Jodi's conclusion. The windowpanes rattled with the group's raucous whoops and hollers, the thud of clamoring feet echoing off the elevated ceiling rafters. He clapped with them, a polite gesture but also one he meant.

He'd come to see so much more in Jodi this week, starting with her tender care of Tyler, the faith she'd shown Sue and how passionate she'd sounded tonight when speaking about the dangers of farm life, her earnestness when suggesting that some of the farming families might enjoy a life with a little more downtime. He respected the thoughtful, articulate adversary she was and realized that her job at Midland was about more than a paycheck. She believed in what she did.

When she'd revealed the mind-boggling price her company would pay per acre, many jaws had dropped. He could practically see those who hadn't heard the news at her field day doing the math in their heads, slow smiles spreading across their tired faces as they realized how much they'd get for selling their farms.

While they'd cheered for him about the benefits of collectively bargaining their health care premiums and setting their milk prices, it hadn't been this loud. In fact, the majority of those who'd clapped were school friends and closer neighbors. Others had looked puzzled when he'd shown them the charts of needed upgrades and had explained that spending money would make them money.

It was a tough sell, especially when the co-op grant wasn't a given. But he'd expected more and felt frustrated that he hadn't reached them as Jodi had. Her dollar signs chased away the sense of community he'd revived at her field day.

The council president shook back a lock of salt-and-pepper hair and stood. "Thanks to you both. Ladies and gentlemen, there are microphones in either aisle. Please form a line behind them and we'll take turns asking questions, starting with the right side."

Daniel marveled when dozens of people scrambled into the aisles. He'd been clear and his data spoke for itself. Besides, he'd emphasized how his plan would preserve their small farms and community. Maybe they needed more clarification from Jodi?

Mrs. Lareau, the local librarian, shifted her feet and tapped the microphone hard enough to make it squeal.

"Ahem," sounded the tiny voice he remembered from trips into town. "Would you both sum up your proposals in one word? Some of us might appreciate a simpler picture."

As they were now seated in the middle of the front row, Jodi's hip brushed his shoulder when she stood. He rubbed the tingling spot, his nose flaring as it caught the tang of her perfume.

"Freedom," she said, then sat again. Her lower eyelid twitch made him wonder if she felt as confident as she appeared.

"Daniel?" prompted the council president.

He shot to his feet. Focus. A word. What word could he choose now that Jodi had taken his? Then a thought struck him and he leaned into his microphone.

"Freedom." He smiled at the stunned faces staring back at him.

Who said they couldn't each have an interpretation of what that meant? If there was a rule about it, he wasn't following it.

"Next!" the president thundered, quieting the muttering crowd. A thin man in patched overalls stepped forward. Jack Gowette.

"I had a different question, but now I've changed it." He adjusted and readjusted his baseball hat's brim. "Could you both explain what you mean by *freedom?* My head's spinning so hard it's like to fall off."

A spontaneous round of clapping broke out followed by a few whistles. Suddenly the friendly crowd felt less welcoming.

He glanced at Jodi, then stood. It was ladies first in his book, but her tightly clasped hands showed she needed time to think.

"Owning your own farm means shaping your life—your future—with your own two hands." His voice echoed back at him over the PA system. "The amount of time you give it, the effort and ingenuity you bring to the table, equals what you get out, plain and simple." He met Sue's eyes and returned her smile. "My co-op would preserve our freedoms because we'd still be our own bosses. No jumping to follow orders from higher-ups."

When he turned, he caught Jodi's wry expression before her thick eyelashes fluttered down to rest on pale, creamy cheeks. "Your turn."

Jodi smoothed a nonexistent wrinkle in her skirt, then walked briskly to the microphone, looking unruffled as ever.

"Selling to Midland will give you the freedom to choose the life you've always wanted instead of the one you inherited." Her soft voice strengthened and rose. "Many of you were raised on the farms you now operate. You were expected—no, commanded—to continue raising crops and animals because your ancestors did it. I don't call that freedom."

Daniel kept his face impassive when her blue eyes darted his way. Note everything, give away nothing, he reminded himself. And his biggest takeaway of the night: Jodi's strength as his opponent came from her intelligence and conviction, not her company's wallet.

She faced the crowd once more and waited while a mother with a wailing baby left and the room quieted again.

"I call that tyranny. With my purchase price, you can start over where you want, doing what you want, for the rest of your life. What's more, you'll be free of the dangers and worries that go with private-operation farming. I hope you'll prefer my kind of freedom to Daniel's. Thank you."

The crowd applauded and Jodi settled beside him. He crossed his ankle over his knee and mulled over how much her family's tragedy factored into her zeal to shut down small farms. It was a different motivation than the one he'd attributed to the profit-driven businesswoman he'd thought she'd become. At the reunion, she'd admitted that her battle to acquire Cedar Bay farms was personal. Was this what she'd meant?

"Anyone?" Larry Eveleth, a farmer as old as Daniel's father, tapped on the microphone, his weather-beaten face creased in confusion. Daniel gave him a startled nod and the man leaned down. "How much experience does each of you have with what you're proposing?" Suddenly Daniel wished his father could have attended. Hearing the presentation might make him stop wishing Daniel would give up farming. Maybe he'd even embrace the co-op idea.

Jodi stepped forward and Daniel joined her. "Sorry about that Mr. ah…" She gave Daniel a questioning look and he whispered, "Eveleth," as he pretended to bend and tie his shoe.

"Mr. Eveleth," Jodi continued, her tone warm. "I've handled hundreds of acquisitions deals with highly satisfied customers. In fact, if you'll add your name to the sign-up sheet being passed around, I'll be happy to supply you with references so that you can speak personally with farmers I've dealt with in the past. As for Daniel's experience creating co-ops, I have my opinion, but I'll defer to him."

The wicked twinkle in her eye made him wish he'd never saved her with the "Eveleth" maneuver.

"My experience with co-ops is largely

through my studies and internships at Cornell University as well as trips I've taken to visit others in the lower half of Vermont and in up-state New York."

Heads came together and a muttering rose from the crowd. Daniel shifted in his tight loafers.

"May I ask a follow-up question, Rich?" asked Mr. Eveleth.

The council president cocked his head, then nodded.

"Why should we trust this co-op? Seems like Jodi's got a lot more experience."

Jodi's smile bloomed.

Daniel relaxed his features and clasped his hands behind his back before leaning into the microphone. "She has more experience forcing people off their property. Better knowledge on how to get farmers to abandon a way of life that preserves individuality, family, community and the America our founders envisioned."

He paused, enjoying the hush that'd descended and Jodi's restless movement beside him.

"She hasn't even seen any of the farms once they were sold to Midland. So the real question is, what is your experience with me? You've known me all your lives. I'm honest, fair, capable and I've made a success of my own farm and will help you do the same with yours. It's a matter of the right kind of experience. Most of all, it's a matter of trust."

Heads came together again and the noise grew loud enough for Rich to bang his gavel. "Quiet please. I'm afraid we only have time for one more question before we get to other town matters. Ms. Spellman?"

Mary, the classmate who'd supported Jodi at his pig roast, stepped forward, her full skirt swinging.

"I just wanted to invite everyone to The Lounge tonight. It's Line Dancing Thursday and I'll take half off the cover charge for everyone here. Jodi and Daniel, you two are my guests of honor."

A roar swept through the back of the crowd where the younger members stood. The older farmers down front smiled and shook their heads as if remembering their own glory days.

Daniel smiled wide. "Better save a dance for me, Mary."

"You'll have to come over, then!" With a wave, she twirled and raced to the doors shouting, "Follow me!"

"Where are you going?"

He turned and looked straight into Jodi's eyes without letting his gaze falter. "To The Lounge. Colton and Sue said they'll handle the morning milking, so I've got the night off to have some fun."

Her nose scrunched, making her upper lip look fuller and more kissable than ever. He forced himself to look away.

"You mean you're taking the night off to talk more people into getting into the co-op."

He shrugged at her accusing tone and propelled himself away from the beauty that drove him to distraction. "If the topic comes up, I won't stop it." He kept his voice light and normal. She'd made it clear in the barn the other day that she didn't want old feelings rekindled. And he didn't trust himself to renew them either, especially when they grew each time he saw her.

Jodi caught up to him and they plunged into the soft summer night. "I can stop it." With her black suit and blond hair, the full moon acting as her backdrop, she resembled an old-fashioned picture of herself. Crickets played their songs in the grass, but they couldn't compete with the jamboree going on across the street.

"Then you'd better hurry, because the Cupid Shuffle is playing."

He strode to a white clapboard building and heard her heels clicking behind him. Beneath Jodi's confidence, he'd detected an edge of desperation tonight. That eye twitch. It always gave her away. Was she getting pressure from work? If so, he was glad. Maybe they'd recall her and send someone who'd give him less of a fight. Although the thought of her leaving didn't fill him with the same satisfaction it had when she'd first arrived.

Foot-stomping music enveloped him the moment he stepped into the dim, rectangular room. When he stopped to wave at the doorman, Jodi bumped into his back. The brief contact made his eyes close in pleasure until a familiar voice had them snapping open again.

"Why, it's Jodi Lynn. You're looking good tonight."

"Ted." Daniel nodded his head in greeting, trying and failing to keep the growl out of his voice.

"Hi, Ted." Jodi smiled, her mouth lifting slightly at the corners. "I'm looking forward to our meeting tomorrow." She cleared her throat. "You don't plan to cancel, do you?"

Daniel peered from her to a beaming Ted. Why would she question the meeting? It flew in the face of her usual confidence. Unless... He glanced around the room, seeing the rueful looks some of the patrons gave her before they returned to playing pool or darts. Had other farmers canceled? If so, that explained the insecurity he'd sensed. All week he'd imagined her signing deals while he'd toiled in the barns. It'd nearly driven him crazy. That and thoughts of kissing her.

"Of course. Ten o'clock on the dot. Been thinking about it, and you, all week." Ted wrapped an arm around Jodi. "Mind if I steal her for a dance, Daniel?"

"I do."

Ted backed off and Jodi's brows came together as she glared Daniel's way.

"Right. Wishful thinking I guess." Ted waved apologetically. "We'll talk more tomorrow, Jodi," he called over his shoulder.

Jodi shook her head at Daniel, and a few wavy strands fell around her face. "I can speak for myself and dance with whomever I wish."

"Then I'll leave you to it and talk to some of those farmers." He nodded to a loud group in a corner. "They look like they could use a pitcher."

Her hand gripped his wrist, her touch a scorching reminder that he was a long way from over her. "I've got to get back to Tyler. This is unfair."

Daniel shrugged, enjoying the sight of his unflappable opponent so flustered. "All's fair in love and war. Except this isn't love, now, is it?"

Her face pinked and her gaze slid out from under his. "Of course not."

The music switched to an old country tune they'd been forced to dance to together in middle school gym class.

"So glad you could make it." Mary shoved her way between them and smiled wide, her silver hoop earrings brushing her shoulders, a small butterfly tattoo visible on her shoulder. "Remember how Mr. Martin made us dance to this? My brother always plays it." She nodded to Steve who stood behind a wall of black boxes and blinking lights. "Brings back great memories. I recall you two being partners. Don't you just miss those days?"

He nodded and Jodi followed suit. Mary was the delta through which all town news flowed. It didn't pay to offend her.

She cupped her hands and hollered "Steve!" so loud he lowered the music and looked up. "What?" he mouthed.

"Can you start that one over? These two want to dance to it."

Everyone, including the bar backs, looked up, and Daniel wished he and Jodi were anywhere but here. Seeing her this past week had brought back feelings he'd thought he'd forgotten. At the reunion, he'd wanted to dance with her to get information. Now he knew he'd focus only on Jodi.

The music began and Mary gave Daniel a little shove. "Have at her. Indulge us for old times' sake. Everyone thought you two would make a great couple when you weren't scrapping."

He looked down at a dismayed Jodi. "Guess we can't disappoint our fans."

She threw her hands up and he swept her into his arms. And just like he thought, the feel of her brought back their middle school days. He recalled his sweaty palms on her tiny waist and how much he'd tripped because, instead of counting the steps, he'd counted the freckles on her nose. Kind of like now.

"Mr. Martin had some crazy taste in music," she surprised him by saying, a far-off look in her eyes. "How did that count as exercise?"

Being around her raised his blood pressure. She was the best cardio he could imagine. They moved across the crowded floor, weaving in and out of other couples.

"No idea." When the tempo changed he twirled and dipped her, their mouths nearly touching as he bent her over his arm for a long, breathless moment. The feel of her made his blood surge.

"Let me up," she said in a rush, and pushed at

his chest, her touch electric. When he straightened, he pulled her closer and smoothed the hair that had come loose from her bun, her locks like silk. He inhaled the light, fresh scent of her and his body tightened against hers. His eyes dropped to her lips and he remembered her taste: honeysuckle and lemon drops. Kissing her had felt like kissing sunshine, and for a moment he lost himself in the glow of that memory.

"Daniel," she whispered, her eyes shimmering up at him, her voice husky. "People are watching."

"Let them."

When she trembled in his arms, he knew she was remembering the afternoons he'd held her this way. How they'd lie snuggled in the deep grass together, the blue sky their only witness. It'd been magic. The ultimate trick, however, had been her disappearing act. The thought sobered him and he loosened his grip. She challenged, exhilarated, frustrated and attracted him like no other. Yet she had crushed him, too, and he sensed that could happen as easily now as it had then if he wasn't careful. He wasn't just at war with her, he also battled himself.

As he guided her through the swaying couples, their bodies moved in perfect sync. Suddenly he thought of her ex and felt a rush of jealousy at the thought of her in another man's arms.

"I'm sorry to hear about your divorce," he said, and felt her stiffen.

"I got through it," she said lightly, her eyes sliding from his.

"Do you still see him?" An irrational need to know how much time she still spent with the man seized him. It didn't matter—or it shouldn't—yet somehow, it did.

A laugh-snort escaped her and her gaze flew to his. "Not since he left."

"What about Tyler?" he blurted. The guy might be a fool for not returning Jodi's love, but he must at least care for his own child.

The music ended and he led her to a table by the window. After pulling out her chair, he straddled his.

Jodi caught her lower lip between her teeth and gazed outside. The sun had set completely and the moon was up, a wedge of creamy white casting its reflection onto the lake. Night wind rattled tree branches, knocking them against one another. "Not Tyler, either," she said at last, her voice sounding empty. Scraped out.

He found her cold fingers beneath the table and wrapped his palms around them. "He's a terrible father." And a horrible person. Who would abandon his wife and child? He'd known she was a single mother, but he'd never known that she was raising her son entirely on her own. After this night of revelations, she'd surprised him again and he admired her even more. What a strong, caring person.

Jodi nodded, her face bleak and beautiful. "Tyler wouldn't stop crying after his dad left until—"

She froze, then yanked her hands away and stood. "I've got to go."

"Jodi." His voice stopped her. "I—I—" He broke off, searching for the right words the way he might grope for a light switch in the dark.

She glanced around the bar, the faraway look gone, her expression sharp. "We shouldn't do this. It's not good for either of us to get this personal. My focus is on Tyler. Not bars. Not men." She gazed at him, her eyes pleading. "Not you."

Before he could stand, she flew out the door, leaving him again.

CHAPTER NINE

"YOU SURE YOU can't stay for lunch?" Ted dropped a handful of sugar cubes in Jodi's freshened coffee the next day and sat beside her at his kitchen table.

She ducked her face and breathed in the caffeine rather than Ted's heavily spiced cologne. Hopefully he'd sign the paperwork and sell her his farm soon. She traced a dark pine knot on the table's surface. He'd been dancing around the issue for almost two hours now. Beneath the table, she slid her aching toes out of her narrow high heels, then squashed them in again.

"Thanks, but it's almost time for me to pick up my son." She angled the purchase agreement toward him. "If you don't have any further questions, would you sign here—"

"Tyler, right?" Ted pushed a ceramic cow creamer her way and reached for a plate of gingersnaps. "Heard he had an affliction. He's ah…um—" He seemed to fumble for the words. "Mute?" A crack sounded as he bit into the cookie.

Jodi stirred in the milk and forced herself to sip her sugary drink before she spoke her mind. In the quiet, a grandfather clock chimed the noon hour. Who was Ted Layhee to label her son? Tyler wasn't mute. He was loving, funny and smart. He just couldn't or wouldn't use words right now. But Wonders Primary would fix that, and the sooner she earned her raise to pay their tuition the better, starting with her first sale—the Layhee farm.

"He's autistic." She lowered her cup and schooled her face into a friendly expression. *Please, Ted. Sell the farm.*

"Heard of kids like that." He spoke while chewing, crumbs dropping to a rooster-patterned table runner.

Kids like that... The words echoed in Jodi's heart. Would the world ever accept children like Tyler? Would his father? Probably not, and the realization made her ache.

Jodi held up her napkin, pretending to blow her nose but dabbing the corners of her eyes instead. "I see. Now, back to the sale of your farm—"

Ted laid a dry, calloused palm over her knuckles. "Do you want more kids, Jodi?"

She yanked her hand back. "Let's focus on business, please." Her tone bordered on abrupt, but she couldn't help it. After hours of listening to him talk in circles, his comments turning personal and even insulting, her control was slipping.

Ted's chipped canine appeared in a wide smile, his dishwater-gray eyes speculative. "Know what? You need less business and more fun in your life, Jodi. And I'm your man. Even if your son is…is—" he reached over to a jar on the nearby counter and threw his snoozing dog a biscuit "—isn't one hundred percent right," he finished lamely.

Not right? Her chair scraped against the linoleum floor as she bolted to her feet. Enough. "Tyler is perfect! He's none of your business, and now neither is this."

She snatched up the purchase agreement, stuffed it in her briefcase and marched out of the house despite Ted's protests.

ON THE DRIVE to Maplewood Farm, Jodi fumed. She could catalog Tyler's differences, every area in which he needed to progress, but no one had a right to point them out. Ted acted as though Tyler was an oddity and her ex pretended Tyler didn't exist. She swatted the cherry-scented air freshener, needing a clearer picture of her world.

The only thing Peter seemed to notice, and resent, was paying child support. She flicked off the droning radio. This morning, she'd torn up the letter she'd received with the upcoming trial date to lower his child support. There was no way she could deal with that when she had so many other things to handle.

Her growing feelings for Daniel being one of them.

She replayed the shock in his eyes when she'd told him how Peter had rejected Tyler. It touched her that he'd been so horrified. Clearly, he'd never do that to his own children, and imagining him as a father filled her with a strange longing.

It amazed her that, despite everything, Daniel could make her open up as she had at The Lounge. Did part of her still trust him? Care for him? The thought unnerved her.

She stomped on the brakes for a dithering squirrel. When he raced back the way he'd come, she wondered if she should do the same. Go home. Quit. Her foot pressed the gas pedal and the car leaped forward. But giving up would mean letting Tyler down.

In a moment too fast to register, she swerved to keep from overshooting Maplewood Farm and plummeted into the ditch next to the driveway. A hissing sound and puff of white appeared from under the front hood. Her chest ached from the air bag's impact and she rested her damp face against it while her chest heaved. Could things get any worse?

The humming sound of an approaching tractor confirmed that, yes, it could. The engine quit and, in an instant, her door was yanked open and Daniel's anxious face appeared.

"Are you okay? What happened?" he asked while he freed her from the seat belt and pulled her out and into his arms.

She could only nod against his chest, his thumping heart loud in her ear. When the trees seemed to tilt, she wrapped her arms around his warm neck and he hoisted her higher, an arm under her legs while another wrapped around her back.

"I've got you," he murmured, his voice both rough and tender.

"Thank you." His solid body quieted her shaking nerves and, after a moment, she was able to look up into his wide hazel eyes. His dark brows were drawn together, a line between them.

"This isn't my day," she confessed when she should have kept up her guard. But she felt rattled to her toes and Daniel's steadiness made her feel safe.

"It's only noon. The second half could get a whole lot better." His faint smile faded when her eyes stung. "Jodi Lynn, whatever it is, we'll fix it."

She shook her head and buried it against his broad chest, humiliated that he, of all people, had witnessed her at her weakest. "Please let me down."

"Of course." And he deposited her on her feet as gently as placing eggs under a warming lamp.

When she stumbled, he caught her around the waist, then let go again when she clutched the car door and waved him off. Her world still spun, but she needed to right it on her own.

"I can pull you out with the tractor."

"I'd appreciate that."

He swung himself into the black bucket seat of the tall green tractor and, in one move, reversed it so its back end abutted her bumper. The easy expertise of his maneuver impressed her. Or perhaps it was Daniel and his athletic beauty, the way he held himself, his shirtsleeves riding up on toned biceps, the lean planes of his stomach revealed when he twisted around to ensure they didn't collide.

Either way, it was a dangerous direction for her mind to travel. When he hopped down and grabbed metal chains from a storage box behind his seat, she averted her eyes. Better not to look at things she couldn't have.

Once he'd hooked her car to the tractor, he waved a hand.

"If you don't mind getting behind the wheel again, I can spare you the walk back to farm. Are you still feeling okay? Not faint? You look pale."

She blew out a long breath. "No. I'm fine. Do you think the car is drivable?"

He rubbed his jaw and eyed it. "The damage looks minor. I'll check when we get to the house and fix what I can."

Jodi sighed in relief. She'd been ready to call AAA forgetting that, like most farmers, Daniel knew a lot about repairing machinery and most anything else. She had to admit, there was something attractive about men that handy. Their ability to fix whatever broke appealed to her. Peter had considered any repair besides replacing lightbulbs to be beneath a financial advisor like him.

"I have another meeting after I get Tyler down for his nap." As shaken as she felt by the accident, another failure frightened her more.

Daniel's lips twisted. "I'll do my best to get you there."

Would he? The unbidden thought made her feel guilty as she slipped back behind the inflated air bag. Last week the answer would have been an emphatic no. Now, after his help today, she wasn't so sure.

"All set!" he yelled, and she reached around the air bag and honked the horn.

The tractor whined, its tires spinning before gaining purchase on the packed dirt lane. Dust and the strong smell of exhaust blew inside her windows and she cranked up the glass as her aunt's sedan was freed with a neck-snapping jerk.

Aunt Grace! She hoped the damage wasn't too severe. Her auto insurance would cover it, but she prayed she and her aunt wouldn't be housebound. It couldn't come at a worse time. After last night's meeting she had a list of people to call and meetings to arrange.

While Daniel towed her up the long lane toward his house, she phoned her cousin.

"Hi, Archie. It's Jodi," she said when he picked up.

"Hey there, Jodi. Bernice is feeling better today and she baked us a raspberry cobbler."

Her stomach rumbled. Bernice's famed desserts were coveted at potluck suppers. She pictured the slender woman with soft curls around her ears, her hands flying as she served up pie, cake, pudding or cobbler. "That sounds great, and please thank Bernice for me. I'm looking forward to seeing you both. Only, I've had some car trouble and I might be a bit late."

Archie made a sympathetic noise. "Are you okay?"

Her eyes stung. How kind they all were here. Even Daniel was giving up his afternoon break to lend her a hand.

"Yes. My car slid into a ditch. I'm being towed now and—"

"Jodi. Let's reschedule. You've had a heck of a day and we can do this anytime."

Her lower eyelid twitched and her abdominal muscles quivered. "No. It's fine. I'm okay. Really. Couldn't be better. And there's no time like the present. We need to seize the day. Carpe—"

"Jodi." Archie's gentle tone was a splash of cool water on her burning cheeks. "You're not yourself. How about tomorrow? Say ten o'clock? We'll keep the cobbler until then. Won't even cut into it."

"Yes, he will!" she heard a voice holler. Bernice. Despite the letdown, she smiled. They'd always been one of her favorite couples.

Archie chuckled. "Okay. Maybe a small piece. So what do you say? Will tomorrow work?"

Jodi's hands shook as she tapped her phone's appointment schedule and saw the empty spot.

"Tomorrow's fine." Only it wasn't. She'd thought Ted and Archie were sure sales. A much-needed boost to her poor record thus far. When she'd made her bed this morning, she'd envisioned slipping under the covers later on, two signed purchase agreements in her brief-case. Now she was empty-handed once more.

She clicked off her phone and rested her throbbing head against the air bag. If she didn't get Archie and the other farmer she'd scheduled for tomorrow to sell, she wouldn't have good news to share with Mr. Williams on Monday. Without solid finance numbers, he might give in and send Brady. She clutched her locket. That couldn't happen.

Goldie bounded out and barked when Daniel rounded the corner of the farmhouse and cut the motor. She noticed his father sitting on a rocker behind a layer of clematis vines, their purple-and-white-striped blooms contrasting with the mint-green leaves.

"Hi, Mr. Gleason!" she called, and rubbed Goldie's shimmying back. The older man's fluttering hand rose in the air, his smile trem-ulous but warm. She did her best to hide her dismay at how much his condition had wors-ened. He'd still been working when he was di-agnosed the year she left Cedar Bay. Now he appeared housebound and that, combined with his wife's defection, saddened her.

"Hey there, Jodi Lynn. Won't you stay for a visit?" His voice wavered, his eyes bright.

Daniel's hand cupped her elbow and he steered her toward the barns.

"She can't, Pop. She's got meetings. Maybe another time."

"Actually, they're canceled. But I've got Tyler. Sorry, Mr. Gleason. Soon, though," she said. If Daniel was away doing barn chores, she'd enjoy sitting out here one morning with his father. He'd always been kind to her when she'd needed it most.

"Scrabble night's still on Saturday." The wistful note in his voice pierced Jodi's heart. "Why don't you join us?"

"I'll be there," she promised on impulse, then regretted it when she caught Daniel's horrified sideways glance. His league bowled tonight, not Saturdays, she recalled with a jolt. She shouldn't have forgotten that. Why had she let sentiment rule her again?

"Supper's at six o'clock!"

Jodi waved and smiled at the older man, happy, at least, that his face looked brighter than when she'd first spied him. "I'll look forward to it."

"You don't have to come over." Daniel

pitched his voice low as they neared Sue's office door, Goldie hot on their heels. "I'll tell Pop something came up."

She pulled the tight bobby pins from her chignon and shook out her hair. "No. I'd like to see him." *And you,* she added silently, then shoved the dangerous thought aside. "But feel free to make other plans."

"I'll be there." His eyes leveled on hers, his stare so direct she couldn't look away.

She forced herself to shrug, breathless under his intense scrutiny. "Suit yourself," she said when she could.

"There's Mom!" exclaimed Sue, surprising them both and breaking the tense moment.

"Hi, Tyler!" Jodi reached for her son but he buried his head in Sue's shoulder. Her relief turned to disappointment.

"Transitions." Sue rubbed Jodi's arm. "They're difficult. Although Tyler's doing a bit better at them, don't you think? No crying."

Jodi nodded. It wasn't his fault, and Sue was right. He didn't do well when switching from one activity or person to another. But it was hard not to take it personally.

"He had a good day," Sue continued, stroking Tyler's fair hair. "He patted one of the alpacas while I held him. Brave boy."

Tyler lifted his head and his eyes lit up behind his glasses when he spotted the tractor. "Gah!"

"That's a tractor," said Sue. "Want to look?"

Tyler strained to get free, but Sue held firm. "Tyler."

When his head finally turned her way, she said, "Do you want to look at the tractor?"

After a moment of head shaking, he nodded at last and Jodi marveled. A real interaction with a relative stranger. Wow.

"Good. Let's go."

They followed Sue and watched as Tyler smacked the rubber tire treads and the smooth, metallic sides.

"Gah!" he shouted, and Jodi smiled.

"'reen," Sue finished, pointing at the engine. Tyler biffed the tractor with Ollie. "Gah!"

"'reen," Sue repeated, then caught the elephant when an exuberant Tyler tossed her skyward.

Jodi's mouthed dropped and when she looked at Daniel and Sue, their faces held the same expression. With Sue's help, he'd progressed toward a word.

"Green!" Sue exclaimed, putting him up on the tractor seat and holding his waist. "It's your favorite color, right? Good job."

But it was more than a good job. It was everything. Jodi's heart beat fast enough to hurt.

He'd said part of a word. Not a random sound, but a purposeful syllable at Sue's encouragement. It was a start. More than she'd ever imagined. Could Sue's organic diet and methods be working?

"Green," Jodi said to Tyler, but he looked away and banged on the steering wheel instead of answering her.

A strong hand descended on her slumped shoulders. "I'm sure he'll say the whole word soon," Daniel murmured, his intuitive encouragement catching her off guard. He'd known what she'd been thinking, feeling, as he always had. After years of trying to explain herself, this silent understanding and support seemed to fit a loose piece of her back in place.

Before she could answer, he boomed, "Let's go for a tractor ride and celebrate. What do you say, Tyler?"

Daniel seemed to take Tyler's shaking head for yes. He turned to Jodi, his half-moon dimples appearing in a wide grin that did something funny to her heart. "Would you like to drive, Jodi? If we head down that way—" he pointed to a dirt path that led past the barns and grazing fields "—I've got a surprise for Tyler."

Jodi hesitated, her mind at war with itself. Her heart divided. Since her father's accident, large equipment frightened her. Yet Tyler's wide eyes and animated expression made it hard to say no. Would her fears keep her son from enjoying his life?

"What about my car?" she stalled.

"I'll check it," called Colton. He emerged from the barn and joined them. "It's good seeing you again."

She returned his friendly smile. "Same here. But please don't go to any bother."

"No trouble at all. I like working on cars. Got a sweet Camaro back home I've been restoring for a few months. In a couple of weeks, I'll have the part I've been saving for and she'll be on the road."

An exclamation had them turning Sue's way, but her hastily lowered face hid her expression. Her sneaker traced a pattern in the dirt.

"Come on, Jodi." Daniel's eyes glowed brighter than the midday sun. "You've driven this model before. It's the oldest one on my farm, but it's reliable. Remember how much you used to like getting behind the wheel? That time you beat me in a race?"

"It was more than once," she muttered, a reluctant smile forming. She had loved driving tractors. She eyed the gears, her memory going over the steps.

"Twice, then." And the way he said it made her laugh. They both knew it'd been a lot more than that and the smile he gave her felt warm and intimate.

"So what do you say?" Daniel pressed.

When she nodded, Daniel handed her up, the feeling of his palm on her back like little fingers of electricity running up her spine. She set Tyler on her lap and he leaned sideways in her arms. "I don't think this is safe enough. He might fall." Her body went cold when she imagined Tyler slipping under the tractor's tires. A belt appeared before she could step down.

"Put this around you both and latch it. It should fit." Jodi hesitated. She was used to keeping Tyler secure in his car seat. But farm kids started riding tractors practically before they could walk. And of course, they'd go very slow. Daniel smiled up at them and she caught herself staring. Who was this caring, giving person? He'd apologized for the past, listened to her marriage problems, rescued her from her car accident and now he wanted to spend time with her son? Was he using his charm to lull her into a false sense of security about their battle for Cedar Bay, or could he be genuine? With Tyler's hands dancing on the wheel, there was no time to speculate.

She cinched the belt, pushed in the clutch and started the engine. But at Tyler's scream, she shut it off again and tugged his hands from his ears. "This won't work. The noise is too much for him."

"Wait!" Sue ran back to her office and Colton's head lifted from under the car hood, his eyes following her.

In the quiet, Tyler settled down and ran his hands over the gearshifts, his legs kicking in excitement.

"Looks like Tyler's taking a liking to farming," Daniel observed as they waited, his eyes more green than yellow against his deep navy T-shirt. Irritation surged at his anything-but-casual remark.

"What he likes and what he needs are two different things," she pointed out, her voice rising enough to make Tyler's hands flap. She held them between her own. "Sorry, baby."

Daniel's steady gaze did something funny to her heart. "They don't have to be mutually exclusive."

"That's usually the case in my experience," she murmured, almost to herself.

He lifted his baseball hat and a puff of summer air blew brown strands around the strong angles of his face. "I'm sorry to hear that. It can't be an easy life, never getting what you really want."

She gasped as Daniel's words hit too close

to home. The insides of her nose burned as if she'd dived into the lake without pinching it. She didn't know how to cope with Daniel's empathy—it overwhelmed her.

"Here," Sue huffed, rejoining them. She held out two pieces of what looked like fluff. "Put them in his ears."

"What is it?" Jodi eyed the soft puff balls skeptically.

"Alpaca wool. Clean and ready for spinning… only now they're Tyler's earplugs. Okay?"

Jodi nodded. It was worth a try, since Tyler would have a tantrum if she took him off his new favorite toy.

He moved his head every which way as she inserted the wool and pulled his eyeglasses band down to hold them in place. At last, off they went with a jerk that made her teeth knock together.

Wow. The thrum of the machine beneath her and the sense of control as she steered filled her with a rush of adrenaline. It'd been such a long time since she'd driven a tractor, and the thrill of it returned to her. The wind whipped her hair behind her, carrying away her fear. Tyler's screeching echoed her own elation and the air she breathed smelled slightly sweet, like growing things.

When she looked over her shoulder, Sue

waved and Daniel jogged beside them. When they rounded the last barn and headed out into lush, open fields, Tyler squealed and she wanted to join him. She hadn't been surrounded by this much unbroken greenery in a long time. Even when she spoke with farmers, she met them in their homes, not on their fields. Perhaps she should have followed up on Midland's purchases and seen the improvements they'd made as Daniel had suggested. She'd actually missed this. When she returned to Aunt Grace's house, she would set up an appointment with a company farm and bring Daniel as promised.

Daniel disappeared for a moment and she thought they'd left him behind until she felt the tractor dip in back and his voice whisper in her ear.

"So far so good."

She shivered in awareness of his proximity as he balanced behind them on the storage box. His fingers rested on her shoulders as he stood to his full height.

Jodi peeked up at him and took in the handsome picture he made. Beltless, low-slung jeans rode on his narrow hips and a thin T-shirt stretched across his well-defined chest. From this angle, his jaw looked more square than ever, his muscular neck rising from broad shoulders. The bright blue sky behind him contrasted with his dark hair and hazel eyes.

Another bone-jarring mud hole made Tyler flap his hands and Jodi return her eyes to the straightaway. And that was when she saw them...

Strawberries.

The sun-kissed rows of plants stretched to a distant tree line, the berries so blood ripe, so rich and lovely, that the invitation to pluck and sink her teeth into them was irresistible. How long since she'd gathered fruit? Delight filled her.

"The local schools and families have picked most of the fields, but this section is unharvested," he hollered over the engine's roar.

"Okay." She slowed the machine, feeling shaky but victorious when it rolled to a stop. Since her father's accident, she'd avoided machinery like this. Now she'd conquered it, and a feeling of lightness grew within her.

Daniel jumped off and held out a hand, his eyes dancing. The sun brought out the lighter brown in his hair and made the yellow flecks in his eyes shine like gold beneath thick lashes. "Ready?"

More than, she thought, her excitement hard to contain. She wanted to rush through the rows of plants, trailing her fingers along the crinkly leaves, inhaling the earthy goodness. Her hands fumbled to take out Tyler's earplugs before she undid the buckle and handed him to Daniel. He held the wiggling boy with one hand and extended another to help her down.

"Thank you. Oh." An idea pulled her up short when her heels sunk into the ground. "What will we put the berries in?"

Daniel grinned, set down Tyler and raised the lid on his storage bin. He dumped some tools from a container and lifted his shirt to wipe it, exposing a toned stomach that Jodi did her best to ignore. She took the container and followed the twosome into the strawberry patch.

The sight of him shuffling beside her son, his large hand enveloping Tyler's as they trod down the plant rows, made her heart skip a beat. Tyler peered up at Daniel the way he'd looked at the tractor. And maybe for him, the two were in the same category. For the past year it'd been just her and Tyler, and now seeing him with Daniel made her wish her son had a strong male role model.

Daniel glanced over his shoulder, his profile outlined by the sun streaming over distant treetops. "How does this look?" He swept his arm in a circle, and all around, plump berries peeked through jagged-edged oval leaves.

"Perfect. I mean, fine." She cleared her throat. "This is good. Thanks." Why was she babbling like a schoolgirl? This was Daniel. Not a man she'd see romantically. Not again.

Daniel got on his knees, pinched off a deep red fruit and handed it to Tyler. "Want one?"

Tyler shoved it in his mouth, then patted Daniel's cheeks.

Daniel smiled up at her. "I'm thinking that's a yes."

She got on her knees beside him and kicked off her horrible shoes. It warmed her from the inside out to see Tyler so excited and interactive. She wouldn't let her rivalry or her conflicting emotions with Daniel spoil this moment.

"I'd say so!" Happiness added a lilt of laughter to her voice and Daniel eyed her, his expression wary. Maybe he was afraid of *her* charms for a change.

She plucked berries and placed them in the container. Daniel followed suit and, to her amazement, Tyler grabbed a few, as well. They might have been squashed, flattened even, but they were the best berries in the world as far as she was concerned.

"These are great, Tyler!" She popped one of his berries in her mouth and felt the tart sweetness explode on her tongue and against the insides of her cheeks.

He kept pulling berries and leaves with them, giving no notice that he'd heard her. Daniel's nod, however, made her feel less ignored. For the first time in a long time, she wished she had someone in her life. She'd been so focused on helping Tyler recover that she'd forgotten what it felt like to have a partner, or even a friend.

Her husband's defection had damaged her confidence in relationships and her ability to have one. Yet the way Tyler held up berries for Daniel's inspection, the smile he wore after he got a nod of approval, showed her how much her son yearned for male attention. She'd vowed to give him back his speech, but what if that wasn't enough? It touched her to see him so caught up in Daniel even as it made her heart ache.

The considerate way Daniel behaved around her son affected her, as well. He genuinely seemed to enjoy Tyler, if his booming laugh was any indication. This charm was not an act. And the sound of her son's belly laugh assured her that the feeling was mutual.

Twenty minutes later, they'd filled the basket with berries. Jodi straightened and shook out her cramped knees. Daniel grabbed Tyler by the waist and tossed him in the air, neatly catching him on the way down.

"No!" she shouted over Tyler's giggles.

Daniel flew him over to Jodi and exchanged Tyler for the bucket. But Tyler strained for Daniel as she strode toward the tractor, thrashing as she struggled to hold him up.

A hard kick to her knee made her stumble in her heels, and Daniel steadied her. He chucked Tyler under the chin and brushed the damp hair from her son's face, his large hands gentle.

"Would you like me to drive?" Daniel suggested, his brows lowering in concern. "I'll hold Tyler if you don't mind climbing on the back."

She hesitated while Tyler's screams kicked up another notch.

"I'd never let anything happen to Tyler, Jodi." Daniel's eyes leveled with hers, his confident expression unwavering.

And just like that, she did trust him. She'd listened to his speech at the town hall the other night when he'd asked the assembly if they trusted him. Now she knew her answer.

He might be on the wrong side of their war, but her answer was yes. He'd grown from the boy who'd withheld his real reasons for keeping their relationship a secret and going along with others who'd put her down. She might not fully trust him with her heart again, but she did believe he'd protect her son.

Tyler wrapped his arms around Daniel's

neck and snuggled against his chest while Jodi scrambled up behind them. She placed the berries in the storage chest and peered at Tyler's already drowsing eyes. Gently, she placed the wool in his ears and felt his cheek fall into her palm. He was a whisper away from sleep.

"All set," she said, and Daniel started the engine. They made good speed around a loop that doubled them back toward the house and around another field.

"Pumpkins?" she yelled in his ear when she spotted the beginnings of vines snaking across the soil.

"The kids like it here in the fall," he shouted back, Tyler's head lolling against his broad shoulder. "Colton and I take turns running them out with the wagon."

"You do a lot for kids," she said, amazed. How much time did that take out of his day? It was another example of the kindhearted man he'd become. He was as busy as—no, busier than—any corporate suit. Yet he found time to make children happy. She glanced at Tyler and smiled.

"Doesn't Midland do that for the local kids?" he asked.

"I don't know. I—I—"

His question caught her off guard. Her company supported hundreds of children's charities. But somehow the simple gesture of taking kids out to pick their own pumpkins moved her more. Tyler would love that. She could imagine him traipsing through the verdant tangle, picking up the first pumpkin he saw—whether it was spotted, green, lopsided or not—because Tyler didn't discriminate. He loved everyone and everything. Maybe the imperfect ones, like his scruffy Ollie, a bit more.

She watched Daniel hoist her slipping son and marveled when he rested his head on top of Tyler's. Her heart expanded at the tender picture, the image banishing the hollowness inside.

Tyler wasn't the only one who didn't judge. Daniel.

He'd never given, through word, look or action, a hint that he expected any more from Tyler than who he was. His straightforward acceptance of her son was touching.

While she toiled to change Tyler, Daniel simply enjoyed him. That was the luxury of a nonparent, though. One she couldn't afford. But perhaps, by spending every free minute looking up the latest autism treatments and trying new therapies, she'd neglected simple times that were just for fun. Like today and the day at the lake.

The thought rattled her brain and shook

loose the notions she'd had when she'd agreed to come home. While she'd planned to return to Chicago and a day care that would help her son, Cedar Bay and Daniel were making her wonder what was really best for Tyler. And best for her. Had she been doing her son a disservice by discounting love in her life? Suddenly her mission wasn't as clear.

She hadn't realized she'd made a sound until a heavy hand gripped hers before returning again to the wheel.

"It's going to be all right, Jodi."

There it was. That intuitive connection they shared returning full force.

And like the sun bursting through cloud cover, she suddenly realized that maybe Daniel was right. She just had to have faith.

CHAPTER TEN

"ARE YOU SURE you have no further questions?"

Jodi glanced from Archie to Bernice across a polished, Queen Anne–style coffee table the next day. The midmorning sun sliced through a bay window and painted columns of golden light against their cedar-planked floors. Like many farmhouses built a couple hundred years ago, their front parlor contained formal furniture, such as the stiff velvet-upholstered chair she sat in. But she barely felt it beneath her, her spirit soaring as she closed in on her first sale.

Archie pulled his glasses out of his shirt pocket, but Bernice swatted his hand.

"No need to read anything." Her warm brown eyes twinkled and she folded her small hands on her lap. "This is Jodi."

"Of course." He put them away and pulled out a pen. "Where do we sign?" When scar tissue rose in place of his eyebrows, Jodi recalled a barn fire during her eighth-grade year and how Archie and others had helped rescue a neighbor's trapped herd.

The memory made her hesitate, her hand refusing to cooperate with her brain and pass over the purchase agreement.

In the brief quiet, an oven timer beeped and Bernice rose, smoothing a yellow summer-weight sweater over her navy skirt. "That's the cookies. If you'll excuse me?"

Archie stood as his wife passed, the simple, courteous gesture striking a lonely chord in her heart. In their golden years, they'd found the rainbow's treasure...and it'd been beside them all along. Each other. What a wonderful job she had, helping good people enjoy the rest of their lives in comfort. Her lips twisted in a smile as she packed up her things. It might not be her fate, but she'd work hard to make it possible for others.

"Jodi? The paper?"

She looked up, confused. "What?"

Archie's smile deepened the creases in his weather-beaten face, the age lines written in laughter rather than distress. "We trust you, but we're supposed to sign that paper you just put away, aren't we?"

Her face warmed and she unclasped her briefcase. Where was her head? "Right. Al-though your signature is all I need since it's your family's property."

His cheeks shook in a nod. "I'd still like Bernice's name on there."

"Of course," Jodi said, his devotion touching. "There's a spot for a witness signature and we can add a note that she's an owner, as well."

Archie beamed and hefted an ankle over his knee. "She's lived here most of her life. Only nineteen years less than I have."

"Seventeen, Archie. Remember? They let us marry that young back then." Bernice returned with a pile of chocolate-chip cookies on a fragile, flower-patterned plate that looked as old and quaint as their cedar-shingled farmhouse. Fluted glasses rimmed in gold and a bottle of something sparkly rested on the tray beside the treats.

"Sorry about the cobbler, Jodi." Bernice shot Archie a sharp look and he lowered his crossed leg. "Turns out Archie's small piece at dessert turned into another for his bedtime snack and then more at breakfast this morning."

"There's still some left," he protested, then took the tray from his wife and set it on the table. He accepted the napkin and cookie she handed him. "Thank you, dear."

"A big man's got to keep up his energy." Bernice patted his leg and Archie's chest puffed, his shirt buttons straining against their holes.

Jodi set the paper down on top of her briefcase and accepted a cookie from Bernice. "Thank you." She inhaled the homey scent of melted chocolate and vanilla. "These look great."

The warm cookie was gone in three bites and she reached for another. "Delicious, as always." The best bakeries in Chicago couldn't compete with homemade desserts. Everything here tasted fresher, the flavors more intense.

Bernice twisted her pearl necklace, a smile playing at the corners of her lips. "It's my pleasure. I'm glad I was able to make them in time to celebrate." She passed them each a glass and poured sparkling apple cider.

"To a fresh start in New Mexico." She lifted her goblet, then lowered it, looking from a motionless Jodi to Archie. "Did I miss something?" She faced her husband. "You signed the papers when I left, didn't you?"

Archie drained his glass and shook his head.

"But we all agreed to the price and terms." Bernice crossed her ankles and looked at Jodi, her expression apologetic. "I'm very sorry. Archie, please sign Jodi's paperwork."

"I can't." His rheumy eyes grew wide when Bernice's lips flattened into a straight line. "She hasn't given it to me."

"What? Why? Did you turn her down?" Bernice's voice rose. "Moving means we'll get to see the grandkids grow up and my arthritis won't ache so."

Jodi moved to the edge of her seat and set her glass down on the table. Goodness. She'd forgotten the paperwork. Again. "This is my fault." She ran a hand over her hair and felt its smooth bun at the base of her neck, the dampness beneath the thick layer. "Archie's been great. I suppose I got distracted." Since her time with Daniel in the strawberry fields, she'd felt disoriented and less focused, her mind churning over the realizations she'd made when she should be nailing down farm sales.

"So—may we sign it now?" Archie's eyes slid to his wife, whose expression had changed from irritated to suspicious. "Please? We don't need to read it over."

A nervous laugh escaped her as she fumbled for the paper that had slid to the floor. She was behaving as if this were her first sale.

"Perhaps Jodi's reluctant to buy our farm." Bernice's speculative glance fell on her and Jodi flinched when she straightened. Deep down, there was some truth to that statement, and she sensed the answer was in those strawberry fields.

"No. Not at all. Cedar Crest Farm is perfect. Exactly what my company would like to acquire." She forced her mind back on her job.

Mr. Williams would be thrilled to hear she'd brought another two hundred and fifty acres under Midland's control. At last, she'd have something good to report during their planned Monday phone call. She should feel excited, but strangely she experienced a faint sense of loss.

"If that's the case, then why do you still have the purchase agreement, dear?" Bernice's gray-brown curls fell away from her jaw when she cocked her head.

Jodi looked down at the paper sheaf. Why hadn't she let it go?

"I think being home is doing something funny to me." Her hands trembled a bit when she laid the documents on the table, her fingers lingering before she forced them to let go.

Bernice nodded as if to say she understood and that it didn't need explaining.

But Archie leaned forward, his gnarled hand patting Jodi's knee. "When I saw you at the field day, I hardly recognized you." His hazy blue eyes crinkled in concern. "And it wasn't the dressy duds or the fancy hair. You talked different. Acted more formal and a little, I don't know, distant-like." He picked up the pen. "But right now, you sound like your old self. Maybe the longer you're in your hometown, the more you're becoming…uh…you." His pen scratched across the paper, and then he slid it to his wife.

Jodi sank back in her chair and considered. Before flying home, the suggestion would have horrified her. But now she wondered if she'd been too hasty to give up on the old her, too quick to discard her previous life.

Yesterday, she'd felt more excited about the five jars of strawberry jam she'd canned with Aunt Grace than the twenty appointments she'd made for next week. When she'd gone to sleep, instead of reviewing sales strategies, she'd pictured Daniel driving them on the tractor, his dark hair mingling with her son's golden strands as he rested his head on top of Tyler's.

Even more telling, she'd awoken thinking about tonight's Scrabble game rather than her sales meetings. It was a sobering thought. Was she here for business or pleasure? Lately it seemed more like the latter. And she wasn't so sure anymore if that was a bad thing.

"Thank you, Jodi. I can't tell you what this means to us." Bernice pulled a tissue from her sleeve and dabbed the corners of her eyes when Archie passed Jodi the signed purchase agreement.

"I've wanted this for a while, but Archie didn't trust those other men from your company enough to sell." She laid her head on her husband's shoulder and his large hand ruffled her curls. "After working two jobs for fifty-five years, he deserves a chance to enjoy life."

Jodi's heart swelled. She might be confused about the best direction for her own life, but she'd helped this couple find the stress-free future they deserved.

Archie kissed his wife's forehead. "As long as I'm with you, I'm always happy."

Bernice's eyes glowed as she swatted him away and leaned forward to replenish his cider.

"To new beginnings." Bernice raised her glass and crystal rang as they touched rims. It heralded a bright future for Bernice and Archie, but a muddled one for Jodi.

DANIEL PACED BEFORE the large window facing the driveway, his eyes searching the early evening's gray gloom for a flash of Jodi's borrowed car. Colton had pronounced the vehicle in good shape except for a dented hood yesterday, so he didn't fear another accident. Yet something held him here, watching.

He peered at the dark bruise of a sky, purple-bottomed clouds blotting out the sun that'd shone earlier. Rain tap-danced across his roof and poured steadily from the gutter that ended beside Sue's hummingbird feeder. How much longer until Jodi arrived? Strange that the concern he'd felt at the airport was replaced now by excitement. He smoothed his unruly waves behind his ears and checked his watch. Five forty-five. With supper at six, she'd be here soon.

He pictured the table he and Sue had set, the wildflower bouquet in an iron watering can, their family's scalloped white china on a navy tablecloth. The smell of roast chicken filled the house, overpowering the apple-scented candles flickering on the brick hearth by the entranceway.

Pop muttered as he napped in the back parlor's recliner, the television's cheering Red Sox crowd having no effect on his buzz saw of a snore. Daniel smiled at his father. With his hearing aids out, he wouldn't hear a tractor if it drove through the front door.

He glanced out the window and watched the sky wring out sheets of rain. There'd be no tractor rides today, but the memory of his time in the strawberry patch with Jodi and Tyler lingered. He'd slogged through his chores earlier, his mind full of Jodi's silvery laugh and Tyler's head snuggled against his shoulder. She'd enjoyed it as much as he had. Had the day reminded her that she'd once loved farming? Had cared for him, too?

When a car approached, he tensed, his senses jangling, until it passed by his driveway. He threw himself into a wooden chair. Its intricately carved arms and slatted seat were too delicate for his size, but it faced the window, at least.

Since their afternoon together, Jodi no longer seemed like his enemy. Her patient, caring and sometimes goofy personality had wiped away her layers of business polish. She'd taken him by surprise with her vulnerability—hiding her fear of driving the tractor and her disappointment when Tyler had rejected her. This felt like the real Jodi. Not a Midland suit and not the girl he'd once known, but someone in between. And he liked that person. If circumstances were different, he'd want to get to know her again.

Was it possible to win his hometown and his girl?

The crunch of tires outside made him stride to the door and out onto the screened-in front porch. When her long legs emerged from the car followed by a lithe body and pretty face he wondered why, of all the girls he'd met in college and at home, she alone attracted him this way.

She opened an umbrella and raced to the house carrying a red jar. His heart hammered out a drumbeat of excitement at her knock.

When their eyes met through the screen, he did his best not to smile, but failed.

"Good evening, Jodi."

He opened the door and the tang of her perfume filled his nose as she breezed by him with unconscious grace, like a cat seeking the best spot in the sun.

"Evening, Daniel," she murmured, and then her face brightened. "Hi, Sue! It's just me tonight. Aunt Grace offered to babysit Tyler. But he helped make some strawberry jam for you."

Sue's gaze flipped from him to Jodi, her speculative eyes taking notes. "That looks great, thanks." She held out a pewter tray of glasses filled with tomato juice and celery sticks. "Would you like a drink? It's organic."

Jodi nodded and shrugged off her raincoat, her white sundress revealing smooth, sun-kissed shoulders. His eyes roamed over her golden skin, his hands lacing behind his back to keep from reaching for what he wanted.

"Daniel?"

"Thanks." He grabbed a glass and bolted it back while Jodi and Sue chattered and sipped. Jodi's loose honey-blond hair and lacy dress contrasted with the faded brick hearth of the original kitchen. When a dab of juice stained her full upper lip, he swallowed hard, wishing for a taste.

"I can't take all the credit for dinner tonight," he heard Sue say as she repositioned her slipping headband. "The juice is my creation, but Daniel's responsible for the rest."

"Daniel cooks?" Jodi's gaze shot his way, her eyebrows curving up.

Sue punched his shoulder. "Come on, big bro. Modern men know their way around a kitchen these days."

He gathered the used glasses and returned them to the tray. "I like cooking. It's not a secret."

"What made you decide to learn?" Jodi asked as they headed for the parlor.

He stopped for a second and looked evenly at her. "Someone had to make Thanksgiving supper after Mom left."

Jodi's eyes rounded. "Oh."

He strode toward Pop and heard Sue say, "I tried learning, too, but I'm better at reading charts than recipes."

"Pop." He shook his father's shoulder gently and his eyes fluttered open.

"Whaaaaat?"

Daniel wiped the wet beside his father's mouth and handed him his hearing aids. He looked back at the women, grateful they had given his dad a moment to get his wits together.

"Jodi's here," he said, once his father had

finished fiddling with the hearing aids. "She came for supper and Scrabble. Remember?"

Pop fumbled for the lever to lower his recliner and Daniel waited, not wanting to interfere unless it went on too long.

At last the La-Z-Boy chair straightened and his father dragged the comb Daniel handed him through his thin silver hair.

"Where is she?" he asked, his eyes brighter now, his head swiveling toward the front parlor, but Daniel blocked his view.

"Taking off her things. She'll be here any minute." He sent a silent thank-you to Jodi and Sue for playing along. "I think I hear her coming now." He cupped his hands around his mouth. "Jodi!"

"Here I am." She appeared beside him, her curls bouncing across her shoulders, her wide smile revealing perfect white teeth. "How are you, Mr. Gleason?"

Daniel unfolded a walker and helped Pop to his feet.

"Better now that you're here." His tremulous smile and shaking head seemed to make no visible impression on Jodi. She gave him a quick hug.

Daniel blew out a long, quiet breath, relieved that Jodi hadn't made Pop feel self-conscious about his worsened Parkinson's. Considerate. It was another layer to the woman who'd returned to buy out his hometown, but might leave with his heart instead. For a moment he imagined what it'd be like if she'd come back for different reasons. They'd line dance at The Lounge and row out onto Lake Champlain and watch shooting stars.

"I'm starving." She wrapped her arm around Pop and squeezed without letting go. "Let's eat." And with that, she guided him into the kitchen.

Daniel trailed, amazed as his father pushed his walker faster than ever, his gait a bit steadier, his head held higher. Jodi might be here to destroy his community, but she did a world of good for his father.

At the table, Sue set out the warm dishes.

"It's been a long time, Jodi," Pop said once Daniel pushed his chair closer to the table. "How are your mother and father?"

Jodi's face seemed to tense at the question. She unfolded the navy-and-white-patterned napkin and smoothed it on her lap before answering.

"They're doing well. My grandmother needed some help, so they moved in with her for now."

"Be sure to tell them I said hello." His father's hands shook too hard to grasp the serving spoon for the glazed carrots and Sue swiped his plate. She loaded it with food, then placed it back in front of him, oblivious to the red staining his hollow cheeks.

"Oh, thanks, Sue." Jodi handed her plate to his sister. "I never know how much to take, either."

Daniel stared at Jodi in surprise, but then he saw his father's smile. Her maneuver had restored his dad's pride. It'd made him feel less embarrassed about depending on his children.

"Does this look good?" Sue handed over Jodi's plate at her nod. He held Jodi's gaze and smiled in thanks. Warmth filled him when she smiled back.

Once Sue sat, Pop spoke up. "Let's join hands tonight when we say grace."

Daniel stretched across the table and felt Jodi's soft hand unfold inside his.

"Thank you for this food you've blessed," Pop began. "Thank you for the friends we've missed. Thank you for our family, too. Thank you for all you've helped us through."

Daniel's fingers tightened around Jodi's, and when her eyes lifted they were luminous, her lashes damp. For a long moment they stared at one another until Sue cleared her throat and they let go. When he picked up his fork, his palm felt empty.

"Saw you and your little boy a few times. Is your ex around much?" Pop lifted a quivering forkful of potato to his mouth and gulped the bite.

Jodi's face paled. "Not since he left us."

Daniel's hands fisted beneath the table. Only a creep would completely abandon his family, especially when Tyler needed both of his parents. The sting of waking up to find his mother's closet emptied, her car gone, returned.

Pop tried passing Jodi a piece of banana bread but half broke off before it reached her plate. "You're better off without someone like that."

She made a fierce little movement with her head, but it was hard to tell if it was in agreement or denial. "Some days I wonder."

Daniel stared until he caught her eye. How could she want a jerk like that around? Then he remembered her struggle with Tyler in the airport. At times, he imagined she'd welcome any help at all.

"I got a divorce, too. The missus took off when the bank rep showed up threatening to foreclose." Pop waved his fork, silencing Jodi's sympathetic response like a conductor. "I should have sold this farm a long time ago. Now Daniel's trapped on it and he's going to end up old and alone like me."

The despair in his father's voice took Daniel aback. He'd thought Pop was over the divorce, and he'd never known he was worried about Daniel's future. And suddenly, a nagging thought took hold. What if his father was right? What if, after sending Jodi back to Chicago and forming the co-op, he would never again have a moment like he'd had on the strawberry fields, holding a boy he was growing attached to, the woman he cared for—despite their differences—riding with him.

It was a lonely thought. Sending Jodi packing felt more like a win-lose than a win-win. He'd win the battle, but lose the girl. He peered at her over the rim of his glass before taking a drink. It was crazy to think this way. Her goals couldn't be further from his own. But what if he could make her feelings for this place, and him, return?

"I guess some people just aren't meant to be together," he heard Sue say. When he looked up from his plate he caught Jodi's gaze on him before she lowered her eyes and took another bite of potato. Did she think they fell into that category? Even if he could get her to care about farming, would she ever care for him again? He swallowed another tasteless bite of chicken.

"My sympathies are with you, raising your son all by yourself like that." Pop leaned down to sip milk from a clear straw. "That's got to be tough. You should move home. Be with Grace and your neighbors. We'd help you."

Jodi looked up from her plate, her eyes awash in tears, and excused herself.

"Pop. Stop. You're making her upset," Sue whispered as Jodi's heels clicked away. "Let's talk about something lighter."

"Like the weather?" Pop peered out at the water running down the kitchen windowpanes. "Still raining. How about the price of tea in China?"

"She's right, Pop." Daniel glanced up at the empty kitchen archway and lowered his voice. "Jodi came here to see you and have fun, not to talk about serious things."

"That's the problem with your generation," his father grumbled. "Always looking for easy times instead of dealing with the hard ones."

Daniel gaped at his father. "And you think saving the farm from bankruptcy, putting Sue through graduate school and trying to keep our community together is me not handling hard times?" Despite his words, he kept the heat out of his tone. He knew Pop would have done the same if his Parkinson's hadn't worsened.

"Not if it means that co-op idea of yours, son." His father grabbed a roll and, with effort, passed it to Daniel, the gesture taking the sting out of his words. "Every man should choose for himself. It's what I fought for in 'Nam. You can't force people to see things the way you do."

Daniel tore the bread apart and buttered it. Why couldn't Pop appreciate his efforts? "But what if it's the right way to think?"

"How do you know?" A coughing fit took hold of his father and instantly Daniel regretted his outburst. "How do you know how people should feel? You can't control the world, son, and the sooner you understand that the better."

A throat cleared from the kitchen archway and Daniel caught Jodi's eye. How much had she heard? More important, did she agree with him or his father? If anything, she was as guilty as he at deciding others' fates.

"Dessert?" asked Sue when Jodi pulled back her chair and sat.

"Sounds good, sweetheart." Pop polished off the last of his potatoes and smiled. "What do we have?"

"We have cheesecake, and Jodi brought homemade strawberry jam. We'll put it on top." Sue strode to the fridge while Daniel stacked dishes in the sink, his mind occupied and his heart heavy. He worked hard to keep his home and town together, and his dad didn't approve.

When he'd cleared the table, Sue put slices

on small plates with a dollop of Jodi's preserves.

"Now, that's good jam." His father's fork scraped against the china. "Thank you for the treat, Jodi."

She smiled over at his father. "This is a treat, Mr. Gleason. I'm glad I came."

His father stopped chewing and fumbled his hand across the table to rest on Jodi's.

"I'm glad you did, too. I always appreciated that letter you sent me after you left."

Daniel felt as if the lightning flickering behind the barns had struck him instead. *What letter?*

"I wanted you to know how much your help that summer meant to me." She gave his father a warm smile and replaced the napkin that'd slid off his lap.

Meant to her? It'd meant a lot to him, too. Daniel forced himself to swallow the bite lodged in his throat. Knowing Jodi had reached out to his family made the floor seem to rise up and drop again. Or maybe that was his stomach. All this time, he'd thought of her complete dismissal of him and his family as callous. Now he needed to rethink not only the new Jodi, but the old.

"I was glad you didn't blame me for the accident." Pop's double chin appeared when his head drooped.

Jodi laced her fingers in his father's. "It was the skid loader, not you. That's why I love buying farms for Midland. Only an industrial farming company like that can make farming safe."

Her words stemmed the tide of sentiment Daniel had felt tonight. She sounded like a corporate mouthpiece. He opened his mouth to insist a co-op could guarantee the same safety features, but his father spoke first.

"No one mentioned that was your line of work." His father's gaze flitted toward Daniel. "Seems like that puts you two on opposite sides of the fence."

Daniel met Jodi's stare, neither of them willing to look away.

"I suppose it does," she said at last, her expression firm, blue eyes unwavering.

"We couldn't be further apart," he agreed, though his heart said otherwise.

"Kind of like the old days, then," Pop chuckled. "Only this time it isn't some childhood game, is it?"

Jodi's gaze bored into his. "No. It's much more."

After a tense silence, Sue spoke up.

"Scrabble, anyone?"

CHAPTER ELEVEN

A FEW DAYS later, Daniel waved goodbye to a wind turbine representative and turned at a plaintive lowing from a small pasture off the back of his barn. One of his heifers was calving today. Fear raised the hairs on his arms. Was she struggling?

Another keening moo sounded and Daniel glanced sharply into the pen. He hustled over, unlatched the gate and strode through the knee-high grass, the area not as shorn as his other pastures since most of his cows had birthed a month ago and grazed with their calves in his other fields. Sandra Dee, however, hadn't gotten pregnant on the first attempt so now she tromped, restless in the field alone, her tail up and neck arched as she called.

In the furnace of midday, he waited for her to turn, then spotted the amniotic sac where it'd been hours ago. A rushing sensation swept through in his gut. She hadn't progressed. For her first pregnancy, he'd expected her to have the calf out in a couple hours, but four... That gave him pause. And where was Colton? His farmhand had been instructed to get him from the turbine meeting if Sandra Dee showed signs of complications.

In the golden light, her body looked massive yet vulnerable, a sheen of sweat along her heaving sides. There'd been a fair share of calves he'd hand delivered through the years, and some lost lives. He hoped today wasn't one of them.

Sandra Dee dropped to her knees and let out another long moo that ended when her head fell against the ground. His pulse pounded hard enough to feel it in his toes. When he pivoted to race to the barn, he pulled up short at the sight of Jodi. After their tense parting on Scrabble night, he was surprised to see her.

She cupped her hands around her mouth. "Is she having trouble?" The wind flung her hair around her pretty, flushed face as she leaned against the fence wearing a dress and heels. "I heard the cow and stopped by to look before getting Tyler."

His nerves grew taut as he took in her business outfit and recalled how she'd shared her pride in working for Midland with Pop the other night. The old Jodi juxtaposed over the new. Which one was she today?

"Looks like. Would you get Colton?"

Without a word, she kicked off her high heels and sprinted through the rear door of his newest barn. A faint smile ghosted across his face. It was the old Jodi, then. He had to hand it to her, she'd always been good under pressure and had never played the damsel in distress. Better yet, she hadn't let their uneasy parting last Friday keep her from jumping in and helping out. There was a lot to like about Jodi when he wasn't busy fighting her every move.

He eyed Sandra Dee as she pushed to her feet again and did a half walk, half jog along the fence perimeter, her head swinging from side to side, her belly moving independent of her feet. When the air stopped flowing, the summer bit again, the heat so humid it felt as if his flesh melted. He had to get Sandra Dee in quick before the burning temperature and her extended labor exhausted her. If she went down and stayed down, there'd be no moving her. He peered into the shadowed barn and wondered how long before Jodi located Colton. He'd give her five minutes and then he'd handle the fractious cow himself.

He stretched his arms overhead and bounced on the balls of his feet. It'd been a long week. While he'd met with and convinced twenty farmers to sign on for his co-op, he'd heard Jodi had been just as busy acquiring property for Midland. He wasn't sure how many farms she'd purchased, but even one was too many. He glanced across the pasture. Strategizing would have to wait for now, however. One of his animals depended on him.

He stalked closer to Sandra Dee, careful not to startle the now-pacing cow. Colton was taking too long and he needed her inside. When the gate creaked behind him, he whirled, relieved. But Jodi stood where his farmhand should have been, clutching her sides, bent at the waist.

"I. Can't. Find. Him," she gasped out, then straightened and strode his way. "I'll help you get her in." He nearly chuckled when she lifted a leg to reveal knee-high barn boots beneath her peach-colored dress. She wasn't serious.

But the set of her chin and her swinging arms said she was. Jodi had helped plenty of times during the summer she'd worked with him, but that was a long time ago. How much would she remember?

"When I drive Sandra Dee close enough, open the latch and use the plywood board over there to direct her toward the barn. I'll be right behind to guide her past you. She's going to charge, but not straight at you. And whatever you do, don't act nervous."

Jodi scrunched her upturned nose. "This isn't my first rodeo, cowboy."

Her challenging expression made him smile. "Then prove it."

He reached Sandra Dee in a few strides but she trotted away. Another few steps had her heading for the gate. Before she overshot it, he dashed past her. He gave Jodi the signal to open the gate, then waved his arms as the cow approached. Just when he expected the storming heifer to mow him over, she swerved through the opening and up toward the barn, thanks to the large wooden board Jodi brandished.

He blew out a long breath and raced after Sandra Dee.

"Nice work," he called as he passed Jodi, the glimpse of her relieved smile staying with him as he plunged inside the dim barn. The cow headed up the corridor and he suspected she sought out her own stall—a little familiar comfort on a painful day.

But he needed her in the birthing pen rigged out with padded walls and a stabilizing headlock. If he got in front of her again, he'd open the gate and force her inside. But with her moving at a fast clip and the corridors not wide enough for him to pass her, he needed a plan B. The timing had to be exact or she'd miss the space and they'd lose precious minutes needed to save the calf. Where on earth was Colton?

Just as they neared the oversize stall, a bellowing Sandra Dee picked up speed. From a connecting corridor, Jodi suddenly lunged in front of one thousand pounds of agonized animal, her plywood board held in front of her, her face set in firm lines. His heart lodged in his throat at the fragile picture she made, her small form directly in Sandra Dee's path, her slender arms holding up a useless shield. It'd shatter, like her, on impact. It'd been risky for her to stand on the sidelines and guide the cow toward the barn. Trying to stop the mother-to-be altogether was suicide.

He leaped forward and yanked open the gate as Jodi herded the cow inside. Success! The animal blew out a long breath and he slumped against the railing as the door clicked shut behind her.

"That was a stupid thing to do, Jodi Lynn. You could have gotten killed." He couldn't keep the anger out of his voice, or blot out the mental picture of her broken and bloodied on the ground. Why would she take such a foolish risk?

"I know what I'm doing, or have you forgotten?" She brushed back a loose curl and he saw that she was as pale as the white post she leaned against. Despite her brave words, she'd been frightened, and he realized he had been, too—for her sake.

"I thought *you'd* forgotten." For a moment they studied one another until Sandra Dee bellowed. Daniel went to the front of the stall and lowered the head hold around the cow's neck, locking her in place. There. No further threat to Jodi as long as she stayed outside the pen.

"Is Dr. Coryer still the vet?" She held up her phone.

Daniel shook his head. "We lost her last year when she moved to Oklahoma." He gave her the new vet's number and headed into the stall.

"Whoa, now, Sandra Dee. It's going to be okay."

The cow twisted her head around at his gentle tone, her large brown eyes showing white all around. He lathered on hand sanitizer from a nearby dispenser and, when the cleansing foam reached past his elbows, he pulled on long rubber gloves.

He sidestepped to avoid Sandra Dee's moving hindquarters and inserted his hand. While stroking her quivering flank, he felt for the calf's position.

His hand encountered something smooth— the calf's side—and he traced its length to see how much turning was needed to get the front legs and face forward. After another minute, he withdrew his arm, heart heavy. He couldn't risk ripping Sandra Dee's uterus, a real possibility given the tight fit and his large hands. That was delicate work if it was possible at all. The calf was not going to make it.

Jodi slipped in beside him, her phone stowed, her arms encased in gloves.

Surprise chased away his dejection. "What are you doing?"

"The doctor's on an emergency call up at Pine Ridge Farm. He can't be here for at least another hour, so unless you can manage on your own, I'm all you've got." Her blue eyes snapped at him and for the first time he admired the new no-nonsense, business side of Jodi.

At his stunned silence, she nudged him aside. "Now keep Sandra Dee still. My hands are smaller than yours, so I'll turn the baby."

"It's too breech. You'll tear up the uterus."

"If I can't, I can't. But I'm not quitting." And her jaw set in a way that told him she meant every word.

Her hands slid inside as he watched, her face taut with concentration, her arm muscles straining. He imagined her delicate fingers performing a task most wouldn't attempt. Her no-fuss manner disproved every judgment he'd made of her when he'd picked her up at the airport. She still cared about farming; it was obvious in the way she'd jumped in to help Sandra Dee. Something else motivated her homecoming besides money or revenge, and now he was determined to figure it out.

"I'm turning it," she gasped quietly. "Almost. There."

He watched her closely, amazed at her single-mindedness, her ability to blot out everything and focus. No wonder she'd done well at a large company like Midland. She'd succeed at anything she set her mind to. He didn't like what she stood for, but he respected that she defended her principles, as misguided as they were. Would he mind losing to the person Jodi had become? With stakes this high—yes. But part of him wondered if there were two sides to this argument and if, by ignoring hers, he'd missed out.

Sandra Dee jittered to the right and he saw Jodi wince when a hoof grazed the side of her foot. But she didn't make a sound, only lifted her ankle once the cow moved and kept shifting her arm slightly in different angles.

"I'm taking over," Daniel said, his voice firm and low. "She's getting more agitated and I want you out of here before you get hurt."

Jodi's eyes narrowed and she gave a sharp

little yank before she stumbled back against the railing, panting.

"See. The calf's too—" Daniel stopped speaking when his hand encountered a pair of hooves and then the outline of a face. He looked at Jodi, stunned, and her elated expression lit him up inside.

"You did it! You turned her."

Sandra Dee fell to her knees, the head holder sliding down on the pulley.

"Daniel, pull that calf out! It's still caught in her pelvis."

He braced his heels on the slippery straw and pulled with all his might. The calf didn't budge and Sandra Dee brayed, her keening wail trailing off to an even more chilling silence.

Arms slid around him from the back. Jodi. "On the count of three," she said. "One. Two. Three."

They strained, grappled and tugged until at last he felt a slight give. All at once the calf tumbled out in a wet heap on the straw, he and Jodi along with it.

"I'll get Sandra Dee loose." She scrambled to her feet and flinched, grabbing the post when she stepped down.

Her foot. If Sandra Dee's full weight had pressed on it, she'd have a broken bone or two. Farm life's dangers had never felt as real

as they did looking at her ashen face. He un-
hitched the anxious new mother and removed
his gloves. Scooping up Jodi, he carried her
out of the pen.

Her head rested against his thudding heart
while they paused to watch Sandra Dee and
her first offspring begin the afterbirth rituals.
After much licking, the calf wobbled to its feet
and they both cheered.

His arms tightened around Jodi. "Jodi, I—"
He was at a loss for words. He looked down at
the beaming face that had occupied many of
his thoughts lately. She was incredible—strong
and tough when she needed to be, loving and
generous when it counted most. His heart expanded, making room for his growing feelings.

Her hand came up and touched his cheek,
igniting a storm of sensation that made him
pull her closer still. "You don't have to say it,
Daniel. It's what neighbors do."

He looked at her in wonder. She'd used his
words against him. And even more astonishing,
she seemed to mean them. Only, he wasn't concerned about neighbors right now as he stared
into her blue eyes. No. What he cared about
most was more personal than he'd ever imagined.

More and more, it felt as though he and Jodi
were a package deal, and he couldn't picture a

better combination. It'd certainly worked when they'd birthed the calf. Yet Jodi would leave him and Cedar Bay soon unless he found a way to stop her. He'd hoped reminding her of her old life would convince her to stop her Midland plans. After today, he knew he needed to make her remember her old feelings for him. To trust him enough to give him a second chance.

Something called her back to Chicago, and he couldn't fight what he didn't understand. At first he would have thought she preferred city life. But after seeing her drive a tractor, birth a calf and make homemade jam, he knew that wasn't true. She'd looked too happy. And lately, he'd felt the same way.

There was a mystery to Jodi's homecoming he needed to solve and if he didn't, he might lose her again. His arms tightened around her. It was a chance he was no longer willing to take.

"Oh, my goodness, what happened?"

Jodi gave Sue a sheepish grin as Daniel carried her over the last stair and onto the loft's landing. He'd wanted to take her to the house, but she'd insisted on the loft instead. Tyler would be worried by her absence. Colton put down a guitar and Tyler looked around, his eyes wide.

"I'm okay," she protested, her face heating more from Daniel's hold than the attention. The ease with which he carried her had made her feel as if she weighed less than a newborn chick, his touch gentle. Only the throb in her foot had distracted her from tracing the biceps encircling her.

Daniel's jaw tightened. "She got stepped on by Sandra Dee."

Colton shot to his feet. "Sorry, Jodi. Broke my big toe that way last year. Lost a nail, too, but that was from a fungus I—"

"Daniel?" Sue cleared her throat. "You can put Jodi down over there." She pointed to the rocking chair.

Daniel gently placed her in the chair, his arms releasing her slowly, as if reluctant to let go. And she felt the same way. His physical absence made her feel alone in a way she hadn't in a long time.

"Let me get you some ice." Sue hurried off and called over her shoulder, "Colton, will you grab the hassock?" A short stool was slid under her foot, its crocheted top a soft cushion that relieved some of the jarring pressure.

Jodi hoped the injury wasn't serious. After her horrible phone call with her boss this morning, she couldn't be out of commission, not even for a moment. Her eyes lingered on her son as he toddled to the rocker on tiptoe, Ollie in hand.

"Hi, Tyler." She smoothed back his soft blond curls and centered Ollie's slipping tiara, her love for him blotting out her tender foot.

When Daniel removed her boot and felt her instep, she tried keeping a brave face but failed.

"Ouch!" Yanking back her ankle only made the pain intensify. Of all the terrible luck. This couldn't have happened at a worse time.

Tyler started to cry and he tugged off his eyeglasses.

"No, sweetie. It's okay." She brushed tears from his round cheeks and replaced the band when Sue handed it to her. "Mommy's okay."

"Now, that's an egg," Colton exclaimed, settling Tyler onto her lap when he tried climbing up himself.

A bag of icy coolness descended on her throbbing arch. "It looks serious." Sue studied her through her rimless glasses, her oval face and sharp features reflecting her concern.

Tyler's flapping hands smacked Jodi face, his knees knocking the air from her stomach. Three pairs of hands descended on him, stroking, patting or tickling until his tears dried up and he looked around. Jodi's heart swelled. For once, she and Tyler were accepted without judgment about his behavior. Her "Bad Mother" marquee blinked once, then dimmed.

But despair returned when she looked at her rapidly swelling foot. How would she ever purchase the five thousand acres she needed for her promotion now? Especially given the curveball her boss had thrown at her this morning. Tyler would never talk again, and it would be her fault.

Aunt Grace could drive her to appointments, but then who would watch Tyler when he wasn't with Sue? The amount of help she'd depended on this summer staggered her. She couldn't ask for more. This was it. She'd reached the end of her fading rainbow.

A small sound escaped her and instantly Daniel's warm hand grasped her calf, hazel eyes peering at her beneath a brush of lashes. "I'll take you to the health center for an X-ray."

"Tyler needs to go down for his nap," she protested. Why did it have to be her right foot? And why was her body as aware of his strong grip as it was of the pain shooting up her leg? Now that the euphoria of birthing the calf had worn off, the reality of her situation returned with a vengeance. And it crushed her more than the cow's hoof. She'd been told by her boss that her colleague, Brady Grayson, was coming to Cedar Bay to "help."

Colton picked up a fussing Tyler and settled him beside his guitar. "Would it be all right if he stayed up a little longer to show you something special? We've been practicing."

Sue clapped her hands and rushed over to kneel by Colton's chair. Jodi nodded, curious as he struck a melodic chord. Daniel shot her an amused glance and her lips quirked in response. It was sweet to see Sue so enamored with something other than her weaving, knitting or reading. But what did the guitar have to do with Tyler? He liked his sound soother, but that was the most he usually tolerated.

A rich baritone filled the room, deeper than she would have expected from Colton.

"Old Macdonald had a farm. E-I-E-I-O." He grinned at Sue and strummed another cord. "And on that farm he had some—" He paused and Sue held up a picture of a chick. They waited a moment and their faces fell when Tyler looked from one to the other without speaking. Had they thought he'd say the word? Hope surged and her heart beat out its own song.

"Chick," Sue supplied at last and nodded at Colton to begin again. She held Tyler's hands and patted them gently together. Her soft soprano blended with Colton's voice as they sang, "with a chick chick here and a chick chick there, here a chick, there a chick, everywhere a chick chick…"

The ice bag slid, and a lance of pain stabbed up her calf as she bent for it. She released a breath she hadn't realized she'd been holding. Would Tyler chime in? Sing a word?

"Stay," Daniel ordered, his murmur so commanding she sank back against the soft cushion. She'd grown independent, but being taken care of felt good, too. Not that she'd let herself get used to it. This morning's news from Midland meant she'd have to work harder than ever, on her own. But if she heard Tyler speak, none of that would matter. Not by a long shot.

The song continued with a pause for every animal, an expectant hush where Jodi could hear her own heartbeat. At last the song ended with a flourish of strums and cheers from Sue, who seemed determined to look optimistic.

"I wish you could have heard him earlier, Jodi. He said *dog* and *chick* and *duck*. Look." Sue held out a folder.

Jodi's hand rose to her locket before she took the file, her pulse stammering in her veins. Tyler had spoken, but not around her. Something about that thought niggled at her, keeping her from being as thrilled as she should be. Of all people, she knew that autistic children were unpredictable and did things on their terms. Yet something about his silence around her suddenly felt purposeful. Sue had mentioned in a previous phone call that he was getting close to speaking full words. Yet now that she was present, he didn't even try. Why? She pushed the thought aside now that Sue's excitement started to fade.

"That's amazing. Did you record it?" She fanned herself with the folder, both euphoric and strangely unsettled.

Sue's chest heaved out a long sigh. "It happened so fast that we didn't have time. But we'll keep working on it, right, Tyler? We were hoping he'd do it in front of you."

Sue's last comment pierced Jodi's heart. When she gasped, Daniel's gaze snapped her way and she released the file to grab her ankle, pretending as though her pain wasn't stemming from some unknowable place.

Colton helped Tyler strum Ollie's trunk across the guitar strings, and the boy didn't turn.

"Oh. Right. Next time." Jodi's voice was a notch above a whisper, disappointment weighing down her buoyant emotions.

To hide her conflicted feelings, she picked up the folder again and studied Sue's dissertation notes, her eyes drawn to what Tyler couldn't do rather than what he had.

"You don't look happy." Sue brought her a juice box, her eyebrows meeting above her glasses.

Colton's earnest face appeared beside Sue's. "I heard him, Jodi. I swear. It was Sue's idea to have me sing to him and he seemed to like it so much he joined in." He looked abashed at Sue's admiring look and hurried on. "After Sue held up the picture card, of course."

Jodi forced a smile and spotted the edge of a sticky note peeking out of her purse pocket. It had the name and number of the afternoon appointment she'd need to cancel. "I'm happy. Really." But for some reason she started to shake, a shudder that seemed to start in her bones. Suddenly it was all too much: her injury, this possible hope for Tyler, her boss's crushing announcement, these relentless, intensifying feelings for Daniel and the fact that her son had spoken, but not in front of her.

"Time for the doctor," Daniel pronounced.

When he scooped her up, she clung to his neck, the familiar scent of him soothing. Sue carried Tyler and they trekked down the stairs and outside to Daniel's truck.

"Sue, bring Tyler to Grace's and we'll be there as soon as we get Jodi looked at," said Daniel.

"I'll go with her." Colton reached to pat Tyler's back but somehow missed and got Sue's shoulder instead. He jerked back as if burned and Sue buried her red face in Tyler's curls.

Daniel's voice was so deep it vibrated beneath her ear. "Stay and check on Sandra Dee and her new calf."

Colton's eyes grew wide and impressed as they reached the truck. "I meant to check on her earlier but Tyler was singing and I hated to leave. Did Jodi help with the birth?"

She nodded. "Though Daniel did the heavy lifting."

Daniel gazed down at her, his expression tender. "If it wasn't for Jodi turning the calf, it wouldn't be alive. Maybe not Sandra Dee, either."

Colton whistled. "I'll be darned. You two make a good team."

A short laugh bubbled out of her. They were a good team at the field day and in the barn, but in real life, not a chance.

Jodi held out her arms to give Tyler and Ollie a smooch. "Love you, baby."

His blue eyes watched her over Sue's shoulder as Sue carried him to Jodi's car and buckled him in.

"Will you be able to use this evidence for your dissertation?" Jodi asked. All signs pointed to her heading home soon and figuring out some way to pay for Tyler's education. Sue shouldn't be another casualty to her misfortune.

Sue sighed as she straightened. "Not until I can record it. But I'm sure I'll get it the next time."

Jodi forced herself to smile at Sue's assumption that Tyler would talk again. It would be a miracle, but now there was no guarantee that Tyler would return. Depending on her diagnosis, she might be doing what she'd promised Daniel when she'd arrived in Cedar Bay: taking the next flight to Chicago.

"Colton. Would you get the door?" Daniel jerked his head toward the truck.

Minutes later, they hit the road. She was nestled in the seat beside Daniel, an old flannel shirt wadded up around her aching foot, when he turned to her.

"Do you want to tell me what really made you upset back there?"

His green-yellow eyes saw too much, and she stared out the window, wondering which of the farms they passed would join Daniel's co-op, which would be sold to Midland and which might remain independent.

"I wished I could have heard Tyler say those words."

"Me, too." His sincere tone touched her. "It's been over a year since he's talked, correct?"

Her stomach bottomed out as she nodded, not trusting herself to speak. Daniel had a way of getting her to see things she'd rather not face. And after her frenetic day, she couldn't handle any more.

"That's a long time to live in silence." He steered the truck away from a pack of biking kids.

She lowered her chin to her chest, her brain absorbing the thought like a thousand needle jabs. Chicago was lonely, her office the only place people spoke to her. A sharp blade of sadness went through her, deep and quick.

"I have my work." She leaned her temple against the window, the heat of the day as powerful as a hand pressing on her head.

Daniel turned on the air-conditioning and cool air rushed across her face. "You don't sound happy about that."

She shot him a look out of the corner of her eye. "Trust me. You don't want to know."

A large hand dropped on top of hers again and squeezed. "I do."

The steady pressure made her want to open up. After all, what did it matter now that the war was lost?

"Midland's sending another executive to

'help' me, but we're actually competing for a promotion based on who acquires five thousand acres first. His name's Brady Grayson and he's a junior executive they've nicknamed The Rainmaker."

Daniel frowned. "He's not better than you."

Her laugh ended on a startled hiccup at his confident tone. "He's had the most sales this year and he's out to break a record. Now that he's coming here and I'm out of commission, I'm sure he'll have no problem getting it."

Despair drummed along the hollow pit of her stomach. If she failed, Tyler would be the one to lose.

"And why are you out of commission?" Daniel's voice rumbled over the pickup's engine as they glided down I-89.

Jodi looked at him, askance, and pointed to her foot. "I'm not going to make appointments now that I can't drive and I need Aunt Grace to watch Tyler."

"I'll drive you."

Jodi blinked at him in surprise. "What did you say?"

"I said I'll drive you. Grace can take you while Tyler's getting therapy, and when he's done I'll drive you to afternoon appointments. We can head out again in the evening, after I do my second milking."

"But why would you do that?" She still couldn't believe her ears. "You'll lose time pitching your co-op. Keeping your own appointments."

"How about this." His eyes slid her way and she stared back at him, shocked. "Let's set up joint appointments, we'll both make our case and whoever signs with us signs. No hard feelings."

Jodi suppressed a groan, her eyes flitting away from his handsome profile. Oh, there were feelings. Just not the kind that went along with business promotions and bonuses.

"But all the appointments I have are for people that want to sell to Midland."

Daniel flicked on the radio, the sound of a screeching guitar filling the cab until he turned down the volume. "Then I'll be there to talk them off the ledge. And when you meet my appointments, you'll have the same chance."

Despite her foot, she had to laugh, and he joined her. Their familiar blend of rivalry, friendship and more returned in a melting rush.

"Good luck." Jodi grinned, happy despite her injury and her earlier uneasiness about Tyler's silence in front of her.

"I won't need it." Daniel tapped his head. "I've got this."

"More like this." Jodi made a talking motion with her fingers and Daniel chuckled.

He turned the volume dial down even farther. "Sounds about right."

After a moment's quiet she added, "You don't need to help. I'll figure something out."

"And let some slick salesman try to take over our hometown." His dark eyebrows rose. "Uh-uh."

Their hometown.

The rightness of that phrase rang in her ears like a battle cry. Only suddenly, she wasn't exactly sure which side she was on.

"We make a good team," Daniel said in the comfortable silence that had descended as they exited off the highway to a rural route.

Jodi thought about how they'd saved a life together today. Two, possibly. He was right. They did work well together. What was more, they felt right together. She needed Daniel's help, there was no way around it, but deep down she knew that things were going to get very complicated. For her, anyway.

"I'm happy Sandra Dee and her calf will be all right," she said, her voice strained as she forced her mind back to normal, everyday topics.

"She's the last of the season which means, thanks to you, I didn't lose one."

She leaned down and rubbed her foot. "And I know how much you hate losing." There. A little bit of their old teasing would put them safely in a friendly category. Nothing more. She could admire him from there, couldn't she?

"Losing only matters when the prize is special." He brushed her damp hair from the side of her face and she thrilled at the feel of his calloused fingers. "Especially if it's something you've lost and want to win back."

Her breath caught at his words. Did he mean her? Them? She'd always wondered why he'd never come after her. Hadn't fought more. Giving up hadn't been like him. But now that she knew about his mother, it made sense. Then again, why dwell on it when it was all too late and impossible?

"We are still talking about cows, right?" she asked, wishing they weren't but knowing it was best.

"If you want to."

It was the safer topic. A thought struck her and she turned toward Daniel. "We forgot to name the calf."

"I didn't." Daniel's half smile revealed dimples on either side of his mouth. "I'm calling him Tyler."

CHAPTER TWELVE

JODI STUDIED HER swathed foot propped on a recliner a few days later, a red afghan covering her bandages. Despite her best navy suit and yellow silk tank, it wasn't the professional image she needed for this sales pitch. But she was fortunate to be in Mr. Donaldson's farmhouse at all. She glanced at Daniel as he discussed his co-op graphs, his muscular physique dwarfing an antique chair.

If he hadn't offered to drive her to her meetings, she might be back in Chicago now. She felt a short, sharp pain in her chest at the thought, the hurt worse than her foot's bruised bones. How strange that her enemy had come to her rescue. He was still clever, wily and competitive, but he'd also grown generous, compassionate and patient. She shifted in her seat, uneasy at her changing feelings.

His naming the newborn calf after Tyler touched her. It was the kind of thing farmers did for friends' children, and the sense of normalcy felt good. Daniel treated her son like any other kid. Better, even. She'd never questioned the way the world viewed Tyler: a difficult child, an object of pity, a challenge to be diagnosed and fixed. Yet Daniel's way of focusing on the good made her feel like a mother whose preschooler did amazing things like recite the alphabet or catch a ball with a glove.

She pushed the strange thought aside and peered around the low-ceilinged room, dark despite the light forcing its way through dusty blinds. It'd been hard to focus on her sales contract's fine print when she'd presented it to Mr. Donaldson. She wondered if the place had been properly cleaned since his wife's passing two years earlier. Sympathy welled as she noticed newspapers, sports magazines, soda cans and overflowing ashtrays littering every surface. A TV tray with an empty microwave meal container rested beside her, a crusted fork and milk-rimmed glass suggesting last night's supper.

The poor man needed help but, given his age and the fact that his children had left Vermont, she doubted Daniel's co-op would be his best option.

Nevertheless, she didn't interrupt. So far, they were deadlocked today with one farmer signing on for the co-op and another agreeing to sell. While they'd been silent in the truck after losing to the other, he'd stayed true to his word, as had she. No hard feelings. Their war had turned into a gentlemen's competition, the real enemy her colleague Brady Grayson.

Since he'd landed in Vermont a couple days ago, she hadn't answered his voice mails. With any luck, she'd evade him altogether; although word had it he'd already purchased a number of farms. She bunched her skirt's fabric, then released it. She and Daniel needed to move fast to lock down the rest of the area, shutting Brady out. Who knew what kinds of unfair deals he might be making with her former neighbors?

"But I have Medicare," she heard Mr. Donaldson say, his high-pitched voice at odds with his loose bulk. "I don't need to worry about health insurance rates. Cookie?"

When he pushed an open carton toward Daniel, she discreetly shook her head. It was kind of the older man to do his best to entertain them. But who knew how many treats he had left? Without his wife, he probably didn't get to the store often.

Daniel widened his eyes so that white showed all around and shrugged with upraised palms as if to say "I have no choice," which of course he did, the scamp. Mr. Donaldson missed the silent interaction while fumbling for napkins and lightness bubbled within her at their secret exchange. It felt good to be working side by side, even if it wasn't together. Though sometimes that didn't feel like enough. She'd caught herself staring at him as they'd driven around the area, imagining her world a different way.

Daniel accepted the limp cookie with a gracious smile, then popped it in his mouth. Jodi tried to frown at him, but the corners of her mouth quirked. She wagged her finger as he leaned forward to take another when Mr. Donaldson answered his phone.

"Stop it," she mouthed, then clamped a hand over her mouth to stifle her giggle. They were acting like children, and this was a business meeting. What was it about Daniel that brought out the carefree girl she'd once been? Part of her personality she'd given up for lost.

"I'll be there with some firewood. See you." Mr. Donaldson dropped the old-fashioned handset back in its receiver. He peered at them, his face sagging as if the bones beneath had melted—a man collapsing in on himself. "Are you two going to the potluck and bonfire before tomorrow night's fireworks?"

Jodi shook her head. She hadn't seen Independence Day fireworks since Tyler's birth, his noise sensitivity preventing it. "I'm leaving after the potluck to put my son down to sleep."

Mr. Donaldson's sunken cheeks drew in farther. "You can't miss out. It's tradition."

"She'll be there," Daniel promised, his eyes leveled on hers. "With me."

"I'll only be around to help my aunt with the food," Jodi corrected firmly. Why was Daniel behaving as if they were a couple? As if the fireworks would be a date? Not that a small part of her didn't thrill at the idea.

"Goodness." Mr. Donaldson threw his hands in the air, then dropped them. "This is all so confusing. I need time to think before giving my answer."

Jodi leaned forward, worried that Brady might get to the wavering farmer first. "But the choices are clear, and we need to know—"

"When you're sure. Perhaps tomorrow," Daniel interrupted when Mr. Donaldson's expression slid from baffled to irascible.

The deep line between the older man's brows lessoned at Daniel's reassuring tone. She shot him a grateful look, impressed. Using a soft sell approach had been a good call.

"May I offer you more refreshments?" Free of the pressure to make a decision, Mr. Donaldson smiled for the first time since they'd arrived, his dentures a startling white against his weather-beaten skin.

"Jodi might like a cookie," Daniel said, a mischievous gleam in his eye.

She sent him a brief glare and waved her hand. "No, thanks, Mr. Donaldson. I just ate."

"But it's noon now." His one functioning eye wandered her way in confusion while the glass one remained fixed. She recalled how he'd always held up one end of the banner for the Veterans of Foreign Wars at the Fourth of July parade and how they'd all scrambled for the candy he'd thrown from a bucket attached to his belt loop. It'd been one of her favorite childhood memories, as anticipated as opening her Christmas Eve present or getting the drumstick on Thanksgiving. Only now she had no one to buy her presents and, since Tyler didn't like turkey, they ate chicken nuggets and watched cartoons on the holiday. Life had certainly changed. For the first time, however, she wondered if it was for the better.

She pressed a hand to her stomach. "It was a big breakfast."

The farmer shrugged, his white tank top drooping beneath a frayed plaid shirt. "Suit yourselves. So are you two a couple again?"

"What?" they both asked, their raised voices registering equal decibels of shock.

The war veteran shrugged. "You two looked

cozy that day I returned Daniel's father's combine."

Jodi flushed at the fire that leaped in Daniel's eyes, the memory of their heated moment ten years ago rushing back. She could almost feel the rough wood of the wall at her back, Daniel's large hands splayed on either side of her face, his muscular arms caging her in a trap she'd had no intention of escaping, the passionate kiss they'd exchanged until Mr. Donaldson had cleared his throat behind them.

"That was a long time ago." She folded her hands in her lap and pushed the recollection back where it belonged—oblivion. Kisses and romance were not a priority. Tyler was. And that would never change.

Mr. Donaldson pulled an inhaler out of his breast pocket, held it up to his mouth and pressed. After a deep breath, he said, "Seems like yesterday."

"Feels like it to me." Daniel's voice was light, his eyes piercing.

"Those were the days." Mr. Donaldson's smile pushed his cheeks so far up into his eyes that he didn't seem to notice their silent, charged exchange. "I used to stack hay bales for hours, but now my torn rotator cuff's got me pretty much laid up."

"I'm sorry to hear that, Mr. Donaldson. You

should get it fixed." Her heart went out to him. He really needed to retire.

He nodded. "That's what my doctor tells me. Except who's going to take care of my cows? I only got the fifty, but still…"

"I'll help out," Daniel offered. "And when we form the co-op, we'll cover for each other to allow for sick time and vacations."

Jodi made a face. So much for the soft sell. If he wanted to play hard ball, then so could she.

"On the other hand," she spoke up, "you could take Midland's offer, get your shoulder fixed and retire in comfort. Maybe near your son in Georgia? I heard he was expecting a child." She arched an eyebrow Daniel's way. She'd done her homework.

Daniel's eyes narrowed and Mr. Donaldson beamed. "It's my first grandchild. A boy. And they're naming him after me." He pulled out a grainy photo on slippery paper and brought it over to her. "This is Arlen Jr." His shortened index finger traced an oval shape in a dark area. "He's due in October."

Jodi studied the picture. "Congratulations. I bet you'll be happy to be there for the birth."

Mr. Donaldson tucked the picture away in his shirt pocket and nodded. "I would."

Jodi pulled out her purchase agreement. "So then, if you'd like to sell—"

The farmer looked around the small living space, his expression far away. In the silence, the only sound came from the whispering of the trees outside and the low ticks and groans from the walls, the usual old-house arthritic noises. The terrier behind her woke, scrambled to its feet and bolted straight into a nearby wall. It shook its head, tottered back to its sleep spot and resumed snoring.

The commotion startled Mr. Donaldson from his thoughts.

"Is he okay?" Jodi peeked around her seat.

"Max? He's fine." He leaned over and rubbed his pet. "Just an old fart like me. Dreams he's running through fields when he can't even keep up with my tractor anymore."

"When you sell your farm, you and Max can take walks whenever you like," Jodi pushed, ignoring Daniel's head shake.

With a sigh, the aging farmer settled on the couch again. "I know. But I'm not sure if I'm ready to leave yet. Lots of good memories here. See that patch on the wall?"

Jodi and Daniel looked.

"My younger brother and I used to pretend we were King Kong and Godzilla. One day I threw him so hard his head went right through the plaster." Mr. Donaldson's breathy laugh sounded. "My mother was so mad she clobbered me over the head so I'd have a bump the same size." He twisted his wedding ring. "Yep. Lots of good memories here."

Daniel rose and extended a hand. "Then it's better not to rush into rash decisions you might regret."

When his eyes flashed her way, she wondered if he had any regrets that included her.

THE SETTING SUN bathed Lake Champlain's sandy shoreline in softest gold the next evening. From a thicket of swaying ash trees, a twilight chorus of starlings rose, the cool breeze rippling the darkening water's surface.

Daniel touched an elongated lighter to citronella lamps dotting the beach, the stringent lemon smell repelling the nagging mosquitoes. The smoke made his eyes burn. He glanced over at the picnic-table area, his eyes searching out Jodi amongst the potluck supper's cleanup crew.

Because of the holiday, there hadn't been any scheduled meetings and he'd missed her. It amazed him how quickly he'd grown used to having her around. Without her, the day had crawled, a hollow feeling overtaking him, even when he'd played fetch with Goldie and fed the barn cats. If he felt this way now, how would he feel when she returned to Chicago? His gut twisted.

As he strode across the damp sand, he glimpsed Jodi before she disappeared from view. Other than greeting him when she'd served him his plate, they hadn't said much to each other. Yet he'd caught her eye a few times when he'd searched for her in the crowd.

Had she missed him, too? When he'd picked her up at the airport weeks ago, she'd seemed distant and changed. But now, after their time together, he'd seen more sides to her. Flashes of the old Jodi mixed with the new, a poised and strong woman who braved a charging heifer and a caring mother who conquered her fear of machinery to take her son on a tractor ride. She was tough and vulnerable, business-minded and caring, funny and a bit sad at times and most of all, intelligent. Her sharp, clever mind attracted him to no end. He appreciated a woman who could put him in his place— when he let her.

He waved to a family heading toward the beach and lit the last torch. When the father settled his son on his shoulders, Daniel felt a pang, wishing he could be that man for Tyler. The determined boy who laughed from his belly and cared for his stuffed toy had also found a place in Daniel's heart. Both son and mother seemed happy here, so what was her real reason for needing to leave?

If it was a custody issue, he could help her negotiate it. It didn't sound like the absentee father would put up much resistance. She needed to trust him enough to confide in him. As strong as she was, he wanted to be there for her. The anchor that would give her family stability, the wall she could lean on, the extra pair of arms that would hold her and Tyler both, a foundation strong enough to support them all.

"Can you give me a hand with the coolers, Daniel?" called his friend Frank.

He headed over, peering once more into the shadows darkening the eating area. Had Jodi left to put Tyler to bed? He hoped she'd changed her mind and stayed. He'd even taken Grace aside earlier and offered to drive Jodi home. From the knowing look she'd given him, he sensed his feelings were more obvious than he thought. But if he couldn't get through to Jodi tonight, then when? He needed to seize the moment before she slipped out of his life again.

Grabbing the nearest cooler, he hefted it, a hand on either handle, and lugged it down to the waterline. They'd have a great view of the fireworks over the lake from here, the coolers doubling as places for kids to stand if they couldn't see.

As he returned for another, he passed a stranger wearing a pressed shirt, dress slacks and a tie. Was this Brady?

"Hello," the man called as he walked by. "Need a hand?"

Daniel looked over the guy's gelled hair, his groomed jaw stubble and gym muscles, and shook his head.

"No, thanks. I've got it."

"I'm quite strong, actually." The man tagged along, his voice reminding Daniel of one of the prep school kids he'd roomed with at Cornell. "I'm glad to help."

Daniel sighed. The stranger was more annoying than the mosquitoes whining by his ear. "Suit yourself. Grab any one you like."

"By myself?"

He lifted another cooler and turned. "I can ask one of the women to help you."

The man's angular jaw worked. "I'm sure I'll handle it. And the name is Brady, by the way."

"I figured," Daniel muttered, his sandals sinking into the cooling sand as he walked back to the lake. Jodi had been dodging the guy for days and now he'd shown up to ambush her. His temperature rose.

A series of non-prep-school-sounding words made him stop and turn. This was a small town, not a truck stop.

"Hey, buddy," he called. "There are kids here. Watch the language."

Brady looked abashed, his arms straining as he inched forward. "My apologies."

"Just put the thing down and I'll come back for it," Daniel grumbled, and continued down to deposit his cooler.

"So who's that guy?" Frank jerked a thumb at the man, who now dragged the cooler.

Daniel filled him in on Brady and his mission, the news making Frank's eyes narrow.

A moment later, Mary dropped a cooler close enough to Daniel's toes to make him dance back. She looked around at the gaping men, her hands on her hips. "What? Who do you think helps out as bar back at The Lounge? This isn't all just looks, you know."

Frank snorted and Ted Layhee lunged and caught her around the waist.

"Back off, Hands." When she stomped on his instep, he released her with a yelp. "Or I'm dropping the next cooler on your head."

Frank and Ted watched her as she walked purposefully back up the beach.

"What a woman," Ted said, then whistled.

"She can handle more coolers than that joker over there." Frank nodded at Brady, who'd progressed less than a yard. "Hey, mister," Frank bellowed, and a red-faced Brady looked up, the cords in his neck visible. "Give it a rest. Mary will get it."

Mary whirled and gave Frank a rude gesture that he pretended to catch and press to his heart.

Despite his worry for Jodi, Daniel laughed at the gang's good-natured ribbing. This was exactly what he loved about living in Cedar Bay, the generations of family and friends, the experiences and traditions that connected them.

Sand sprayed as a cooler thudded beside him. "That's one," said Brady, his shirt damp under the arms, his hair spiking in every direction. "Does anyone here know Jodi Chapman?"

"Did someone say my name?"

Daniel whirled alongside Brady, his eyes drinking in her impish grin, her face framed by a cloud of pale, tousled hair.

He couldn't help staring. He'd grown used to seeing her in formal clothes, her demeanor just as reserved. Tonight, though, she seemed more relaxed. Almost dreamy. And so beautiful in a light blue sundress that matched her eyes.

"Hello, Jodi." When Brady stepped forward, her eyes turned cold. "You haven't returned my calls."

"I've been busy making sales." And the assertiveness in her tone, the firm set of her features, made Daniel admire her business persona all over again.

Brady's smile revealed perfect teeth.

"Caps," he heard Mary mutter to Frank.

Brady ignored the comment and stepped closer to Jodi. "Is there somewhere we can talk?"

She caught Daniel's eye. "There's nothing you have to say that my friends can't hear."

Brady looked around the group. "Friends?"

Mary linked her arm through Jodi's. "Yes. Friends. So you were saying?"

Daniel flanked Jodi's other side, his fingers lacing through hers. "Say what you've come to say. Fireworks are on in ten minutes."

"I'm doing a Midland family picnic," Brady began, his dark eyes on Jodi. "And I'll need your help to set up. I'm meeting a farmer at eleven, but the caterers are arriving at ten in the town hall, so—"

"A picnic inside a building?" Mary snorted. "Makes sense."

Frank gave her shoulder a light punch and guffawed.

"Either way," Brady breezed along, "the weather tomorrow is inclement so I'm arranging a series of indoor entertainments. I'll need you there to supervise the setup."

Daniel tightened his hand around Jodi's and

he felt a surge of pleasure when her fingers curled through his.

"I won't be able to help. I've already made an appointment with Spencer Tisdale."

"Tisdale? The farmer with all the lakefront property?" Brady's eyes widened and his cocky expression slipped. "Well. Well. Nice work. Heard he was a bit of a recluse."

Jodi's jewel-toned eyes shot toward Daniel and he smiled back at her. "Yes, well. I have connections." And she did. He'd personally arranged the meeting, for both of them.

"Then lend me a hand tomorrow and I'll help you out on that appointment." Brady's broad smile smeared the words with honey.

"No, thanks."

"But we're on the same team." His friendly expression collapsed into a pout.

"Not the way I see it. Goodbye, Brady." She caught Daniel's eye, angled her head to the left and limped away in her boot.

When she stumbled on a rock, he was there, his arm around her waist, a hand under her elbow.

"Thank you," she said, her blue eyes shining up at him.

A few minutes later, they'd found a secluded rock a distance from the growing crowd. Daniel's pulse thrummed. Here was the opening he'd wanted. The chance to convince her to trust him again. And to get the answers he needed from her at last.

They settled on the stone's wide surface; every accidental brushing of skin against skin made him feel potent, alive and grateful for the opportunity to spend time alone with her.

"Brady seems nice," he joked to wipe the pensive look off her face.

"If you put rattlesnakes in that category." Her uncertain laugh faded away. "I've got to reach my sales quota before he does."

"You will," he reassured her. "I heard he's only gotten verbal agreements. He's rubbing a lot of people the wrong way."

"Good." Jodi's shoulders lowered and she sighed as they gazed out at the vibrant sky.

It was a midsummer's twilight. The kind an artist would want to paint—a blood-orange sun dripping behind banks of cloud washed with colors ranging from a pale pink to ink-blue. But none of it matched the beauty beside him.

"And I'll get Frank and Mary to go to the picnic. Stir things up. He won't get a sale and you might add the Tisdale farm to Midland's acquisitions. That should get you closer to the five thousand you need." She'd been quiet about how much acreage she'd acquired, but from the sales he'd seen her make this week, and the ones he'd heard of, she had to be closing in.

She looked at him sharply. "Aren't you going there to persuade the man yourself?"

He stared at her, struck dumb by the realization that he'd thought only of her. Had forgotten the co-op, what Cedar Bay needed. But what about what he needed?

He flipped her hand over in his, spreading her fingers out to expose her palm. "See? It's written here. 'Tisdale is selling to Midland.'"

"Since when are you on board with Midland?" She looked at him, puzzled.

He pulled her hand closer, his fingers running over the mound at the base of her thumb and up toward the underside of her wrist where the skin was almost translucent. He felt her shiver under the caress, his gut tightening in awareness. "I'm not. But I'm on board with you."

"Oh," she said, and her hair fell in front of her lowered face like a golden waterfall.

"MAY I ASK you something?" Daniel's deep voice jolted Jodi from her thoughts.

She tensed. "Okay."

He looked at her, his gaze steady and measured. "What was in the letter you sent my dad?"

She relaxed. Safer topic. "Just that I was grateful for everything, appreciated all that he'd done to help, that he'd made what could have been the worst summer of life better and I wished it hadn't had to end."

His fingers skimmed along her sensitive forearm, the touch sending a tiny current buzzing through her. "And were you sorry that *we* ended?"

She cleared her throat as emotions battled each other: confusion, regret, shame, hope.

"I never wanted things to happen the way they did," she admitted in a croaky whisper.

"Then why did you leave without saying anything?" His voice sounded as ragged as a battlefield flag. "You wrote my dad a letter, which I appreciate, but you never gave me any warning."

Her pulse leaped. Did he still care? "You admitted you pitied me and I didn't want your charity. You only dated me because you felt sorry for me. What more was there to say?"

"That I loved you."

After a moment of shock and pleasure, something else worked its way to the surface—a dull feeling of disappointment. And stubbornness. Part of her still doubted him.

"I didn't know."

"Now you do." He smiled unevenly.

"But that was a long time ago." She didn't trust herself to follow this line of thinking.

"Was it?" His eyes moved over her face and the breath whooshed out of her lungs, everything freezing for a second.

She dragged her gaze away, dazzled, her vision clouded by floating black spots. Was he suggesting that he still cared for her? Impossible. And even if he did, it changed nothing. So many people she'd trusted, thought she could count on, had eventually disappointed her. A disturbing sensation pounded through her. That category most likely included her, as well. A sinking sensation made her limbs feel heavy, her foot throb.

"I have Tyler to think about now," she said over the throaty song of crickets in the brush behind them.

He was quiet for a moment as they watched the crowd swell farther down the beach. A few sparklers flared to life and children splashed through the lake's edge, tracing sizzling light patterns in the evening sky.

"And there's no room for anyone else?" His tone was calm, but the shoulder that brushed Jodi's was stiff with tension.

Her throat squeezed closed and she shook her head, her mind spinning like wheels on ice. Wishing for Daniel was like wishing for another reality. "Tyler's my priority." How strange that guilt accompanied that thought more often than joy. Ever since he'd spoken in front of Sue, she'd had the fleeting sense that there was a reason he hadn't done so around her. Yet whenever her mind got too close to an answer it shied away like a skittish calf.

"Couldn't he be someone else's priority, too?" Daniel asked, his voice quiet, steady as a heartbeat.

Now it was her turn to be silent. Questions crowded her brain at once, a fog that had rolled off Lake Champlain and settled there.

"I can't imagine it." And that much was true. If Tyler's father couldn't love him, then who?

He cupped her shoulders gently and turned her to face him. Goose bumps pricked up over her arms. "I can."

"Oh." In her head, her pulse tapped out the passing of time. *Let me stay here forever,* she thought. Then the reality of their situation wouldn't drag them apart again.

"If anything's bothering you, some problem back home that you need help with, tell me." Concern darkened his hazel eyes to emerald. "We're on opposite sides about Cedar Bay, but otherwise I'm with you all the way. Or want to be."

She laughed, the sound light but unconvincing. "There's nothing wrong that a few more sales and a flight home won't fix."

His palm held her chin, gently lifting it so that she met his earnest eyes. "Jodi, trust me. I want to help."

As the first bloom of color exploded above them, she pulled away and gazed skyward.

"I don't need it. But thanks," she said. For some reason, she couldn't bring herself to open up about this last secret—her need to raise the tuition for Wonders Primary. She'd told Daniel so much, yet there was something about her desperate need to get Tyler there, a feeling that had strangely intensified since he'd started verbalizing, that she couldn't explain. Even to herself.

As a rocket shrieked into the sky, she wished she could scream along with it, release the frustration inside her. She'd come to Cedar Bay to find redemption for Tyler, not herself.

Red, pink, yellow and purple flashed as she watched fireworks paint colorful patterns against black velvet. Her mouth trembled when she felt his eyes on her. "Daniel. Aren't you going to watch the show?"

"When I see something more beautiful, I will."

She looked at him then, her mouth parted in surprise and, as if unable to resist, he pulled her against him. The feel of him drove away rational thought, the drumbeat of her heart registering in her stomach.

"Daniel. No," she murmured, but couldn't move from such warm arms, every breath drawing in his faint smell of musk and fresh air, her heart full of him.

He laid his cheek against hers. "Why?" he whispered in her ear, his voice rough.

"You know why," she whispered back, though there was no one to hear them; the distant crowd more focused on the sky. It was getting harder and harder to remember her reasons for resisting him.

Her gaze drank in the shape of him—the breadth and contours of his chest, the sharp line of his widow's peak that her fingers had traced so many times, and his eyes—above all, his incredible eyes. Confronted with his nearness, Jodi understood that she was fighting familiarity, a profound kind of recognition.

He stroked the back of her head. "I know the timing is lousy, but if we—"

"But we're not. It makes no sense when I imagine it," she said, almost to herself, and pulled away. His absence registered, the way it had once before, as cold rushing in to fill the void.

"So you do think about it." His eyes lit up. "About us."

Her sigh felt as though it came from the deepest part of her. "Oh, Daniel."

He cupped her cheeks. "We can make this work."

Her brows came together. "Impossible. We both have too much to lose."

He seemed ready to argue, opening his mouth and then closing it at her firm head shake. At last, he pulled her close instead. "Our loss, yes."

The thought caught in her soul as he let her go.

She rose unsteadily, an impressive display of pyrotechnics signaling the show's end.

"I'd better get back in case Tyler wakes."

They looked at each other. She didn't want to go, the thought of leaving him and this beautiful moment behind an almost physical ache.

"If you're sure."

"I'm sure," she said, her trembling voice giving her away. There was nothing more to say. Or too much.

They waited for the crowd to disperse, darkness falling on them like a warm cloak. Elation that Daniel cared about her, saw a future for them, warred with disappointment that it could never be.

He led her through the lingering locals, her hand clasped in his. She'd resisted him tonight, but how much longer could her heart hold out? The sooner she got the sales needed for her promotion and left, the faster Daniel could get on with his co-op and they'd return to their old lives.

It was for the best. But no matter how many times she repeated it, the hollowness in her stomach didn't go away. And ridiculous as it was, she couldn't shake the feeling that she'd forgotten something, or missed something, or lost something forever....

CHAPTER THIRTEEN

THE AIR WAS stifling and the sky sack heavy with rain as Jodi rode beside Daniel to the Tisdale farm the next day. It felt too hot to move, too hot to think, almost too hot to conduct this critical meeting. She plucked at the green knit dress sticking to her thighs and leaned her head out of the window. She needed to cool her restless mind and focus on acquiring this coveted property.

Had she worked with Brady at his indoor picnic event, she might have made a sale or two. But her pleased boss had told her this morning that purchasing Tisdale's acreage would give her the numbers needed to guarantee her promotion. She'd beat Brady unless he snapped up more land today. Worry clutched at her until she forced it away. Daniel had assured her that she'd make the sale, or, at the very least, that it wouldn't fall into Brady's hands. Her mind marveled at his reassurance...and the other confessions he'd made last night.

"You're quiet today." Daniel's deep voice broke into her thoughts and made her jump.

She glanced at him quickly, her stomach doing a weird twist, then back out at the birch-and-poplar-lined road. "Just thinking."

"About?" In her peripheral vision, she caught the sparkle of his eyes and pressed her brief-case to her jumpy stomach.

"Work."

"I see," he said, then turned off the classic-rock channel he'd been playing. "So you can think." She didn't need to look to know he was smiling.

She picked off her nail polish, her mind re-playing their conversation at the fireworks. Her feelings for Daniel had grown, yet she hadn't guessed he felt the same way. It seemed like a tangible presence that sat between them, arms crossed, foot tapping, waiting for—what? She wanted to tell him that she'd loved him once, too.

She wouldn't let herself take that risk again, yet it'd felt so right to be in his arms. Even if it could work out, did she deserve that kind of happiness? She caught her reflection in the side mirror and frowned. A second letter from Pe-ter's attorney had arrived today and she'd put it in the garbage—where it belonged.

To distract herself, she grabbed the carton

of fruit Sue had sent. The last of the season's strawberries melted like honey in her mouth. If only life could be this simple and sweet. But she'd made too many mistakes, had changed too much to ever go back to the girl who'd stolen embraces with Daniel behind barn doors and spent more time kissing in the grass than haying it.

When a few drops splattered against her hand she cranked the window closed. Summer storms in New England arrived out of nowhere—a sudden rising of wind shunting in fat-bellied clouds and letting loose sheets of rain that caused flash floods and rivers to overflow their banks.

Water dropped from a dark gray sky with increasing frequency until Daniel clicked on the windshield wipers. Through the blur, she made out a farm she'd purchased last week, Willow Park, and knew they were near. Her heart leaped. It was now or never. If she lost this deal, Brady might pass her in numbers and she'd return to Chicago defeated.

As Daniel turned onto the downward sloping driveway, his truck seemed to shudder and she heard him groan.

"What's wrong?"

He scrubbed a hand across his eyes and steered them downhill. "Out of gas."

She looked at the gauge. The orange needle pointed at *E*. "You're kidding."

"Wish I was."

She shoved her Post-it note in her briefcase's outer pocket and looked at her foot brace in despair. There'd be no walking home. "Didn't you check it before you came?"

"I had other things on my mind, Jodi." His eyes lingered on her, then returned to the winding drive.

"What are we going to do?"

He slowed the rolling truck to a halt before a brick home that looked more like a country estate than a farmhouse.

"We'll ask Tisdale for some gas. He'll have some. Don't worry." When his hand covered hers, she pulled away, shocked by the fierce leap of her heart at his touch.

She peered through the torrential rain and noticed crumbling stonework, a broken basement window and collapsed barn roofs. Her anxiety lifted. Mr. Tisdale would sell and she'd buy tickets to Chicago tomorrow. The sooner she escaped Daniel and Cedar Bay the better. They were finding the place in her heart that had never fully healed.

He opened the door and the whipping wind yanked it out of his grasp. "Let's go!" he hollered over the rising gale.

Jodi tucked her briefcase under her arm and deployed her umbrella once she stepped out into the storm. But by the time she'd clomped her way up the cracked sidewalk, Daniel's hand on her back, they were both a bedraggled mess. She hadn't seen such an intense storm since she'd moved away.

Daniel rang the bell as the rain turned into hailstones, big as marbles, driven sideways by the tempest. Her umbrella turned inside out, then flew from her grasp, skittering across the backyard's long grass and lifting in a draft to fall upon Lake Champlain. Daniel pounded on the door as rain flattened her hair and clothes.

"Wait here," he shouted over the howling wind, and sprinted around the house.

Jodi shivered and stepped beneath the shallow overhang above the front door, her briefcase clutched to her chest. Where was Mr. Tisdale? Daniel had promised. If not for his word, she'd be at the Midland picnic picking up more referrals. She doused a flicker of doubt. He wouldn't have fooled her again, would he? Used his charm to distract her from Brady's offer, then brought her to this isolated spot and—her temperature rose—run out of gas!

"He's not here," Daniel panted when he jogged back, his polo shirt and khaki shorts a second skin, his hair pushed forward like a Roman general's.

Lightning tore a jagged hole in the sky, and a thunderclap arrived at exactly the same moment, exploding directly overhead. It was so loud, Jodi cried out. On the roof of a nearby barn, the bolt scored a direct hit, bringing down a tilted weathervane.

"Hold on!" he yelled, and reached to scoop her up. But she checked his momentum by pushing hard against his chest; his touch melted her when she needed to stay firm. Resist.

"I can do this."

He shook his head, grabbed her around the middle and threw her over his shoulder.

She pummeled his back and thrashed. "Put me down."

"Stop. You'll hurt yourself," he called as he trotted toward the truck.

Another crack of lightning hit a tall oak nearby and a limb crashed to the ground. She screamed and Daniel swerved to a rocky outcropping that jutted onto Lake Champlain.

"Are you crazy? Let's get in the truck." Her rising voice competed with the howling wind.

"Not with all those trees around." With a bang, he kicked open the door to an old abandoned lighthouse. "We'll wait out the storm in here. Check for gas cans, too, though they're probably stored in the barns."

"You planned this!" She pounded on his shoulder as he strode across the space. "You knew Tisdale wouldn't be here, made sure you ran out of gas, so that I wouldn't make the sale."

"Is that what you think?"

His eyes delved into hers as he deposited her gently on a wooden bench that encircled the damp, musty interior. They studied each other and, after a moment where only their harsh breaths sounded in the still space, she shook her head. Daniel was a tough competitor, but he always played fair. It was easy to blame past trouble for current problems.

"I'm sorry, Daniel." She bit her lip and couldn't look away. "It's been a tough few days and I'm taking it out on you."

"Apology accepted." His dimples appeared and his eyes gleamed, and suddenly she was very aware of their aloneness.

Rain pounded on glass windows fifty feet above them while water trickled from the octagon-shaped roof. A large light was mounted at the top of a long spiral staircase. Tarnished brass ornamented the space with reflective panels glinting in the meager illumination, making it feel like the inside of a jewelry box.

"I forgot about this place." She looked around

in wonder, remembering the fun of exploring these out-of-commission lighthouses. "This is Windmill Point, isn't it?"

Daniel's eyes lit up. "We came here once. Remember?" He sat beside her and took her hand.

"Stop." And she needed him to. She was losing this war with her heart.

His insistent eyes met hers. "When I heard you were coming home, I never thought I'd feel this way again. But I can't help it. I care for you and Tyler. It's how I feel. I might wish I didn't, but it would be like asking the sun not to rise."

To her consternation, her voice trembled. "How do you know anything about me, Daniel? You say you care, but you don't know who I am now or what I need. For you, in the end, I am just another player in your game to control everything and everyone."

He pressed her hand to his pounding heart. "That might have been true once. But it's not anymore. I care about you, the old Jodi and the new." His eyes searched hers. "Tell me you feel the same way. That something else is coming between us. Because whatever it is, I can fix it." His fierce tone made her eyes prick with tears.

"You thought of me as a charity case once," she said with a catch in her voice. "I don't want your pity again and won't repeat the past."

He flinched, but didn't let go when she jerked her hands free. The charm he wore like armor had vanished and he looked wounded and vulnerable. "You think I don't understand what I did to you? Did to myself?" He stopped, as if realizing how close to being out of control he sounded. "I drove you away once because I didn't open up and share what I was going through. I thought I could handle it on my own. But, Jodi, you can tell me anything. You're not a charity case and we weren't together because I felt sorry for you. You're strong, caring and, after seeing you with Tyler, I know you're the best mother."

His last words pierced her heart, an arrow shot at point-blank. Her mind staggered backward, stopping on a long-suppressed memory.

"Daddy? Daddy home? Daddy? Daddy home? Daddy..." She smoothed a hand over Tyler's wet face and pulled him away from the front door. Her temples throbbed from his ceaseless cries and his refusal to sleep in case his father came home. She wanted to scream along with Tyler, furious at her callous husband, who'd checked into a hotel and out of their lives a week earlier, leaving her to explain the unexplainable.

"Sweetie. Daddy is gone away and..." Her voice trailed off when she thought of her many

unanswered voice mails and texts. She had no idea when Peter would return to say goodbye to Tyler, or visit him. She'd tried making sense of this to Tyler all week, but without hearing further from Peter, none of it made sense to her, either.

"Daddy! Daddy home!" Tyler's voice rose another decibel. He launched out of her arms and flung himself at the front door, banging his head against it with each word. "Daddy! Daddy home! Daddy! Daddy home!"

"Hush! Stop! Tyler, be quiet!" she screamed, panicked at the red lump swelling on his forehead, frustrated that, after a week of asking for his father, Tyler still believed Peter cared enough to answer his call.

Tyler stopped and turned to her, his big blue eyes full of fear. She'd never spoken that harshly to him before, and she ached that she'd hurt him. But she didn't know how else to get him to stop pining for something he'd never have again. To stop hurting himself.

"Let's go to bed, okay, baby?"

His limp body fell against her, his mouth moving without making a sound as his eyes closed.

If she'd known that it'd be the last time he'd speak, she would have apologized then instead of waiting until morning. She'd thought, mistakenly, that Tyler had needed sleep when he'd really needed her. She'd let down a lot of people in her life—her father, Daniel and, unforgivably, Tyler.

Daniel had hit on the real reason she would never love again or give him another chance. A truth she'd buried until Daniel's faith had brought it to the surface. The pain made her gasp, and she pulled away and scrambled to her feet. Despite her footgear, she headed for the iron staircase.

"Where are you going?" he called.

"I need to be alone. To think." Her eyes stung and the world in front of her went watery, colors and shapes sloshing together.

She didn't look down when she'd reached the top and pulled open a door that led to a narrow walkway surrounding the lighthouse.

"Jodi, don't go out there. It's dangerous. Wait!"

But she ignored him and slipped outside. The rain had tapered to a downpour, the thunderstorm moving farther west over the Green Mountains. Drenched anyway, she paced, her hand trailing along the soft wooden rail topper. Down below, Lake Champlain was white and gray, colored by storm clouds and chaffing waves. It reflected her mood. She knew that she wasn't a good mother.

She stood against the rail, caught in a vortex of grief, fear and yearning. How had she kept this secret from herself all these months? It explained so much. The wind whistled around the lighthouse.

"Jodi!" Daniel took a step toward her. His gaze was fastened to her face as if he couldn't look away.

"Go away." The wind tore the words from her mouth and sent them skittering across the churning lake.

He took another step, and now he was close enough to touch her. She jerked back and a hand cupped her arm when she tottered, leaning over the ledge. He pulled her against him. "Come inside." The gray day turned his insistent eyes more green than yellow. "These boards are hundreds of years old."

Despite the one creaking under her foot, she shook her head. She felt the strength of his muscles beneath his drenched shirt and wished, with all her might, that she could lean on him and never feel alone again. But she needed him gone. Daniel was a light that illuminated all of her shadows, and what she saw was unbearable.

"Please." She stepped back and extended her arms, palms up. Her heart was beating so hard it made her dizzy. "Please go," she repeated.

When he stroked her cheeks, she trembled

and a tear escaped, followed by another. The grief poured out, blackening the air and weighing on her chest so that she couldn't breathe properly.

"Shh. Hush," he murmured, pulling her close, rocking her back and forth. "Whatever it is, no one will hurt you in any way. I would never let that happen."

She wished she could move, wished she could reach out and hug him back, but she couldn't. Her arms felt frozen at her sides. His face was close to hers, so close that she could see her own reflection in his eyes.

"It's not me," she gasped, her words sounding as watery as the air. "It's Tyler." She pushed away from him and looked out at the foggy air ghosting across the lake's surface.

"What's wrong with Tyler?"

The absolute sincerity in his voice finally undid her. He saw only the good in Tyler, and lately, in her. She owed him the truth, no matter the damage it inflicted. He'd kept his true feelings from her once to devastating effect. It'd be hypocritical if she did the same.

"He doesn't speak."

"Sue said he stopped when his father walked out. When I meet the jerk, I'll—"

She pressed a trembling finger to his full

lips. "I'm the jerk." The pain of her admission ripped through her.

"What?" His spiked lashes blinked at her through the misting rain.

"It's me. I'm the reason Tyler doesn't talk anymore. Not his father. Me." Her chest heaved and for a moment she struggled to speak. Daniel reached out but she stepped back. She didn't want his pity. Didn't deserve his solace.

"When Peter left, Tyler kept asking for his father. Over and over." She lowered a shaking hand from her mouth. "And over."

Understanding dawned in Daniel's eyes. "You told him to stop talking."

Jodi nodded, beyond words, as tears mingled with the rain streaming down her cheeks. It was her greatest failure since the day she hadn't helped her father. Impulsive, just like her mother said. She'd lost control of her frustration and her son had lost his speech.

"And he hasn't spoken since. Not to me." The words burst out and with them came sobs, gulps of pain. Daniel pulled her to him and held her tight, and she gave in to him, burying her head in his chest as she wept. "Sue says he talks," she said when she could. "But I'll never hear it. I'm a bad mother."

The more she tried to contain herself, the more she broke down, as if the tears were all the things that she could never say—the humiliation, the strain of living with this guilt she'd hidden from herself, of blaming herself.

Her tears flooded Daniel's shirt, her skin cold and clammy against the cloth. She had always felt safe in his arms, this beautiful, strong childhood rival then boyfriend.

His hand slid over her hair—long, gentle strokes. As the storm subsided, within and without, he moved her away from him a little, his eyes fixed on hers. "You are not a bad mother. I've seen you with Tyler, on the tractor, in the strawberry fields, at the field day. You love him, and he'll get better. At his pace. And if that's not fast enough for some people, then they can—" He stopped himself and wiped away a few soggy strands of hair that had become plastered to her face. "No. Their opinions don't count. All that matters is how you and Tyler feel. Your own happiness. And from now on, that's what I care about, too."

"But after what I did—"

"You were under pressure and snapped. It doesn't make you a bad person or a bad mother. No parent is perfect. No family is the Waltons. Look at mine. But what's important is that you're working hard to make things better."

She stared at his earnest face, marveling at his faith in her. His support. "That's why I need to get him into Wonders Primary. I made him stop talking and it's up to me to help him get better."

Daniel crossed his arms. "Then why aren't you there now?"

Jodi took a steadying breath. She'd told him this much and he hadn't pitied her. In fact, he admired her. She could trust him with the rest. "The tuition is too much. When my boss offered me Cedar Bay I turned it down, until he promised a promotion and bonus if I got enough farmland."

Daniel was quiet for so long, his face frozen, that she wondered if he'd heard her until he asked, "And you believe this is the only way to help Tyler?"

She nodded. "Sue's wonderful. But these are experts with proved results to help him fully regain his speech."

Daniel rubbed his jaw and eyed her. "Help Tyler or help you?"

Her stomach contracted as though she'd been sucker punched. "What?" Had she been wrong to let down her guard?

"Jodi, Tyler is fine whatever he does or doesn't do. You're the one who's not okay with it."

Breath rushed out of her. "Of course I'm

not okay with it. I'm his mother and he needs to be—"

"The amazing person he is," Daniel interrupted her, then gathered her back in his arms. "Like his mother."

Could it be true? Something about Daniel's tone made her want to believe, but she needed time to process.

"Daniel?" she said on a half breath, just before he lowered his mouth to kiss her. His lips whispered against hers but she put her hand against his drumming heart and pushed. "No."

Abruptly he let her go and she backed away from him. He leaned against the lighthouse, the mist making his handsome face glisten. She stared, her breath coming in fits and starts.

"It's not that I don't have feelings for you," she admitted, and Daniel's eyes lit up. "But I don't see how this—" she gestured between the farm and them "—could work."

"It can." He looked at his watch. "I've got to find some gas so I can get home for chores. Will you meet me tonight and we'll talk about it?"

"I have Tyler."

"I'll come to you."

Her heart tumbled at his determined tone. After all this, he still wanted her. It made her head swim.

He gathered her to him again. "Ten o'clock."

Her cheek slid against his, their hearts pounding together as she nodded. "Ten o'clock."

Though her words were light, there was something in her that was not. She moved to the door as if in a semitrance. When Daniel guided her down the stairs, she lifted her fingers to her mouth and held them there, imagining how his kiss would have felt.

JODI PACED ALONG the stripes of moonlight filtering through her blinds, both wishing and dreading ten o'clock. What would she say to Daniel when she hadn't sorted out her own feelings?

Her bare feet slid across her aunt's oak flooring, her mind and heart torn. Daniel's acceptance of her confession made her care for, no—she'd admit it now—love him more than she ever had. But the thought scared her. This could only be a summer romance with a painful ending...again. Could she subject them to that for the sake of a few stolen weeks of happiness?

Her pulse leaped at the base of her throat and she clutched her locket, the cool metal a reminder that she needed to consider Tyler. She couldn't let him get attached to Daniel, see him as a father figure. If she did, he'd feel abandoned again when they returned to Chicago. And after her painful phone conversation with Peter, that was more of a must than ever.

When she hadn't responded to his lawyer's letters, he'd called her himself tonight, his news a shock. He couldn't help with Wonders Primary, was suing to lower his child support, because he'd lost his job and had been ashamed to admit it. In fact, his wedding was also off since his fiancée couldn't handle his financial issues. Oh, how she'd felt the irony of that.

Yet despite his treatment of their son, she'd heard him out and agreed that, until he found employment, he could stop the payments. But that made her need for the promotion greater than ever. And Daniel, and now Brady, stood in her way. Did she dare give in to personal feelings when she so desperately needed to keep her focus on Tyler?

Then again, hadn't Daniel shown her that she deserved happiness, too? She remembered the feel of his arms around her and hugged herself as she peered at the clock. Nine forty-five. He'd be here in fifteen minutes, but suddenly that seemed much too long.

A pebble pinged against her screen and she grinned, her heart galloping too fast for her breath to keep up. Daniel. Like always, their feelings were in sync. Was he as conflicted as she, or did he have a clear picture of how this—how they—could work?

She flung open the sash and leaned out. Below her stood Daniel, his eyes so full of delight she couldn't help but smile back, despite her nerves.

"You're early," she whispered sternly, her expression anything but.

The corners of his mouth lifted, his dimples deepening as he laughed at himself. "I've been out here since nine." His face sobered. "I was worried you might have changed your mind."

"Only about a hundred times," she admitted, relieved he'd been as uncertain as she. These were tricky waters to navigate. They might not find their way to each other. "Give me a minute and I'll meet you by the dock."

She watched as he strode away and the ache of him leaving made her call out. He turned at his name, his eyes lit with a hope she felt, too. "I'm not dreaming this, am I?" Although she meant it as a joke, deep down, she struggled to believe that this beautiful moment was real.

He returned and pressed a kiss to the hand she dangled from the ledge. "If you are, don't wake either of us. Now hurry, sweetheart."

Sweetheart. Her heart pounded and swelled with a surge of hope that she feared more than anything. The blinds fell to the window ledge and she grabbed Tyler's monitor, placed it in her aunt's room as they'd arranged and raced to Tyler's room.

He slept curled on his side, Ollie tucked beneath his arms, his eyeglasses on the table beside him. His cheeks were flushed and his mouth moved, the sight striking a poignant chord in her heart. Her sleeping prince spoke in his dreams. She put a hand to her face and was surprised to find it damp; she'd been crying without knowing it.

But they were happy tears, and she dashed outside in such a hurry that it wasn't until she felt a splinter that she realized she'd run all the way to the dock without shoes.

At the end of the pier sat Daniel, his broad back tapering to his lean waist. Beyond him, the full moon's reflection danced on the glass-like surface of the lake. Their stormy afternoon had blown away, leaving a still, fresh summer night pregnant with possibilities.

The evening could go in many different directions, though her heart sank when she considered that the summer could end with only one: her leaving. The thought was so painful even her teeth ached at it.

As she tiptoed toward Daniel, she watched the reflection of the stars pull into long, dancing streaks on the moving surface of the water.

The scope of that glittering sky had a way of making her problems seem smaller, more manageable, and she relished the feeling that perhaps she could control her destiny.

Was it wrong to want this night with Daniel? To talk and see if they could figure out a way to be together? And if they did, to have the affections of such a good man, one who lifted her up, supported her, cared for her son? If they were clear about managing their expectations, and she kept Tyler from getting too attached, then perhaps she could have this summer of love. Without Tisdale's farm in her pocket, she'd need to acquire several smaller properties, which would give her more time with Daniel. It would last her through the winter of the rest of her life.

"Daniel?" Jodi called, and he whirled, his face alight.

He shot to his feet but kept his arms at his sides. She respected his restraint when she longed to fling herself at him, to trace the muscular curves, to feel the beat of his heart beneath her cheek as she had at the lighthouse.

But with so much still to say, she held herself back. Instead of rushing to him, she admired how handsome he looked in a T-shirt that fit his lithe form and shorts that revealed his strong thighs and calves. It was hard not to stare as she slowly closed the distance between them.

When she reached him, his smile broadened. "I'm glad we're going to talk."

She nodded. "I'm glad, too. It's beautiful out here," she said lightly over the pounding pulse in her ears.

"Yes, it is," he said, but kept his eyes on her.

She cuffed his shoulder and laughed. "We're supposed to be talking about the night."

"I'd rather talk about us."

She nodded, her smile fading. Truth time. Would he accept what she had to say? "Let's take the rowboat out, watch the stars from the water."

At least, stuck out in the middle of the lake, he couldn't walk away if he didn't like what she proposed. A summer-only romance. It was that or nothing, and she hoped, with all her heart, that he'd agree. Her life was in Chicago and his was in Cedar Bay. Though their feelings had changed, those facts had not.

His eyes were more brilliant than the stars when he smiled. "Okay."

He stepped into the small red boat tied to the edge of the dock, balanced himself as it rocked beneath his feet then helped her on board. After untying them, he pushed off and rowed them a ways offshore.

Her pulse raced along with the boat. A pair of ducks started as they cleaved the water and took off with a squawk, their feet skimming the surface, wings beating until they were airborne.

Finally he stopped and watched her, his eyes intent. The passion she glimpsed made her lose her nerve. She peered down at the water, making out the black shapes of tiny darting fish moving just beneath the surface in the bright starlight.

"Jodi." The way he said her name, soft and tender, made it feel like a kiss. She looked up and met his gaze. "If you're not ready to talk, we don't have to."

Everything froze. The blood stopped flowing in her veins. Her breath quit coming. For a moment, even the sound of the water lapping against the boat and the rustling of the trees along the shore fell away. She had to speak now or she might lose him. Lose this chance.

"I care for you, Daniel," she said slowly, each word feeling like a step toward the edge of a cliff.

His smile faded but his eyes stayed bright. "Why do I hear a 'but' in there?"

She laughed, disarmed by his humor as always. Even in the most difficult situations, he knew how to put her at ease.

"But we have to agree that we can only be together—" she swallowed over what felt like shards of glass in her throat "—until I go home."

"But you are home, Jodi Lynn," he murmured, his voice tender and serious.

She thought of how much she'd love to live in Cedar Bay again, marveling at how foreign that idea would have felt before she'd left Chicago. "I can't sacrifice Tyler's future for my own. Plus, my job is there."

Daniel was quiet for a long time as he gazed at the shadowed outline of New York's Adirondack Mountains. In the silence, her heart counted out each second that passed.

"Let's lie in the bottom of the boat," he said at last. "Stargaze."

"Is that what they call it these days?" She couldn't resist lightening the moment as she slid off her seat and curled up on her side in the bottom of the boat, facing him.

"I forgot how beautiful a star-filled sky looks," she said quietly. "We can't see the stars in Chicago."

With care, Daniel settled in next to her and put an arm around her shoulders, the feel of his skin electric. "When do you think you'll go back?" She could hear a forlorn note in his voice and second-guessed herself. Was she right to propose this temporary arrangement? Give in to feelings that would be hard to end?

When she looked at him, their noses touched. "As soon as I reach my acreage quota."

Daniel caressed her cheek, his calloused touch making her squirm and forget her misgivings. "Sue's new advisor gave her the go-ahead to present her dissertation."

She inhaled sharply. "That's wonderful. She's helped Tyler, Daniel. You have to know how much I appreciate that."

"Enough for you to let her keep working with him?" His expression looked wistful.

"As long as I'm here." She snuggled against him, loving the feel of his hard chest beneath her cheek.

"So forever, then."

She gave a half laugh. He was incorrigible. A stubborn optimist.

"I'm going to make you change your mind, Jodi." The confident ring in his voice seemed to echo around the still water.

"Oh, Daniel," she sighed, and brought her hand up to his smooth cheek. "I don't want anyone to be hurt."

He pressed her palm to his face, then kissed it. "Let's not borrow tomorrow's trouble. We'll take it day by day."

"How many clichés did you just fit into that sentence?"

He chuckled, the deep rumble vibrating against her ear. "I mean them, though. I'm not going to ask anything more than you can give."

She felt her joints loosen and she relaxed against him. "So you're okay with us being together just for this summer?"

He tucked a curl behind her ear, and the feel of his touch made her shiver. It was so quiet, she could hear every breath he took, felt it vibrate through him in the cramped bottom of the boat.

"Let's enjoy every moment together until it's our last."

"But that moment isn't today," she said, so grateful that he'd agreed. She wanted to be with him until she couldn't. It was that simple.

His hand smoothed the length of her hair as he gazed into her eyes, his expression tender and full of longing. "No. It's not." The words sounded so reverent they could have been a prayer.

His fingers trailed down her cheek to her lips, outlining the shape of her mouth. He bent down, his lips against her cheek, brushing it lightly. Shivers ran through her whole body, making her tremble. He brushed his mouth against the hollow of her temple, then traced the line of her jawbone.

The aching anticipation for his kiss was suddenly too much and she reached up and pulled his mouth to hers. He kissed her gently, carefully, but it wasn't gentleness she wanted, not when time was fleeting. She knotted her fists in his shirt and pulled him closer. He groaned softly, low in his throat, and then his arms circled her, gathering her against him as the boat rocked beneath them. The small possibility of falling into the water vanished as soon as it occurred to her.

All that existed was Daniel. She could feel his warmth burning through his clothes and hers. She ran her fingers along his arm—soft skin over lean muscle, a scar like a thin wire on his biceps. It was an imperfection that made him seem even more perfect. He fumbled as he pushed her heavy hair aside to kiss her ear. She didn't think she'd ever seen his hands unsteady before.

She trailed her nose across his jaw, inhaling the clean smell of summer countryside, of him. He released a pent-up breath, the sound like music. Her pulse tapped a fast beat and her breath quickened with it. She stroked his cheek and kissed every inch of his neck until he moaned again. Or maybe she'd made the sound; they seemed to share each breath, each heartbeat. It felt as if the universe disappeared and all that remained was the two of them, holding each other close.

"I forgot it was like this," she said when Daniel pulled back and looked down at her. It seemed as if the stars hurtled down around her head like a rain of silver tinsel.

"It wasn't." He kissed her nose, then traced the line of her cheek with his fingertip, a dreamlike intensity in his gaze. "This is better."

And she never wanted it to end. She felt feverishly alive, every nerve ending jangling as they watched the sky, enjoying the private moment.

"I agree," she sighed, nestling against his side. "I wish we could stay like this forever." When he toyed with her earlobe, she tried, unsuccessfully, to settle her heart back in her body. She watched the stars shimmer above and it also felt as though they were celebrating.

"Me, too," he said softly in her ear. He captured her lips in a kiss so fierce and full of longing that it felt like a love song.

A few minutes later she pulled away and squeezed his hand. "I should go back and make sure Aunt Grace and Tyler are still asleep."

He tipped an imaginary hat, then pressed a quick kiss to her nose before reseating himself.

"Happy to oblige." He gripped the sides of the boat, holding it steady as she did the same.

"Home, ma'am?" Daniel dipped the oars into the satin water and they slid forward. She hated to end the night, but hopefully it'd be the first of several before she'd have to leave. The thought filled her with a strange mixture of excitement and sorrow.

She leaned back on her hands and studied the stars again.

"I'm not even sure where that is anymore."

CHAPTER FOURTEEN

"SUE SENT HER apologies, Jodi," Daniel said, not feeling sorry about the situation at all, as he drove them toward a Midland-operated farm a week later. "Her professors had a department meeting yesterday afternoon and they agreed to hear her present first thing this morning. She flew to New Jersey last night."

After adjusting her elastic bandage, Jodi smiled at him. "It's okay. It turns out 'wunderkind' Brady isn't so wonderful in Cedar Bay. Since he hasn't made any sales, I'm still ahead. And after hearing from Mr. Tisdale that he'll be gone for a month on his Alaskan cruise, I'll need lots more acquisitions to get the acreage I need. It's too bad he'd mixed up the appointment dates, but at least it gives us more time here. Tyler and I might as well take a day off together."

Her golden hair gleamed in the midmorning light when she twisted around. "Right, Tyler?"

Tyler's thumping feet signaled that he agreed and Daniel grinned as he checked the tyke in his rearview mirror. The boy had a way of communicating that cut right to the chase.

Although Jodi wanted to keep their relationship a secret, he couldn't resist a quick kiss after she'd strapped Tyler into the back of Sue's car. He respected her wish to keep Tyler separate from their temporary relationship. It was the temporary part he couldn't accept, deep down.

He glanced at her pert profile, the bright blue sky behind her matching her eyes. After this week of stolen kisses and hidden hand holds, his heart couldn't feel fuller as his eyes darted from the beautiful woman beside him to the boy he wished to make his son someday. The rightness of it settled inside him, patching up the potholes he'd swerved by these past ten years. He registered a lightness, a happiness, even; the contentment of someone who has, at last, found his match. Now, how to keep her when she was set on leaving?

His grumbling father had passed on phone messages from co-op converts hoping to meet with him. Adding the number of calls to his growing list, he already had two-thirds of the area convinced—as much as he'd hoped to get. Enough to apply for the Organic Farming Upgrades grant. Better yet, it blocked a Midland takeover.

But before she and Brady divided up the rest, he needed to build his case and convince her to stay. This industrial farm tour would be a start. The farm's conditions would surely open her eyes to what she was selling, and selling out.

Tyler hummed the "Old MacDonald" tune and he fought the urge to hold Jodi's hand when he glimpsed her eyes brighten with hope. If she heard him speak, she might give Sue a chance. But deep down, he knew Jodi needed more. As much as she said this was all for Tyler, he suspected she needed to prove herself, too. But she didn't have to be in Chicago to do it.

"How would you like to be the director of the Cedar Bay Co-op?" The question charged out of him before he'd given it the go-ahead.

She gaped at him. "Come again?"

He felt the small hairs on the back of his neck rise. It was now or never. Time to put every persuasive skill he had to use. The stakes couldn't be higher.

"Jodi, you're the right person to lead the co-op and the board would agree."

"The board?" she echoed, her voice faint, her eyes wide.

He strove to keep his tone light but confident. "The co-op elected a governing body on Monday and now we need a director. You."

"I—I didn't know you'd made that much

progress." Her voice sounded suspicious, a hint of fear flavoring it. "Why didn't you tell me?"

"I'm not supposed to discuss this with anyone until we get our grant," he said, wondering why he'd opened his mouth in the first place. But he needed to get her thinking about it. Give her a reason to see that she could help the community and her family without Midland or Chicago—especially now that Sue would have her Ph.D. and could continue working with Tyler. Jodi had to see that there was another way, one that included him in her future.

"I see." She rubbed her temples and peered at him. "And what happens if your grant is turned down?"

Anxiety forked, lighting quick in his gut. "That won't happen. Especially if you're working with us."

Jodi glanced up at the mirror in her visor. Checking on her son, he imagined.

"I already have a job."

His fingers brushed hers for an electric moment, then withdrew. "But not here. Not with me."

She brought her foot up to rest on her seat and hugged her knee to her chest. "I can't work here."

"Can't or won't?" He glanced at her sharply but she gazed back steadily, her eyes clear.

"Wonders Primary is in Chicago."

Tyler switched up his humming to another tune. "Bingo." Daniel glanced in the mirror as the child danced Ollie to the beat; he was a smart kid. "What makes you sure that's the best route for him?"

Her back straightened. "I'm his mother."

Case closed. For now. Time to switch tactics.

"You could fly in on weekends, handle weekly business from Chicago." But even as he said it, he knew it wouldn't work.

Her extended sigh signaled that she agreed. "Daniel, directing a co-op is a hands-on job. You've got an MBA. Why don't you do it?"

"Because I want to work outdoors, not in an office."

"That's my world," she drawled as they passed a sign that said Welcome to Bennington.

"It doesn't have to be, Jodi. At least not in Chicago. Think about it." He looked her way, his voice strengthening. "You can still use your MBA, but in your hometown, doing something that will help farmers. You heard what I had to say at the town hall. You have to see the good in this plan. Plus, who better to handle Midland than an ex-employee?"

Her eyes narrowed, her features gathered in a pucker. "And you've been thinking about this for how long?"

"Since we set up the board meeting," he said, then wished he could smack his head. Idiot.

"I see," she said slowly. "And this has nothing to do with what's going on between us?"

He glanced in the rearview mirror, noted a preoccupied Tyler prancing Ollie in the air, and touched her cheek. "They're separate. My feelings have nothing to do with this."

Or everything, he added silently. But how to untangle one from the other? Either way, he needed her here, and if that also meant her brilliant mind managed the co-op, then it was the win-win he hoped for.

He put his hand back on the wheel when she turned away. "I want you and Tyler in my life. Period. We'll make it work."

"We agreed on a summer-only relationship. And even if we took things further, we could only see each other on holidays and my vacation. Would you be okay with that?" she asked.

His mouth dried and he found it hard to swallow. It was painful to imagine, but a future without her at all? Not a chance.

"Yes," he said as he spotted the right exit and slowed. "Though I like my idea better." Besides, once she got a look at how an industrial farm really operated, she'd want to leave her job and work for an organization that valued animals' and owners' rights.

"It's better not to want what's impossible," she said, her sad tone echoing his mood. If they only had the rest of this summer together and a sporadic future, it still wouldn't be enough. He'd only be kidding himself if he thought that was true.

"You look beautiful today," he said lightly. And she did, especially when her cheeks pinked at his compliment, her beauty a knife to his heart. How much longer would he get to see her? The way her blond ponytail showed her graceful neck and the delicate jaw that he couldn't stop kissing made it hard to look away. He could still taste the peach of her skin and planned to get her alone tonight after they had supper at her aunt's house. Never before had he considered time as he did now, both treasuring it when it came, resenting it when it passed.

"You look nice, too." Her sidelong glance and the upward tilt of her lips made him sit a little straighter.

"Ollie's the best dressed." He returned her smile, his fingers gripping the wheel as he fought to keep his mind on the road instead of on his concerns for their future.

"I think a candy necklace is the perfect accessory for a leopard-print unitard."

Daniel nodded, solemn. "Good thing I didn't wear the same outfit today."

They laughed together, the sound filling the car. If only he could store it in his memory, bring it out to hold close on the lonely winter nights ahead.

"There it is!" Jodi pointed, her voice rising, and he spotted a massive compound in the distance. "Those are Midland colors."

The barns were painted a navy blue, the metal-sided silos emblazoned with a yellow logo so bright it outshone the sun. A decent enough looking fence of white boards and electrical wire ran along either side of the road. But without crops inside he wondered, did cows graze out here?

From the piles of droppings, he'd say yes, yet he'd heard a different story about these industrial farms. That the cows rotated from milking to their stalls and back again until they were dried up and sold to slaughter. He hated thinking of anyone mistreating animals. Just as he wouldn't be penned up inside an office, he wouldn't make his cows stay indoors unless the temperature dropped too low. Even in winter they were quick to head out when they could, jostling until they got their pecking order right before passing through the gate.

Tyler's humming quit when Daniel clicked on the blinker and turned up the paved driveway. He imagined the cows' hooves striking this hard surface and shook his head until he spied the barn's massive side doorway that opened to a beaten path and pastures. Jersey cows grazed at a distance. Yet their calves were penned separately rather than free to roam with their mothers. Jodi frowned at the sight of the calves, but she kept her voice neutral as she spoke over her shoulder.

"Tyler. This is Mommy's work," she said as Daniel pulled into a visitor parking spot. "The company, I mean," she corrected herself. "It looks...decent." The uncertainty was audible in her voice. Had she been worried? His jaw clenched. She'd have plenty more second thoughts once they got inside.

But instead of heading into the barn, she pointed to a separate building with a shingled roof and windows with geranium-filled flower boxes. What was next? Hansel and Gretel?

"That's the main office. Jeff said he'd be in there."

Jeff? Who was Jeff? He imagined a guy in a suit with perfectly styled hair, and pushed the pinch of jealousy away. Jodi cared about him, not some office jockey. Still, there'd be plenty of Jeffs in Chicago when she returned, while he stayed behind in Cedar Bay, his mind too full of Jodi to consider anyone else.

He shoved the thought off for another time

and lifted Tyler from his seat. After adjusting the boy's askew eyeglasses band, he set him on his feet, careful to shorten his strides so the youngster didn't trip to keep up with him. Lately, he'd taken to dogging Daniel's footsteps. And Daniel enjoyed every minute of it.

A bell jangled as Jodi limped across the doorway, him and Tyler right behind her. To his discomfort, a man about their age rose from his desk and seemed to keep on rising, his imposing height making Daniel step back rather than look up. Why wasn't this guy on a basketball court instead of working on a corporate farm?

"Hi. I'm Jodi from central office. We spoke on the phone." Her hand was engulfed in the Goliath's paw and Daniel ground his teeth when the man held on a moment too long.

"Jeff." He stepped around his desk and gave Daniel a nod that he returned with a brief jerk of his chin. "It's nice to see our salespeople out on the field. Thanks for taking the time to stop by."

His voice was pleasant enough, but Daniel wasn't fooled. The guy was clearly impressed with Jodi. And by the way he kept smiling at her, he had more on his mind than showing her around the farm.

"And who might this little guy be?" Jeff

turned to Tyler. "What's your name? Would you like to see some cows?"

Jodi's horrified glance met Daniel's when Tyler buried his head in Daniel's leg and whimpered, hands flapping.

"Did I scare him?" Jeff looked at them, confused. "I have some lollipops."

Daniel put his arm around the shaking boy. "He's not one to warm up to strangers right away. We'll see the farm now, thanks."

Jeff shrugged and his congenial expression returned. "Have you ever been on a farm?"

Jodi's snort turned into a cough and she turned away, red-faced. Daniel shrugged. "One or two."

Jeff clapped him on the shoulder. "You're in for a treat, then. There are no farms in the world like Midland's. It's the best place to work." And with that he led them outside, leaving Daniel to wonder how this guy felt the same way he did about his job.

At least now the whole aw-shucks act was about to end. The barn loomed.

Jodi pointed to the calves as they walked past their pen. "Why aren't they with their mothers?"

"Company policy. Males are picked up for slaughter on the first of every month."

Daniel covered Tyler's ears and the boy

shook, as if understanding what he'd heard. Male calves were sold to slaughter, but his conscience demanded that he give their shorter lives some happiness by allowing them time with their mothers. Separating them this young was traumatic. Disgust filled Daniel. What a place. What further inhumane scenes awaited them?

But as they ducked inside the cavernous space, the length of it about as long as half a football field, he spotted empty stalls being raked out by robotic arms and hoses letting loose powerful cleansing spray that misted and freshened the air. Massive fans dotted the outside wall, drawing out the heat and keeping the air circulating. Inside the cool, dim space, the summer's roar faded.

He felt the dry rushes of hay underfoot as he strode deeper inside. Each step released a fresh, sweet smell.

"Where are the cows?" Jodi asked as she walked alongside Jeff, her head barely up to his shoulders.

Tyler reached his hands up and Daniel swung him onto his shoulders to the boy's laughing delight. Jodi turned and her eyelid twitched.

"Don't let him fall."

He lowered his chin and shot her a significant look. He would never let any harm come to

Tyler or Jodi. But how to guarantee that when she returned to Chicago? What if Wonders Primary wasn't so wonderful? What if they made Tyler feel worse about himself instead of better? The way he perceived the world might be different from others, but that didn't make it wrong.

He tightened his grip on Tyler's hands and marveled at the boy's improving balance. He might not be speaking except for occasional words to Sue, but he was progressing in lots of other ways. Plenty of people talked a lot of nonsense that no one heard. If Tyler spoke few words, then they were worth paying attention to. Jodi needed to listen to Tyler's mood and body language. See how much the kid liked spending time on the farm, had even started brushing the alpacas, his hand-eye coordination growing, too. Wonders Primary might help him "progress," but would they make him happy? And when it came down to it, wasn't happiness more important in life than anything? Why couldn't Jodi see a different path for her son?

Tyler beat the top of his head and he looked around the space he was grudgingly starting to admire, with the exception of the veal calves. Wasn't he guilty of the same tunnel vision? Believing all industrial farms were bad and, until now, never giving them a chance? He'd never considered other viewpoints but now he wondered—what if he had tried figuring out why Jodi had run off without a word ten years ago instead of letting her go? Where would they be now? On the other hand, Tyler wouldn't be here, so he'd take the ten-year break if it meant this amazing kid was in his life.

"This looks very nice," he overheard Jodi say as they passed cows stepping onto one of several revolving milking stations, electronic arms bringing the tubes under the cows' udders, workers below guiding them into position. "Orderly."

Jeff nodded, his grin so wide it seemed to split his face. "Everything revolves around a schedule. Sections of cows alternate between feeding, eating, milking and grazing. They grow up with it, so they crowd to come back in when they know it's time."

Daniel had to give him that. Cows were creatures of habit. He could see they'd like this setup, though it lacked the personal touches his farm had. And he'd never create "downed calves" by chaining them up. Keeping them from standing and walking crippled them. They might be destined for the slaughterhouse, but even a short life deserved dignity.

When they'd reached the end of the first

barn, Jodi gasped at an outdoor pen holding a sow and her litter of piglets.

"Daniel would you let him down? Tyler, baby, you'll want to see this."

He lowered the boy, but Tyler clung to his leg again. "He doesn't want to look that close, Jodi. Let me put him back up and he can see them from there."

Her lips firmed. "He's my son, Daniel. He just needs a chance."

When she peeled Tyler off his leg he squealed louder than the pigs. He kicked and flailed in Jodi's arms, beating his head against a wooden beam until she gave him back to Daniel, her eyes bright with unshed tears.

Daniel scowled until Jeff closed his gaping mouth. "He's autistic." He pulled out one of the cards he'd ordered for Sue after spotting Jodi's and handed it to Jeff. "Everything's spelled out on the card. Let's go, Jodi," he said over Tyler's sobs, the child's arms, and Ollie, flung around his neck.

She looked down at her feet and, after a small sound that could have been a sniffle, she said, "I agree. Time to leave."

THE RIDE HOME was silent as Tyler napped and Jodi leaned her head against the window, her mind twisting the facts around until they made less sense than ever. Midland farms were every bit as high quality as she'd suspected. Despite the lonely calves, the equipment had looked new, the animals generally well cared for, the farm run as efficiently as a business. Yet she'd missed something indefinable there. She couldn't put her finger on it. Something about the place seemed too well-oiled, too precise, impersonal. It hadn't felt like a home, and no matter how she tried, it was growing harder to separate farming from that sentiment.

Beside her, Daniel tapped out some rhythm on the steering wheel as she stared at the familiar landmarks near Maplewood Farm. She'd wanted to stop and check in on Sue. Find out how she'd made out this morning after her quick flight home. She lowered her window to release some of the heat from the car's interior—the day was baking hot.

As they drove, she noticed that the hillside lambs looked bigger now, their bodies filling out as they gamboled farther away from their grazing mothers. Would she ever feel that way about Tyler? Secure that he could safely roam without her? Besides Sue, Wonders Primary was the only place that made her feel that way. If only it wasn't thousands of miles from the man she'd fallen for. The thought made her stomach clench.

Tyler startled awake when they stopped behind Daniel's house. He looked in every direction until he pointed at the green tractor.

"Gah!" he shouted with a smile, and she reached back and patted his knee.

"Home," said Daniel, his tone wistful, his gaze on her.

She forced herself to look away. How would she ever leave this incredible man? She wished this was home, but what she wanted and what she needed weren't the same thing. She had to think about Tyler. What was best for him.

Sue rushed outside as they shut the car doors, Colton a step behind her. Jodi's heart leaped. She must have good news.

"I did it, I did it! They approved my dissertation."

Delighted, Jodi rushed to give her a hug before Daniel stepped in and swung his sister around. He set her back on her feet with a kiss on the cheek. "Dr. Gleason, I presume?"

Sue grinned. "Nice eleven-point word, Sherlock. Too bad we aren't playing Scrabble tonight."

Daniel turned to Jodi. "Stay and we'll celebrate. I made a cake last night and—"

Sue's elbow to Colton's ribs cut off his guffaw. "He likes to cook. You like to sing. Can we agree that men do more things than stare at their belly buttons?"

Jodi snorted. She loved no-nonsense Sue who'd fought to get her Ph.D. by believing in herself and Tyler, and might have gotten her man to boot.

"Are you kids coming inside?" Daniel's father called from the kitchen window.

"Be right there, Pop." Daniel put a hand under Jodi's elbow and guided her up the steps as though she'd trip at any time. Honestly. But when her tender foot caught on the top step, she stumbled and he was there to catch her before the thought of falling had fully formed.

Yes. That was Daniel. He was that extra pair of arms she needed, for her and Tyler. If only she could keep them.

They burst into the kitchen, Daniel's hands on her waist, and Sue behind them with Colton carrying Tyler. It wasn't until she noticed Mr. Gleason's elated grin, Sue's knowing look and Colton's confused expression that she realized they'd given themselves away.

"Here's the happy couple now." Daniel's father rolled his walker ahead and shuffled forward. "Knew you two would get back together."

"I—I—" Jodi stammered and shifted away

from Daniel. How horrible that they'd discovered a relationship that had to end.

"You two were a thing?" Colton set Tyler on his feet and her son tottered over to Goldie and grabbed the sleeping dog's tail.

"No," Daniel protested, and she knew, without him saying it, what he meant. They were never just a thing. It'd been more than that then, just as it was now. An unfurled rose, an unopened present, an uncut pie. The painful thought cut through her—she'd never know the promise their relationship held.

Sue nudged him in the arm. "Come on, you two. We all knew what was going on that summer. We're just glad you came to your senses and have a second chance."

Jodi met Daniel's eyes, dismayed that their secret was out. The more people involved, the more who would be affected when she left. They followed the rest of the family over to the table as Tyler alternated between stroking and batting a wriggling Goldie. Thank goodness he appeared not to have noticed the exchange. Hopefully he hadn't grown too attached and wouldn't miss Daniel as much as she would. The thought of going through the motions of her life without his teasing smile, his banter, his intuitive understanding made her feel hollow and scraped out.

KAREN ROCK343

The smell of rich buttercream frosting and chocolate filled the room. A three-layer fudge cake wobbled as Daniel set it down. *Dr. Gleason* was spelled out in looping letters that grabbed her heart and wouldn't let go. What a good brother. She watched him as he served his father the first slice. A great son. Her gaze drifted to Tyler. Someday he'd make an amazing father, too, and the thought made her stomach drop. He'd be a dad someday, just not to Tyler.

Now that she'd visited a Midland farm, had seen how attached Tyler had grown to Daniel, she realized how much in danger he was of getting hurt. If she stayed much longer, Tyler would grow so close to Daniel that leaving him might bring on the same reaction he'd had when his father disappeared. She recoiled from the thought. Although she'd made mistakes as a parent, she wouldn't make that one. Tyler deserved better from her, no matter that she'd wound herself to protect him.

She swallowed a bite of cake, tasting only despair. Their relationship couldn't work. Even from a distance. Every time they saw each other, Tyler would find it harder to say goodbye, to understand why people he cared about kept vanishing from his life. She couldn't do that to him. The pain of what she'd need to do lanced through her as she forced a smile at Daniel.

"Here's to Sue," Colton said. He lifted his glass of milk and they followed suit. "Here's to you." He angled his drink toward Jodi and Daniel. "Here's to Pop." The older man's eyes disappeared into his laugh lines. "And here's hoping we bring in a good crop."

They all clinked glasses and Jodi noticed that Colton and Sue saved each other for last, their eyes meeting as they each took a sip. How sweet. That was how life should be. Straightforward and uncomplicated. Yet hers had taken so many turns she barely knew the way, or where, exactly she was heading.

Mr. Gleason's glass rose again and wavered, the milk shimmering up the sides. "I'm awfully proud of my little girl. I wish you'd had your mother longer. Wish I'd been around more, too." When his voice broke, Sue rushed to his side and laid her head on his sloped shoulder.

"No, Pop. You did what you could. You had the farm to run. And with Mom gone, well— I could have helped out more instead of doing so much schoolwork."

Daniel's father lowered his glass and patted his daughter's cheek. "No, sweetheart. That was your way out of this life. Now you can have a real family. Not be a slave to this farm."

Jodi saw Daniel flinch and her heart went out to him. Was his father proud of him, too? Of the sacrifices he'd made? Of his ingenuity in saving the farm and working to save his hometown? He should be. Daniel was an amazing man.

"I don't plan on leaving." Sue's eyes flashed to Colton. "Not soon anyway."

"That's what I was afraid of." The older man pointed to a folder on the counter. "Would you give that to Jodi?"

Jodi looked at him in surprise. "Me?"

He nodded slowly as Sue passed her the large envelope full of papers, her expression puzzled. Daniel, however, looked horrified. When she opened it and spotted the farm's deed, she understood why and her lungs seized.

"Jodi, I'm selling my farm to Midland."

"No!" Daniel's chair toppled backward when he shot to his feet. Tyler screamed, the noise startling him.

With the envelope under her arm, she hurried over and scooped him up, settling him on her hip. Her mind struggled to understand what Mr. Gleason had just done. The hurt he'd inflicted on his son. Her vision swam as though she'd been hit in the head. If she took this gift, it'd save her son and destroy Daniel.

"This is my inheritance." Daniel's eyes gave off green sparks as he spoke through his teeth.

"We've got more acres than anyone else in this county. With that money, you can do whatever you want. Put me in a nursing home and move to Chicago with Jodi. You'll have the family you deserve."

"No!" Sue and Daniel bellowed at the same time, though Jodi disagreed. Daniel should have a family.

Mr. Gleason waved his hands. "Look. I've lived my life. Wasted it, more like, and now it's over. At least give this old man the pleasure of seeing both his children happy."

"I am happy," Daniel protested, looking anything but. She wished she could hold him, wipe the pain from his eyes. "And it's never been about the money." When his gaze slid to Jodi, she shook. She couldn't say the same. Guilt twisted her insides until they were a ball of searing pain.

His father studied him until Daniel's eyes dropped. "You're only fooling yourself if you say that."

Jodi's heart pounded. Was it possible? Would Daniel move to Chicago with her? Give up the farm the way he'd asked her to give up her job and Wonders Primary?

Daniel blew out a noisy breath and her hopes sunk. "I'll never leave."

She swallowed hard. There it was, simple and clear. Daniel cared more about farming than her and Tyler, and her son deserved a father who put him first.

"You won't have a choice."

"Then I'll buy another farm. Start over."

Pinpricks of tears stung Jodi's eyes as sorrow rolled through her like a thunderclap. Why couldn't Daniel see a future outside of farming? Care enough about her and Tyler to take this chance and start over with them?

But as soon as she thought it, she realized she was as guilty of that as he, wanting only Wonders Primary for Tyler. And if she accepted this deed, she'd be ripping away the only life Daniel had known.

She set Tyler down when he struggled and tightened her grip on the folder. The acreage she'd glimpsed on the form meant she'd have acquired enough to return to Chicago, earn her promotion and get Tyler the help he needed. Perhaps, if she focused on that, she could get through this. Deal Daniel this mortal wound, although it'd nearly kill her, as well.

Daniel's anguished eyes caught hers and she returned his pleading look, wishing she could give him the reassurance he needed. He knew she had to take this offer.

Unwilling to drag out this unbearable time for Daniel, she said, "Mr. Gleason, I'll need you to sign a purchase agreement."

But the old farmer waved her off. "Some chaw-bacon came over here while you two were at that other farm. He shoved one of those papers at me. What was his name? Brandon, Bradley…"

"Brady," Daniel rasped, his voice jagged and furious. She flinched. "You didn't sign for him." It sounded like an accusation rather than a question.

"No. But I took it so I could sign it and give it to Jodi." His thin lips stretched into a faint smile. "It's in the folder, darlin'."

"Thank you, Mr. Gleason," she murmured, her voice barely a notch above a whisper. How could she do this to Daniel? She glanced at Tyler. How could she not?

Daniel held a hand out to her. "Tell me you're not taking my farm."

She found herself stepping away, as if propelled against her will by the intensity of his gaze. Their mutual pain was too much.

"I have no choice, Daniel." She brushed

away Tyler's tears, her fingers trembling. She couldn't bypass the brass ring before her.

She didn't flinch, but confronted Daniel's angry grief. She opened her mouth to tell him that everything she'd done she had done because Tyler needed her. But after meeting his tormented eyes, she saw that she couldn't make more excuses. Better that he hate her than lose both his farm and the woman he thought he cared for.

Tyler's fussing turned into thrashing. "I'm sorry. He didn't get to finish his nap. I should go," she said, wishing she could stay but knowing the door to Maplewood Farm was forever closed to her. She felt the slam of it echo where her heart had been.

Mr. Gleason looked from her to a stone-faced Daniel. "Will you drive her home, son? Seems like you two have a lot to talk about."

There was a little silence between them, as if they observed the death of their hopes.

"I'm done speaking," Daniel said at last, his voice as cold as a stab. She winced at his meaning, intentional or not. Either way, she deserved it for stealing his home. At least there was some comfort that she hadn't stolen his heart.

"Goodbye," she said, and couldn't help

herself—she looked at him and she ached, knowing she would never again touch him or see him smile.

CHAPTER FIFTEEN

DANIEL POURED WARM milk into the cat trough the next morning and stepped away from the crowding, meowing felines.

He spotted the rag-doll cat but didn't grab it for a belly rub, ignoring the one-eyed Tom butting against his leg for a head scratch. Instead, he watched them as he might an old family movie, one that was already fading, the tape's end snapping against the reel.

What would happen to them once Midland took over? He hadn't seen any cats at their industrial farm. Would they be trapped, caged and shipped to animal shelters? Turned out of their home? He leaned against a support beam and tipped his baseball cap's brim low over his stinging eyes. He could relate.

Since his father had sold the farm to Jodi, he and Pop hadn't spoken. He'd brought him his morning coffee, but hadn't answered his dad's request to talk. There wasn't anything more to say. His father had given away his childhood home, his life and his future. Although he'd never stop loving his dad, it'd be a long time before he could forgive.

He hunched his shoulders against the burning in his chest and watched dust motes swirl in the midmorning light. How could his pop be so misguided, or Jodi betray him? He'd been fixing everyone's problems and had missed the trouble brewing in his own backyard. His fingers tightened around the milk canister's handle as he rinsed it out, then set it down. Fate had thrown him a wild pitch and he hadn't spotted it fast enough to duck.

"Thought I'd knock off early," Colton said beside him, his silent approach startling Daniel from his thoughts. "Help Sue with the alpacas. She's pretty broken up."

Daniel nodded since he didn't trust himself to speak. Colton turned to leave and stopped to look back, his overgrown bangs falling across his forehead. "Sorry about all this, Daniel. That's a tough break."

"Yep." He forced the word out over the swelling in his tight throat.

"Are you going to be all right?" The young man flicked the hair out of his gray eyes, revealing dark rings beneath them. Daniel wasn't the only one who'd lost sleep last night.

He pinched the bridge of his nose and nodded. "I'll survive."

And he would, he thought, as he listened to Colton's work boots clomp away. But surviving wasn't living. He'd have enough money to start over. Go anywhere he wanted, but the only place he wished for was no longer his. And neither was Jodi.

He grabbed a bag of feed before heading to the chicken yard. The roaming chickens' clucking echoed in his hollow chest as he stepped outside. He fumbled with the poultry feeder top before lifting it and pouring in grain, hens pecking at his ankles until he backed out of their way. He smiled faintly at the bossy animals. Their pushy, independent spirit appealed to him.

Over in the chick area, he filled the smaller feeder and watched them wobble his way, some tripping in a flurry of feathers and wings to reach him first. He wondered what destiny held for them. Like him, they were at the mercy of others. He'd wanted a life molded by his own two hands, but Jodi and his father had tied them.

He thought of Mr. Donaldson's hesitance to sell and understood why he'd decided, in the end, to join the co-op. When farming was all you knew, it was tough to imagine your life any other way. Maplewood Farm was his home, and no matter where he moved, it'd always remain that way in his mind.

After refreshing the chickens' water, he latched the gates, looked for any holes in the wired enclosure then headed back inside. Jodi had been a part of how he'd once seen his life. They'd grown up together, teased, tormented and fought until they'd given in to feelings that, for him, had never faded. Had he been waiting all this time for her to come home? If so, he'd been a fool.

He released a long breath as he walked, heavy-footed, down the empty barn—the cows were outside enjoying the fresh midsummer air. He passed the birthing pen, recalling Jodi's courage that day, her elation in helping him birth the calf, Tyler, an animal he'd intended to raise as a herd bull for backup breeding. She'd been as exhilarated as he. They'd made a good team and with her son, they'd have made a good family, too. Yet she hadn't trusted him enough, couldn't see the possibilities beyond Wonders Primary. And in the end, when it'd come to choosing between the two of them, she'd chosen Tyler.

The thought crushed him. She'd warned him Tyler would come first and he didn't disagree. But why hadn't she refused the deed and looked for other sales? Or followed a different path altogether—one that led to him instead of Midland? The only answer was that she hadn't cared enough to fight for them. Of course, if she had refused the deed, his determined father would have sought out Brady anyway.

He may have won the battle for Cedar Bay, but she'd laid waste to his heart. Like his mother, she'd pursued her needs and hadn't considered the ruined lives she'd left behind.

Before exiting the barn, he paused at the empty infirmary pen and leaned against the railing, his slack arms dangling, his head falling to rest on them. Jodi's leg had healed, and the elderly cow now grazed with the rest of the herd. His stomach dropped when he imagined what Midland would do with an older, nonproductive cow. A profit-driven ranch made no allowances for sentiment.

As he headed outside, a breeze twirled the tire swing he'd once pushed Jodi on, ruffling the petals in his grandmother's rose garden and sending a stray burlap sack tumbling along the ground. The world seemed to slow, spinning around him. All this would be gone. Disappeared like Jodi and Tyler as they flew to Chicago. According to Sue, Jodi's flight would be taking off now. He scanned the clear sky, his eyelids gummy as he searched for her plane.

He'd kept most of Cedar Bay intact, and

she'd gotten enough sales to earn her promotion and pay for Tyler's preschool. A win-win, yet he struggled to breathe over the weight crushing his lungs. While fighting for others, he'd left his home and heart undefended, and he'd lost both. He hadn't truly imagined she'd leave him again. Not this way.

"Daniel?" Thin arms slipped around his waist and squeezed. When he looked down, Sue's glasses were fogged, her nose red, her cheeks damp. "What are you going to do?"

He clasped her to his side and watched the oak tree they'd loved to climb sway. Its long leaves rustled, the noise sounding like showering coins.

"I'm out of options, Sue." His face felt wooden, his blood sluggish in his veins. "Dad owned the farm and sold it. When I hear from Midland, I'll start shutting things down."

Sue polished her glasses on her shirt and pushed them back over her nose before looking up at him. "I meant about Jodi."

He opened his mouth but his tight throat muted him, pieces of his broken heart ripping through his chest.

"You've got to do something." Sue twined her hand in his. "You love her. And Tyler." Her fingers curled around his. "Don't deny it."

His eyes squeezed shut, pressing back the

rushing damp that rose at her suggestion. "If I do, it doesn't change anything."

Sue's jaw angled forward. "If you still love her, that changes everything. You have to go to her."

He imagined the crowded, noisy, concrete of Chicago and distaste pinched his gut. "She betrayed me, Sue. I can't forgive her for that."

Sue raked a hand threw her short hair. "No. But you could try to understand. She's a mom who's doing what she thinks is best for her son."

"I'm best for him and so are you." The words burst out of him.

"What matters is what she thinks."

"And you're not offended that she didn't believe you could help him?"

"I did help him. And Wonders Primary will help him, too. Tyler is what's most important. Not my ego. Not anything else." She gestured around the farm and he winced.

In that brother-sister way of theirs, he knew what she suggested, though he wouldn't accept it. Farming was the only life he'd known and he wouldn't give it up. Maybe he could buy Mr. Tisdale's farm when the man returned from his Alaskan cruise.

"Jodi would never be happy in Cedar Bay and I'd never live in Chicago. Once she got what she wanted, she was done with me and her hometown."

"If you think that, you're wrong." Sue poked his chest, her eyes filled with cold fury. How could she be mad at him when Jodi had stolen their farm?

"She fooled me, Sue."

"Get over your ego, Daniel. She fooled herself." Sue's voice lowered and she suddenly sounded tired instead of angry. "And I bet she's regretting it," Sue continued. "I saw how she looked at you, how you were together. She made this sacrifice for Tyler, but she's hurting as much as you are. Trust me."

He hugged her, kissed the top of her head, then headed toward the house. "I wish I could, Sue," he called over his shoulder. "But in this instance, *you're* wrong."

"I'm not." The yellow specks in her eyes glowed when he turned at the porch steps. "Go after her, Daniel. This farm is no substitute for love. And besides, you don't even own it anymore. So what do you have? Nothing."

Her words sucker punched him. Another blow he hadn't expected. He'd thought Sue would be on his side, but instead she glared at him, her arms crossed over her narrow torso.

"Then I'd better enjoy it while I can," he said, and stomped up the stairs, the third tread creaking like always. Would they tear it down? Turn it into one of those gingerbread-looking "offices" that Jeff ran? He thought about the parts of the home that had been added over the years, the additions as families grew, though their finances fell. Yet through it all, they'd survived...until now.

He burst into the kitchen and saw spots as his eyes adjusted to the dim interior. For the first time in his life, he had no idea where he was going, and it scared the hell out of him.

"Daniel," his father called from the table.

When he passed by with only a nod, a hand grabbed his wrist, the grip hard and shaking. "Let's talk, son," Pop said. "Have a seat."

"I need a shower. We'll talk later." What could they say that wouldn't end in a shouting match? His words would only upset his ailing father who, despite it all, he didn't want to hurt.

"No. Now, Daniel."

He responded automatically to his father's commanding tone, pulling out a chair and sitting. How would he hold his temper in check?

He poured himself a cup of orange juice from a pitcher and gulped, the cold citrus tang doing little to smother the burn turning his insides to ash.

"What's left to say, Pop?" He topped off his dad's glass and refilled his own. "You don't like farming, wish you'd sold out. Now you're giving me the chance you never had. I get it."

"I don't think you do." His father's head shook more than usual and concern filled him.

"Then tell me where I have it wrong."

"After I got out of the service, farming was exactly the quiet life I needed. I'd seen too much of the world and I wanted a place to escape. To hide until I worked through some stuff."

Daniel nodded. His father's veteran status had always filled him with deep pride. If he hadn't been needed on the farm so soon, he would have enlisted himself. Suddenly, he saw an example where farming had shaped his destiny rather than him controlling it.

"But you hated farming. Or at least, that's what you said." Daniel buttered a piece of banana bread and passed it to his father. As for him, his knotted stomach was tied too tight for food.

His father nodded, his wrinkles mapping out his sorrow. "Eventually my hiding spot felt like a trap. But by the time I wanted something else, I already had a family depending on me."

"Why didn't you sell then?" Daniel leaned forward, his reticent father had never opened up like this before.

"Who'd buy a failing farm like mine? And

the more I tried to make the best of it, loaning equipment to neighbors, helping others where I could, the more stressful it got. Especially for your hardworking mother, who handled the finances." His father's eyes turned wistful—a faint smile vanished almost as soon as it appeared.

"You still love her," Daniel marveled. He shook out a napkin and passed it to his father.

Pop nodded. "Always will. My biggest regret was that I didn't listen to her when she begged me to cut our losses and move away. The hours I put into running the place, plus my postal run, made her feel lonely as she struggled to keep us afloat. We drifted apart."

Daniel nodded, remembering how hard his father had worked when they'd teetered on the brink of bankruptcy. His own contribution had been a paper route along with his farm chores. Those years had been tough. He knew his stoic father had been hurt when their mother left. But he'd never known that Pop blamed himself. Was Daniel repeating history with Jodi? He'd been at fault the first time she'd left. But that wasn't the case now. Jodi had grabbed the first opportunity to leave Cedar Bay and him, her heartless act destroying his life.

"She left us because of the money," Daniel said, thinking of Jodi more than his mother.

Pop's green eyes pierced Daniel's. "She left because I didn't make this her home. Because I didn't put her first."

The words knocked the air out of Daniel. "Of course this was her home. She decorated it, bought appliances, painted and planted flowers before she left. Quit."

"Home is where the heart is, son." His father brushed at the tears gathering in the corners of his eyes. "Four walls and a roof don't make a home. I learned that too late. I should have sold out like she wanted or I wouldn't have lost the love of my life. And I didn't want you to suffer the same future."

"But I'm not," Daniel protested, though he felt something shift inside of him. It was as if his father held a kaleidoscope up to his eye, each revelation accompanied with a twist that changed the way he viewed his past, present and future.

With effort, his father got both elbows on the table and dropped his chin in his cupped hands. "You are. Since Jodi came home, I saw a change in you, son. I stopped hearing the morning alarm because you were already out the door, doing your chores so you could see her when she dropped off her boy. I knew you'd cared for her once, and I could see you'd fallen for her again. Harder, even."

Daniel flinched, wondering how much his father had witnessed sitting on the back porch, especially this past week, when he and Jodi had given in to their feelings. Their attempt to keep the relationship a secret had failed.

"You love her. If your heart's with her, then your home is, too. That's what matters in life."

Daniel pushed back his chair and stood. "She left me, Pop."

His father sighed and patted Daniel's hand before he trudged upstairs to shower.

Fifteen minutes later, he was clean but not refreshed. He headed for the front porch and the soothing rockers it held. But before he sat, he spied an envelope slipped beneath the porch door and picked it up.

His hand shook as he read Jodi's handwriting on the front. If it was an "I'm sorry" letter, he wanted none of it. His fingers tightened around the paper, but something made him stop before tearing it apart.

Instead, he opened the flap, pulled out the contents and blinked in surprise.

It wasn't a guilty apology. It was Maplewood's deed.

THE MAN IN the plane seat ahead of Tyler turned and scowled at Jodi as her son kicked and thrashed.

"Lady. Can you please control your kid?"

"Sorry," she mumbled, her head feeling heavy and thick, her eyes bleary from lack of sleep. She tried pulling a resisting Tyler onto her lap but stopped when the seat belt sign flashed on with a beep. Great. Perfect timing.

Tyler wailed as she buckled him in, his stomach arching against the restraint, his fingers plucking at the silver clasp. Ollie soaked up most of his tears, her sleep shirt wet from the outburst that'd begun after they'd boarded the long-delayed plane. Jodi's wretchedness was a gnawing thing and she wanted to cry with him. It was taking her in bits. But for Tyler's sake she rolled her sorrow up into a small, tight ball and swallowed it down deep inside her. Leaving Daniel again was harder than the first time. But crying was futile. It changed nothing.

She blew her nose and then held down Tyler's legs when the disgruntled passenger glared again.

"Tyler, sweetheart." She wiped his nose. "Stay still."

Her poor son; without words, it was his only way of expressing his feelings. From the moment they'd packed this morning, he'd looked as confused and upset as she felt. Aunt Grace had seemed just as hurt and bemused. And when Jodi had returned from her errand to

Daniel's farm, Tyler had been agitated, sensing what he couldn't know.

When they'd finally boarded the delayed plane, he'd sobbed the way he had when Peter had walked out. Tyler's reaction erased any doubts about her need to separate him from Daniel, to enroll him at Wonders Primary, to get his life back on its usual track. Order and routine. Tyler did best with it, and that was what mattered.

When she got back to Chicago, she'd find a way to raise the money somehow. Another job, grant funds, maybe a last-minute Cedar Bay sale. Mr. Tisdale had phoned her and apologized for the missed meeting. Perhaps he might sell after all. Anything but taking away what Daniel loved most. She couldn't live with that. She'd returned Daniel's deed after a long night of wrestling with her conscience. Ultimately, she'd known she couldn't leave him with nothing, nor could she stay. She'd already made up her mind to end their relationship, to separate him and Tyler after their Midland farm visit.

Tyler's screams ratcheted up another decibel and this time the couple across the aisle clucked their tongues and looked her way before putting their heads together to whisper. She would have asked Tyler to be quiet, but didn't have the heart when she wanted to scream, too. Plus, she couldn't bring herself to do anything that might make him retreat further into his silence.

These were the outbursts Wonders Primary would help Tyler to overcome. They'd spelled it out in his treatment plan. Her mind drifted back to his last tantrum, realizing just how long it'd been. Since coming to her hometown, Tyler's behavior had improved and her focus on sales, and Daniel, had kept her from seeing it, she realized. What else had she missed?

Cedar Bay, to start with. She slumped in her seat, recalling the fun of Field Day, Daniel's living family tree, line dancing at Mary's Lounge, helping Aunt Grace serve potluck at the Independence Day celebration, strawberry picking. They were warm memories she'd hold tight in the lonely nights ahead.

And she hadn't noticed her growing feelings for Daniel until they'd been too strong to resist. He'd helped her through her distress over Tyler, making her see that she wasn't a bad mother. She'd just made mistakes, like everyone else.

When the woman who sat diagonally ahead of her whipped around, Jodi mustered enough strength to glare. No one was perfect. Not her and not Tyler. He hadn't asked to be born with autism. So why did she pressure her son to be like other kids? Did she think he wasn't great just the way he was? Lovable? Daniel certainly seemed to think so. As his parent, she should feel the same way.

Wonders Primary had diagnosed his faults and made plans to fix him. And, since his autism diagnosis, she had, too. His failure felt like hers and she'd blamed herself. Yet Daniel had shown her that she and Tyler didn't need to be perfect for someone to care about them. The world would and should love her son for who he was. That was the lesson he needed to learn, she realized. And perhaps, she needed to believe it, too. If she had, would she have left Daniel? Her hometown?

"Ma'am, I'm sorry." An earnest-looking stewardess leaned down, her brightly painted mouth twisted in apology. "But is there any way that you could control your son? He's upsetting the other passengers."

Jodi flushed red. "They're upset?" The words tore from her throat, nearly a shriek.

Oh, this was rich. She and Tyler were miserable and the passengers couldn't stick in some earbuds? Their selfishness stunned her. She'd paid for tickets, too. Did they think she was unaffected by Tyler's screams? Cared so little or was so inept that she wouldn't help him if she could? Each cry shredded her tattered heart.

"Yes, ma'am. There are rules about noise and your son is not following our code of conduct." The woman shifted on her heels, looking very young.

"He's four," Jodi snapped, her hands tightening on the cold, metal hand rests. "He couldn't spell code of conduct, let alone understand what it means."

"Just tell him to quit making so much noise," hollered one of the passengers, and a few cheered. "Keep him quiet like everyone else."

Jodi unbuckled herself and stood, rules be darned, and pulled out a thick pack of small cards. She shoved them at the flight attendant. "Please give one of these to everyone on this plane."

The uniformed woman paled as she read the word *autism* on the front.

"My son is autistic," Jodi shouted, her voice so loud that even Tyler's cries dwindled into a watery gulp. The passengers turned and many who'd looked at her in anger now seemed surprised and a bit embarrassed.

"If you want to know more about autism, please read the cards that—" she peered at the stewardess's nameplate "—Jamie is passing out." The woman hurried off and began handing out the cards, moving down the now-silent aisle.

Jodi shoved back her disheveled hair. "I expect every one of you to read it. Educate yourselves so that you don't judge a child for behavior he or she may not be able to control." She eyed the man who'd complained until he looked down, his Adam's apple bobbing.

"My son isn't perfect," she said, her gaze falling on her wide-eyed boy. "And I love him, no matter what. If you can't accept him, then that is your problem. Not mine. Not his."

She unbuckled Tyler's seat belt and pulled him onto her lap. "I love you, Tyler." She tickled his nose with hers, then gave him butterfly kisses, her eyelashes sweeping his cheeks.

He held out Ollie and she kissed the elephant's torn snout. "I love you, too, Ollie."

"Love."

Her breath caught as she stared at her son in disbelief.

"Love?" she asked, her voice hoarse. It couldn't be. But from the grin smeared across his wet face, the glow in his eyes as he looked from her to Ollie, she knew she'd heard his first word in over a year. And it'd taken her acceptance, not her pushing, to make it happen. Daniel's way. Why hadn't she listened to him? Trusted him?

"Do you love me, too, Tyler?"

He pushed Ollie into her face, making the elephant kiss her cheeks, slick with tears, and nodded. "Love," he repeated.

The happiness in her heart spilled over into laughter as she clutched him.

The intercom crackled. "Ladies and gentlemen, we're now at twenty thousand feet over Chicago and making our descent. It's eighty-one degrees and partly cloudy. Please stow your loose belongings and prepare for landing. For the lucky Chicagoans on the plane, welcome home."

Applause broke out but Jodi didn't join in. After this tumultuous plane ride, she realized that Chicago wasn't her home. It never had been. Home was where you were loved, accepted, wanted for who you were. And there was only one person who'd ever made her and Tyler feel that way. Daniel. She should never have left.

She'd do what she'd proposed the day she'd arrived in Cedar Bay—get on the next plane and go home. She doubted Daniel would forgive her for leaving him again, but she owed him an explanation and an apology. As for her and Tyler, she'd stay at Aunt Grace's house, enroll him in Sue's practice and apply for a local Midland job like Jeff's, only she wouldn't separate the calves from their mothers. It wasn't the happy life Daniel had offered her, but after her lack of faith, she didn't deserve it.

Twenty minutes later, she and Tyler disembarked.

"Gah!" Tyler shouted, jumping up and down and pulling away from her.

She tightened her hold and gasped when she followed his pointing finger. There, standing amidst a group of suited men, was Daniel in a plaid shirt and jeans, his belt buckle gleaming, holding a sign with the handwritten words *Jodi Lynn*. Her knees went weak and her pulse leaped like a horse charging out of the starting gate. How she had hated that sign when she'd first seen it. But now it felt like home. He was her home. Had he forgiven her for leaving?

Butterflies took wing in her stomach and flew to her throat, lodging there. Tyler tore loose from her slack grip and raced on tiptoes, Daniel closing the distance before dropping the sign and sweeping her son into a bear hug. He shrieked and smacked Daniel with Ollie until Daniel hugged the elephant, too.

"Love," Tyler said, and Daniel's hazel eyes widened as they met hers, the golden flecks in them shimmering against brilliant green.

"Did he just say—"

Jodi nodded, pride taking the place of her jittering nerves. "Yes. He said it on the plane, too. But how did you... Why are you..." She couldn't process that he was here. Her heart thundered.

"Hey, there!" Sue popped up beside her brother, an impish grin spreading across her narrow face.

Tyler squirmed and Daniel set him down so he could run to Sue.

"Frank had room on his prop plane for me and I came so you two could talk alone. Lucky for us your plane was delayed so we could get here ahead of you." She laid a hand on Tyler's head as he clutched her knees. "Mind if I take Tyler and meet Frank in the food court?"

Jodi nodded and watched the two head toward a McDonald's. When her eyes slid Daniel's way, his smile made her melt.

"Daniel—"

"Jodi—"

They began at the same time and laughed, the sound mingling with the chattering streams of people.

"Can we go somewhere more private?"

Jodi's heart soared when he put his hand on her elbow and steered her to a corner near a large window overlooking the runways.

The sun burnished his dark hair and her breath caught at the thought that this handsome, incredible man had traveled all this way to speak to her. Was it simply to thank her for the deed? Or was there more? She hoped it was more.

His eyes leveled on hers, steady. Being looked at by Daniel was like standing in the sun, the warmth a caress on her skin.

He ran his hands up her arm and she shivered, her nerves waking at his touch. "Jodi. I know Cedar Bay's not your home. But I flew here to tell you that you are mine."

Her hand flew to her locket, her heart pounding beneath her fingertips. "What do you mean?"

"I mean that wherever you and Tyler are is where I want to be."

"But I gave you back the deed. You can have your old life back. Your dad will come around and sign the farm over to you. He's a good man. He just needs to time to realize he was wrong." Her voice came out unevenly—he was standing very close, near enough that she could feel the warmth of him, smell the dark, rich scent of earth and fresh air.

Daniel's hands slid down and twined in hers. "I don't want it. I was stubborn, shortsighted, didn't see that I don't need a hometown to feel that I'm home. I just need you and Tyler."

"Daniel." Her pulse thundered and she could barely hear her own voice. "I—I don't know what to say. You see, I—"

"Say you'll forgive me, Jodi." His insistent gaze nearly undid her.

"Forgive you?" she choked out. "I nearly destroyed your life."

"But you didn't. You gave it back, and that makes you the most selfless, strong woman I know. I love you, Jodi." Excitement radiated off him like an electric force.

Tears flowed as her heart surged with joy.

"I'll get a job here," Daniel continued. "Pay Tyler's tuition at Wonders Primary. Please, Jodi. Make me the happiest man and tell me that you love me, too."

Surprise flooded her. He would sacrifice so much to be with her. It meant everything, but she wouldn't let him do it. It wasn't right for him, Tyler or her. They belonged in Cedar Bay.

"No."

His hands dropped hers and he jerked away as if stung.

"I see," he said, his voice sounding less sure than she'd ever heard it. Defeated. He smiled faintly and bowed his head. "Then I'll find Sue and Frank and we'll fly home. I won't trouble you again."

She grabbed his arm and he turned sharply on his heel, hope filling his eyes at her smile.

"I meant no, I don't want you to move to Chicago. I'd already planned to fly back to Cedar Bay."

"You were coming home to me." His voice was rough and soft, his eyes blazing.

"Or your cooking," she laughed, her happiness beyond containing.

"I'll make you shepherd's pie." He swept her into his arms and her pulse stuttered.

"I love you, Daniel."

His gaze on her felt like a warm caress. "I've waited a long time to hear those words."

"Ten years—"

He pressed his forehead to hers. "Longer than that. Since you beat me for best show-and-tell in kindergarten."

"The albino frog," she whispered, marveling that he might have cared that long.

"I love you, Jodi." His voice was firm and sure and it drove out any lingering doubt. "Wherever you are, that's my home."

Tears of joy blurred Daniel's handsome face. A beautiful mirage that she had to touch to make sure was real. She stroked his thick hair, the swell of muscles under the short sleeves of his T-shirt, the broad curve of his back. Waves of energy filled her until she felt dizzy.

"I love you, too," she said again, thinking she couldn't say it enough times. "You're what's

best for me and Tyler. I don't want to be anywhere that you aren't."

"But what about Wonders Primary?"

"Tyler needs a loving family that accepts
him. He'll have that in Cedar Bay."

"We'll work together with him, and no matter what, love him just the way he is," Daniel
said with absolute clarity before brushing a kiss
along her cheekbone. It was a kiss as light as
a blown leaf, but she felt a shiver far down in
her bones.

His mouth captured hers in an aching, tender caress that was light at first, and her lips
opened automatically beneath the pressure. She
forgot the crowd and felt herself go fluid and
pliant, stretching upward to twine her arms
around his neck. His arms slid around her, his
hands knotting in her hair.

Jodi heard the sound of the crowd behind
them, a wave of noise, but it meant nothing
and was lost in the rush of blood through her
veins, the dizzying sense of weightlessness in
her body. Daniel's hands moved from her hair,
slid down her spine; she felt the hard press of
his palms against her shoulder blades. At last
he pulled away, gently disengaging himself,
drawing her hand from his neck and stepping
back. For a moment Jodi thought she might fall;
she felt as if something essential had been torn

away from her, and she stared at Daniel, her longtime rival who'd won her heart.

"Let's get Tyler," he said, and she was touched that he'd want to spend this special moment with her son.

"There's Mommy—" Frank and Sue led a teary Tyler their way, his hand clutching a broken Happy Meal toy, the other holding Ollie.

Tyler's face puckered when he spotted them and he held out the beheaded action figure.

"He wanted Hello Kitty, but the cashier wouldn't let him have it because he's a boy and... Hey, are you two together?" Sue looked up from their clasped hands and grinned.

Daniel tightened his fingers around Jodi's. "Yes. But we needed to ask Tyler something first." He let go and squatted before her son. "Tyler, would you like to go back to the farm?"

"Gah!" he shouted and threw the action figure at the window.

"I'll take that as a yes." Daniel chuckled, scooping up Tyler with one arm and reaching for Jodi with the other.

Sue's eyes twinkled. "I'm so glad you're coming back, Jodi. Both you and Tyler."

The PA system crackled. "Last call for luggage from Flight 279. Carousel 6."

Frank slapped Daniel on the back. "I'll take Sue home since there's not enough room for all of us. But it looks like you're doing fine on your own."

"Thanks, Frank," she and Daniel chorused, and then after giving Sue a hug they watched the pair disappear into the throng.

"Let's get your bags," Daniel said, his long-legged stride making the crowd part as they headed for the shuttle. "And then we're going back for Hello Kitty."

Tyler's head whipped around for that, and when he smiled, Jodi's heart swelled.

"Can they put the bags on the next flight home?"

"They'd better," Daniel growled, and he tickled Tyler's belly, their laughter filling her with joy.

When Daniel stopped suddenly, she bumped into his back.

"I almost forgot." He handed her Tyler, then reached into a small knapsack and produced something pink and familiar.

Her heart fluttered. It couldn't be, but it was: the lost flower she'd worn to their class reunion.

He handed her the rose, his hazel eyes aglow.

"Welcome home, Jodi Lynn."

* * * * *

LARGER-PRINT BOOKS!

GET 2 FREE LARGER-PRINT NOVELS PLUS 2 FREE MYSTERY GIFTS

Love Inspired™

Larger-print novels are now available...